FORBIDDEN

EMMA NICHOLS

Britain's Next
BESTSELLER

First published in 2018 by:

Britain's Next Bestseller
An imprint of Live It Publishing
27 Old Gloucester Road
London, United Kingdom.
WC1N 3AX

www.bnbsbooks.co.uk

All enquiries should be addressed to Britain's Next Bestseller.

ISBN: 9781980642879

Other books by Emma Nichols...

To keep in touch with the latest news from Emma Nichols
and her writing please visit:

www.emmanicholsauthor.com
www.facebook.com/EmmaNicholsAuthor
www.twitter.com/ENichols_Author

Thanks

I would not have been able to write this book without the significant contributions of a few amazing people.

Eddy - for your wonderful stories of expat living and painting a picture of the beautiful country of Syria before the atrocities of recent times.

Nadège - for your generosity, and engineering expertise. I feel as if I have actually worked on an oil rig for years!

Mu - for your unwavering support, ideas, and amazing book cover designs.

Bev, Valden and Tara - for painstakingly reading through my words, many times, and helping me to make sense of them. Your feedback has been invaluable.

To you, the reader, I thank you for taking a leap of faith. I hope you enjoy the journey.

With love, Emma x

Dedication

To all the women in this world who dare to break
the rules, customs, and beliefs, that would have
their love denied, or even punished.

To the women in this world who are unable to openly express
their love for each other, for fear of breaking the rules,
customs and beliefs that would have such love punished.
May the world wake up one day and set you free.

1.

Ashley sighed, dumped the UK post-marked, envelope onto the wooden food tray, and rattled it along the metal bench rails of the food counter. She stopped briefly, her eyes scanning the stewed fava beans, fattet hummus, and scrambled eggs. Her eyes drew back to the envelope and her stomach lurched, taking her appetite with it. She ambled down the counter to the coffee machine. Pouring a large mug of the hot black liquid, her hand suddenly jerked, and she stopped, the pot suspended in mid-air, her heart racing.

'Hey birthday girl.' Craig's southern drawl had boomed across the room and elicited curious glances from the oilfield workers already eating breakfast.

She winced, sensing the heat rising into her cheeks. Turning, he bounded into her path, and she couldn't help but smile at the gaping grin, revealing his uneven bottom row of teeth.

He ruffled his short dark hair with one hand and handed over the small parcel held tightly in his other. 'Happy birthday darlin',' he said, in a quieter voice.

'Thanks bud.' She took the gift and placed it next to the envelope, slapping him lightly on the arm. She finished pouring her coffee, added a dash of milk and picked up two sugar sleeves. 'You eating?' she asked, her eyes indicating to an empty table, next to the window at the back of the restaurant.

'Hell yeah,' he said, reaching for a tray and loading it with a plate of scrambled eggs and stewed beans. He moved down the food counter, his eyes appealing to his taste buds.

Ashley picked up her tray and rucksack and sidled between protruding chairs and poorly positioned tables, to get to the one she had spotted. She placed her tray on the hard plastic surface, hooked the rucksack over the back of the chair, and slumped into the hard seat. Leaning back and tilting her head into the cool breeze of the air conditioning, her eyelids fluttered. One eye on the tall Texan as he added fruit and pastries to his tray, she smiled to herself. She hadn't expected him to remember her birthday; she hadn't reminded him. She hadn't wanted to! She'd hoped to get through the day quietly, avoiding the truth.

Her thirty-second birthday had hit her hard, but more distressing than that was the fact that her love life hadn't changed since her arrival at Deir ez-Zor, more than a year ago. She hated being single and stuck in the middle of the Syrian desert. The only female in a group of sixteen expats from her own company and over two hundred men at the base made up of locals and expats from other companies. At least that would change today with the arrival of Katherine Blackwell, their new base manager. At least the thought of having female company brought with it a pleasant fluttering sensation in her stomach. *And, what if she were a lesbian too?* She smiled at the thought. *What would be the chances of that?* She tried to dismiss her wishful thinking, but the butterflies continued to dance optimistically.

Striding across the room, covering the space effortlessly with his long gait, Craig approached the table and landed his tray with a thud, silencing the room. He didn't notice. Ashley chuckled, rocking her head back and forth at his quirky ineptitude. He might be able to weld an electric circuit board with his eyes shut, but landing a tray on a table that was too low for him, seemed beyond his capabilities. She watched him squeeze into the chair opposite her.

'So what's up?' he asked, wiggling in the standard-sized seat and banging his knees on the underside of the table.

'Fuckin' thing's built for kids,' he mumbled, not seeking a response.

Her eyes flicked between the gift box and the card, sitting side-by-side on the tray in front of her. 'Nothing,' she lied.

'Uh huh.' A wry smile appeared on his face. He shoved a forkful of beans in his mouth and seemed to swallow without chewing. 'Yer lookin' all worked up 'bout somethin',' he said, with a laugh. 'Ya should be celebratin'.'

Ashley twisted the mug in her hands.

'And ya need t' eat. It's real good. So much better with the new cook,' he said, pointing his fork at Ashley's empty tray.

Ash's stomach rumbled. 'You're right.' She made her way to the counter and returned with a plate of eggs and beans. The subtle flavours danced on her taste buds and stole her attention from her gloomy thoughts. 'This is good,' she said, nodding as she ate. Downing her fork, she straightened her back in the chair and sipped at her coffee, staring at the tray, her eyes flitting between the envelope and the box. Returning the mug to the tray, she picked up the box and unwrapped it with increasing enthusiasm. 'Wow, thanks bud,' she said, smiling at his excited eyes. Holding up the bright green bottle of Envy for Men, she pulled open the lid and breathed in the woody scent. 'How did you know?' she asked, fighting the burning sensation at the back of her eyes.

He shrugged. 'I recognised it on ya. I mean, it is for guys,' he said, a ruddy glow darkening his face. His eyes darted towards his food, his fork poised for the next assault.

Ashley wiped the heel of her hands across her eyes, leant across the table and placed a kiss on his warm cheek. 'You didn't strike me as a cologne kinda guy,' she said, with a tilt of her head. Her brows furrowed as she eyed him suspiciously.

'And ya had a near-empty bottle of it in yer shower room,' he added, starting to laugh.

She slapped him firmly on the arm but couldn't stop the grin forming, or the chuckle that followed.

'So, party tonight,' he said, rubbing his hands together. It wasn't a question, and he didn't get a response. He picked up a mini-pastry and devoured it in one bite, eyeing her inquisitively. The smile had fallen from her lips, and her previously rosy cheeks had lost their shine. She was staring over his right shoulder towards the food counter, her mouth agape and her eyes wide.

No! Ash blinked, trying to make sense of the redhead at the counter.

Craig frowned and craned his neck. He stopped chewing and swallowed hard. *Shoot!*

The perfectly coiffured red-hair swayed from side to side, an empty tray resting on the rails in front of her. Even the tilt of the woman's head had an aura about it that was drawing the attention of more than one man in the room. A low wolf whistle came from the table to Ashley's right. She tutted, and glared at Zack and Dan who continued staring open-mouthed. By the time Ashley turned back, the woman was looking straight into the room. Her heart missed a beat, and she struggled to swallow past the lump in her throat. *You have got to be kidding me!* She immediately slunk into her chair, using Craig as the physical barrier that he was. She picked up her mug and finished her coffee in one slug; heat flaming in her chest, she prayed Kate hadn't seen her.

'Well, well,' Craig muttered to himself, with a wry smile, oblivious to Ashley's reaction to the presence of their new base manager, and his new line manager. Katherine Blackwell! *Well, shoot! She's gone 'n' got married!*

'Fuck me, she's fucking hot ass.' Zack Leighton's blue eyes were popping out of his twenty-four-year-old, clean-shaven, face. He had risen two inches in his seat, his fingers instinctively grooming his short dark hair.

'Shut the fuck up, Leighton,' Dan responded, digging the younger man in the ribs. Daniel Baas lowered his eyes and carried on eating.

'She fucking is,' Zack muttered, slumping back in his seat. He continued to mumble as he bit into a sweet pastry and picked up his coffee.

Heat flushed Ash's face, memories of the woman attracting the attention of every man in the room, flooding her mind. She slunk further down into the seat and placed her hand over her face. Kate, with her distinctive wavy red locks and almost arrogant disposition, navigated the restaurant effortlessly, finding a single table, obscured from Ash's view by the single pillar in the room. Ash shifted across in her seat sufficiently to remain tucked out of sight and sat up. She released a breath and rubbed at her temples. It had been a long time since their paths had crossed, but the heat passing through her now, tracking south at pace, wrestled with the tightness in her chest and the alarmed voices in her head. She puffed out hard. *Fuck!*

'Ya okay?' Craig asked, assessing Ashley with a frown. He finished the last of his food, wiped his cuff across his mouth, and picked up his coffee. 'Ya sure is aggravated,' he said, shaking his head, but there was also a concern in his tone.

'I'm fine,' Ashley responded, her attention distracted by the concealed corner of the restaurant. Pocketing the unopened card and placing the gift in her rucksack, she stood and slapped him on the shoulder. 'Thanks for the birthday present bud,' she said, swiftly ducking out through the side door, which led to the rear of the building. She didn't look back.

Craig was still shaking his head as he rose from the table. *Yup, aggravated 'bout somethin'!* His thoughts shifted to

5

the redhead. He could have sworn Katherine's eyes had spied him, but he deliberately hadn't responded. Unable to reconcile Ashley's uncharacteristic behaviour, and seeing Katherine again after so many years, had stirred something in him he hadn't expected when he made his way to breakfast just half-an-hour earlier. He cleared his throat and scratched at his rugged face. 'C'mon y'all, we got work t' be doin',' he said, pointing at his two junior crew. Zack and Dan downed their coffee, stood, and followed their boss.

*

Ashley stood outside the rear door of the restaurant and leaned against the wall, her heart thumping and her breath catching in the dry, early morning heat. She reached into her jeans pocket and pulled out the packet of tobacco and papers. She released one paper and pocketed the rest. With shaking hands, she laid out a thin line of tobacco and rolled the paper around it. Pocketing the pouch, she fixed the roll-up between her lips, lit it and dragged the smoke deeply into her lungs. She released the smoke slowly, spat out a loose strand of tobacco and dragged again. Kate Davidson! Her ex's name bounced around her mind. *Happy fucking birthday!* She inhaled too hard and spluttered.

Holding the roll-up between her lips, squinting as the smoke drifted into her eyes, she took the envelope out of her pocket and opened it. Pulling out the contents, she noted the Our Darling Daughter message embossed in pink glitter on the front and scowled. It couldn't be any more inappropriate if they tried! She opened the card. Three ten-pound notes slid down the inside, and she removed them to reveal the words her mother had written.

Happy Birthday, Ashley,

Love Sandra and Jason x

She placed the money back inside the card, folded it into a quarter of its original size, and put it back in her pocket. She sucked slowly on the roll-up and blew out hard. Throwing the cigarette to the ground, she trod it down, screwing forcefully with her foot. Today was already turning out to be a shit day, and it wasn't even 7am.

She gazed around, briefly distracted by the merging of the deep blue sky and expansive desert to the west, and the tooting horns and general bustling noises from the city of Deir ez-Zor to the northeast. Beads of sweat had already started to form at her temples. It was going to be a hot one; too fucking hot. She ran her fingers through her hair, pinning the short platinum-blonde bob behind her right ear, leaning her head slightly to keep it in place. Kate's image appeared, and she studied her fingernails, picking at the loose skin around the nail bed, unconsciously clearing her throat. She could face the woman, or she could try and avoid her at all costs. She hadn't decided what to do before Craig's voice grabbed her from her musings.

'C'mon, let's go.'

'Right. Coming.' Turning to face him, she planted a fake smile.

Craig had already disappeared back into the building by the time she moved from the spot. She glanced around the restaurant and breathed deeply. Kate had gone. Her heart thumped with every cautious step back through the restaurant to the main door, answering her question. Avoid Kate at all costs!

The doors behind the food counter swung open suddenly, clattering against the wall. Ashley jumped, and her breath stalled. She pressed her hand to her chest. 'Fuck.' The word was out before she could suppress it.

'Sorry, I didn't mean to startle you.' Dressed in a pristine white uniform, Iman dashed into Ash's path. She held out a large off-white cardboard box, her light-brown eyes lighting up her face. 'This is for you. Happy birthday,' she said, with a kind smile.

Ash couldn't prevent the excitement of the new cook touching her own eyes. Iman may have only worked at the hotel for a short time, but she had already captured the hearts of the oilfield workers with her passion for food and her unique cuisine. 'Thank you.' She took the box, tentatively resting it on the one hand, and opened the lid a fraction. Peeking inside, the birthday cake pictured a small 3D bottle of champagne at its centre point. Coloured sugar paper had been cut up to make the small pieces of confetti that lay sprinkled around the bottle, and the words, 'Happy Birthday Ash', were elegantly written in rich-coloured icing. 'This looks extraordinary,' she said, looking up, a warm glow colouring her cheeks.

'I hope you have a lovely day.' Iman said, the kind smile broadening across her cheeks. Turning on her heels, she dashed back through the door into the kitchen.

Ash stood, staring at the lid of the box, taken aback by Iman's generosity. *It must have taken ages to make.* She juggled the rucksack that was beginning to slip from her shoulder while balancing the cake in the box. There was only one problem! What the hell was she going to do with a huge birthday cake? Now everyone would know. There would be no escaping a party later.

She released a weighty sigh, and made her way out of the building, juggling the box in her hands as she eyed her feet, carefully taking the steps down towards the parked vehicles.

A loud cheer went up, followed swiftly by male voices breaking into song. 'Happy birthday to you...'

Jeez! Craig's operatic tenor voice rendered her motionless before she reached the bottom step. Zack and Dan were trying their best to sing, struggling not to laugh at the stunned look on her face. Positioning the cake safely on the low wall, she started waving her arms, orchestrating the song, trying, but failing, to hide her embarrassment. *Bastards. Nothing was a secret in this place!* 'Fuck off you lot,' she said, with more than a hint of affection, as their rendition came to a squeaky end, her cheeks prickling with warmth.

She picked up the box, turned then stopped suddenly. Goose bumps raced down her spine. *Kate!* Her eyes darted around; the small group, the vehicles, over her shoulder to the main hotel entrance, and then out to the front again, across to the row of expat houses adjacent to the hotel. Her heart raced at the idea of having to face her ex. Was Kate watching her? Her eyes widened as she scanned. Her breathing was speeding up and her already tight chest tightening. She tried to release the air slowly, but it came out more like a pant.

'C'mon,' Craig said, interrupting her panicked thoughts. He opened the door to the 4x4 and leapt into the driver's seat.

2.

Ashley puffed out a deep breath, her heart still racing; placed the cake box carefully on the central seat and her rucksack into the foot-well. She climbed in, slammed the door behind her and slumped, digging frantically into her jeans pocket for her tobacco.

Craig was already belted up and slammed his foot down hard on the accelerator. The older of the company vehicles responded sluggishly, and he raised his eyebrows. 'Darn heap o' crap,' he said, beeping his horn at Zack, who was overtaking them and giving them the middle finger, a broad grin plastered on his smug face. Craig huffed jovially and responded with his salute. 'Fuckin' kids!'

Ignoring the banter, Ashley pulled out a thin sheet of paper and tried to position the small line of tobacco down its centre. The land-cruiser bumped and shook its way along the dusty road, and she tutted as the tobacco fell to the floor. Dipping her hand deep into the pouch, she started the process again. She handed over the completed cigarette to Craig and flicked her lighter at its tip.

'Thanks,' he said, drawing in the smoke and blowing out rings.

She pulled out another paper and filled it, cursing as she was thrown heavily against the door. Lighting the roll-up, she drew down deeply, willing its relaxing effect to eliminate the tension that had taken up residence in her mind.

Craig eased into the rhythm of the Deir ez-Zor rush-hour, one arm swinging casually out his door window; his other hand tapping rhythmically on the steering wheel. 'So, c'mon, what's got ya all worked up?' He glanced sideways for too long, and nearly back ended the taxi in front of him. Braking hard, he started laughing.

Ashley held out an arm and braced herself against the dashboard, the other reaching for the cake box, as the 4x4 lurched. 'You need to keep your eyes on the road, bud,' she said, sucking through her teeth, holding back on the chuckle that was trying to surface.

'So, what 'bout our new boss then?' he asked, changing the subject.

Ashley winced.

'The redhead,' he continued, his eyes firmly on the road. She looked out the side window. 'The new woman at breakfast! Katherine Blackwell, the new boss.' He persisted, raising his hands and drum-rolling enthusiastically on the steering wheel.

'I know, no need to keep fucking repeating,' she blurted, her tone less fervent.

Craig frowned.

Katherine Blackwell. She repeated the unfamiliar name slowly, trying to reconcile the fact that the woman she had known intimately was not only their boss but also married.

'I know her as Davidson,' Craig continued. 'Katherine Davidson.'

Ashley's jaw dropped at his casual admission, and she could feel the heat instantly hit her cheeks. It hadn't occurred to her that anyone at the base might know Kate, but of course, they were all in the oil business! Even though she hadn't seen Kate on the rigs she had been on, paths often crossed. She and Craig had worked together on and off for the last few years. She had joined Schlumberger a year after him, and they had become good friends since. It was entirely plausible other engineers would know Kate Davidson or Katherine Blackwell. 'Where do you know her from?' she asked, her curiosity piqued.

'Houston,' he said. 'We worked together for a bit. She was on some kinda temporary reassignment, 'n' then went fast-track-management. Not sure what happened after that. It was short but real, real sweet.' His mouth twitched, and he sucked noisily on his upper lip.

Ashley clenched her teeth, and her face flared, but not for the reasons that he might have surmised. Her legs tensed in the seat, just as the 4x4 bounced, but it didn't stop her banging her head against the metal back-bar. 'Fuck,' she shouted.

'What?' Craig asked, in a voice close to falsetto. 'She's hot,' he added, with a shrug of his shoulders. 'Can't blame a guy,' he continued, oblivious to Ashley's discomfort, grinning at his recollections.

Ashley took a long drag on the cigarette, before throwing the last of it out the window. She was trying to process Craig's confession while fighting the pressure in her chest that was making it hard for her to breathe. *Fuck, Fuck, Fuck!* This was officially the worst day in hell. She cleared her throat and tried to control the spinning sensation consuming her head. 'Right,' was all that she could say, through clenched teeth.

'What, you don't think she's hot?' Craig persisted, totally unaware the impact his revelation was having on his buddy. He started to whistle, chirpily.

'Fuck off, Craig.' Ashley spat out the words, causing him to turn sharply and face her.

'Seriously, Ash! What ya hissy fittin' 'bout?' He flicked the last of his roll-up out the window and turned his attention to the road, muttering incomprehensibly. He switched on the radio and cranked up the volume, the noise penetrating the silence that hung heavily between them.

Ashley breathed out deeply, her eyes set on the Deir ez-Zor suspension bridge in the near distance, her body rocking with the bouncing of the vehicle. 'Sorry,' she shouted, over the music. She flicked her hair behind her ear, pinched the bridge of her nose, and squeezed at her tear ducts. She watched the side of his head and followed the line of his jaw, and his rugged stubbly chin, as his mouth moved with the words of the song playing on the radio. Betrayal burned in her chest. She needed space. Thinking of him with Kate, the woman she had fallen in love with, touched something deep inside, something very uncomfortable, something lingering. Was she still in love with Kate? She breathed in deeply and rubbed at the tears that had started down her cheeks. She needed to get to work, and quickly.

Craig pulled the vehicle to a sudden halt. 'Ya okay?' he asked. The compassion in his tone didn't go unnoticed, and Ashley put on a brave smile.

'I'm okay,' she said. 'Just don't like the feeling of getting older,' she added, deflecting the conversation from her real concerns.

'Ah huh,' he said, unconvinced.

She avoided his gaze. 'Got a card from my parents,' she added, continuing to stare vacantly.

'Ah huh,' he said nodding. He reached across and punched her affectionately on the arm. 'Damn, that sucks, babe!' he said.

'It's okay. I'll send it back. They'll get the message eventually,' she said, tilting her head.

'Shoot!' He paused. 'We need a few drinks later t' celebrate,' he said, in a more upbeat tone. 'You be at my place at eight, got it?' There was no question in his tone.

'Sure,' she said, rubbing her arm, a tight smile on her face. 'I'm good, honest. Come on; we've got kit to pressure test before it needs to go to the rig.' She pointed at the road to direct Craig's attention.

'Ah huh, ain't that a fact,' he said with a tilt of his head and a slight smile. There was a loud crunching sound as he rammed the stick into first gear. He slammed his foot on the accelerator, bouncing them both up and down in their seats as the 4x4 pitched forward, leaving a trail of dust in its wake. It wasn't long before the base came into view - a series of portacabin structures of varying sizes - encased in a giant wave of heat emerging from the desert sand. 'Gonna be hot as hell today,' he remarked.

'Yep,' she responded, but she was still thinking about Kate. She hadn't realised her ex was bi when they were together at Imperial College. The year that had ended, for her, with her heart broken. Seeing the redhead again at breakfast had brought back a strong sense of desire. Her mouth dried and she tried to swallow. Kate had clearly moved on, if she had ever been into her in the first place? Ashley's chest constricted, and she pushed the unwelcome thought to the back of her mind. She had work to do, and that, thankfully, would require her full attention.

*

Niomi placed the large tray of lamb kebabs in tomato sauce onto the middle shelf of the oven. 'What are you making those for?' she asked abruptly, wiping at her forehead.

Iman was working in a dreamlike state, delicately folding the semolina dough around the homemade sweet walnut paste. Her soft features twitched at the unexpected challenge. Craig had asked if she would prepare something for Ash's birthday party and she had agreed willingly. But, it was supposed to be a surprise, so she hadn't involved Niomi, instead, leaving her to get on with preparing the kebabs and vegetables for the restaurant's evening meal. 'It's for a birthday party for Ash,' she said, wanting to keep the conversation short.

Niomi huffed at the mention of the engineer's name, rolled her eyes and slammed the oven door. Iman always seemed too joyful and enthusiastic when talking about Ash, in a way that she had never been about Rifat. Yet, Rifat was a good-looking man and a wealthy one too. He had been very keen to date Iman, but she had always been distant with him. 'How is Rifat?' she asked, forcing Iman's attention away from the engineer.

Iman ignored the question, lost in the softness of the dough playing through her fingers. She had only ever agreed to chaperone Niomi and Joram for trips and meals so that the young couple could go out together. Rifat, Joram's brother, had joined the three of them occasionally for reasons she didn't care to understand. And she certainly hadn't ever considered herself to be on a date with him. More to the point, she hadn't seen Rifat for a long time now, and she knew Niomi knew that too. Her heart dulled with the image of Rifat that was now planted in her mind and she cursed Niomi for invading her reverie. Yes, he was a good man with an excellent job. But, she wanted someone who made her heart sing. 'I don't know how Rifat is,' she said, finally answering the question. 'And, you know he's not the one for me,' she added, glaring at her friend. She felt a strong urge to close the conversation. She didn't want to think about Rifat. Not now. Not ever.

'You never know,' Niomi continued, in a more jovial tone, poking Iman on the arm, taunting her.

Iman forced a smile, but Niomi's young mind was too lost in its world of deep romance to notice. 'Just because you've found love already,' Iman said, steering the conversation to the more comfortable topic of her friend's love life.

Niomi floated around the kitchen, consumed by her dream world. She was in love, but not with Joram. Not anymore. Iman didn't know that though, and she hadn't worked out how to tell her yet either. Heat flushed her face as Zack's deep blue eyes and short dark hair entered her mind's eye, sending a trail of goose bumps down her spine. She played with the towel in her hands as the prohibited thought caused a wave of confusing sensations to pass through her. If her parents found out that she had strong feelings for Zack she could be ostracised. Embarrassed at the idea of bringing her family into disrepute, she cleared her throat to shake off the thought. She pulled out a bag of onions and started cutting one into thin slices. 'Ouch!' She dropped the knife with a clang and pressed her apron to her finger.

Iman looked up from the workbench. 'You okay?' she asked, holding back a snigger. A small nick on the finger was an everyday occurrence in their job.

'Fine.' Niomi responded curtly, heading for the plasters.

Iman continued to manipulate the dough into triangle shaped cakes. No matter how much she tried to think of Rifat that way, it just felt wrong. She sighed and her pace of working slowed. *What if she never found someone to make her feel that way? Or worse still, what if she found someone who didn't feel that way about her?* She finished preparing the sweet cakes, adding her touch of crushed pistachios on the top, and wiped her hands on the apron hanging from her waist. She moved the completed tray to the side and pulled out a jar of flour to start on the pastry. As she began to work the butter into the dry mixture, an image of Ash's brightly coloured birthday cake came to mind, and she smiled. Making the cake had given her such pleasure. She blushed, disconcerted by the fluttering sensation in her stomach that rippled throughout her body. She shook the image from her mind and concentrated on working up the dough in her hands.

Niomi noticed the shift in colour in her friend's cheeks and the soft smile on her lips. 'See, you like him! You're hot for him,' she mocked.

Iman's cheeks burned, and she stopped working. Excusing herself, she walked calmly out of the kitchen and into the adjoining restroom. She stood, staring into the smeary mirror, waiting for her heart to settle in her chest. *What is wrong with me?*

*

Katherine yawned and stretched, her eyes scanning the L-shaped first-floor room; from the oak-style writing desk to the matching coffee table in front of the dark-brown leather two-seater sofa; from the king-sized bed with its coffee and chocolate coloured duvet, to the small box-shaped television which sat on a cabinet. She hated having a tv in her bedroom, and this room wasn't styled in her colours either, but the expat houses were set up like any other hotel room in which she had stayed. It was clean enough, austere, with whitewashed walls and small square windows that let in the light, and too much heat. She switched on the air conditioning.

She yawned again, fatigue rapidly catching up with her. The early flight in and a shift in the time zone were taking effect, and she would also need time to adjust to the persistent heat. She nodded to herself. Declining the birthday party had been the right decision, and not just for the reason that she was exhausted!

Wiping the sweat that was cooling on her forehead, she sought out the en-suite bathroom, contemplated skipping supper and grabbing an early night. Maybe she would explore the downstairs kitchen for food. The large garden and house's private swimming pool would have to wait until tomorrow.

She stared out the small window and sighed. *Ashley Roberts.* She had seen the organisation chart before she took the job of course. Their paths crossing had been inevitable. But, she hadn't expected the rush of heat and quivering in her stomach that had made breakfast impossible to swallow. She hadn't expected her heart to thump through her chest. The feeling had been even more disturbing than when she had briefed a group of cynical engineers in her first role after leaving the management school. She hadn't expected her heart to flutter, or the sharp pain that pricked at her awareness. She fiddled with the indentation at the base of her ring finger. *So much has happened.* She sighed.

Stepping into the shower, she turned the knob. Nothing. *Shit!* She stepped out of the shower and tried the sink taps. Nothing. Throwing on her jeans and t-shirt, she headed downstairs to the kitchen. No water there either. Looking under the kitchen sink, she turned what seemed like the mains stopcock. Nothing. She stood and ruffled her hair, irritation flaring in her chest. She ran back up the stairs, grabbed her bag and headed for the hotel.

'We need to put you in another house tonight.' Lars Eriksen said into the phone. 'The manager can't get a plumber out until tomorrow, and they have no idea what the problem might be. I'm so sorry Katherine, this shouldn't have happened. The hotel is already full otherwise I'd suggest that you stay there. Ashley's house has a spare room, so you'll be in good company.'

Kate gulped into the crackling line. 'I'm sure we will be fine,' she said.

'The hotel has a spare key,' he added. 'Can you give Ashley my apology, please? Your place should have been checked, and we shouldn't be in this position,' he continued, muttering crossly at the apparent incompetence. As the company's country manager he had more important issues to worry about than dealing with routine administration.

Kate shuddered. 'Sure.'

'Kate.'

'Yes.'

'Thank you. I can assure you; we'll have you in your place as soon as possible,' he added, apologetically.

'Sure. I'll see you tomorrow.' She turned, returned the handset, and took in a deep breath. The receptionist was holding out the key with an apologetic smile on his face. 'Is there anywhere I can get a drink?' she asked.

'Yes, there is a bar to the right. There's a breath-taking view from the terrace, out over the desert.' He smiled warmly and indicated towards the back of the hotel. 'Your drinks this evening will be on the company,' he added.

'Thanks.' she responded with a tired smile. *I so need that drink!*

3.

Ashley ambled down the dusty street to the fifth of the nine detached properties that housed the expat staff working for Schlumberger. Although refreshed from lazing in the pool since returning from the base, and the long cool shower and brief nap that followed, the late evening heat still left a light sheen on her skin. The sun, descending over the horizon, firing red flames from the white ball at its centre and creating shades of purple where it merged with the darkness, attracted her attention.

Adhan, the call to prayer, started and she stood still. Chanting voices drifted across the night sky and echoed around the houses, as the minarets throughout the city joined together, their tones blending effortlessly, drawing in their people. Ashley's thoughts silenced, compelled to listen and moved by the haunting resonance that consumed the space around her. The voices eventually faded, then stopped.

She glanced around, suddenly. *Kate!* Curiosity piqued, she wondered what Kate might be doing. She hadn't seen her at the base all day, and that thought should have brought a sense of light relief. It didn't. She glanced towards the manager's house, but there weren't any lights on. Her eyes drifted to the windows of the rooms inside the hotel, drawn to the slightest movement, the rising intensity serving only to heighten the anxiety nestling in her stomach. The last thing she felt ready for was bumping into Kate. Some birthday treat that would be!

She stood at the door to number five and turned the handle slowly. Craig's front door was never locked; every day was an open house. Heavy bass thumped into the street, even though the music wasn't that loud. It felt crude: intrusive. She stepped into the hallway to find a bottle of beer thrust into her hand.

Craig bounded past her and up the stairs. 'Wait there,' he commanded, his index finger indicating to the spot her feet occupied.

She craned her neck to see what was going on in the living room, but other than the thumping sound assaulting her ears, she couldn't hear or see anything, or anyone. She sipped the beer, enjoying the fresh sensation in her mouth, and brushed at the reddish dust off her tan-chinos that had accumulated from the short walk.

Craig bounded down the stairs and leaned in to kiss her on the cheek. 'You smell reeal nice,' he said, with a smirk on his face. She slapped him on the arm. 'C'mon darlin', yer the birthday girl.' He opened the living room door and all but pushed Ashley to the room. Again, voices boomed out 'Happy birthday to you,' and she squirmed, sipping from the bottle of beer.

Three cheers went up, clapping Mexican wave style moved around the room full of men, and a final resounding cheer brought proceedings to a halt. 'Thanks, everyone.' Ashley raised her hand in appreciation, and followed Craig, clinking her bottle with the glasses she passed, heat beating through her cheeks. She would kill him! She smiled at the man who was like a big brother to her. He had drafted in the locals they worked with as well as the expats, and fortunately no sign of a redhead. She smiled. Maybe after another couple of beers, she wouldn't give a shit anyway.

'Hey Ash, happy birthday.' Tarek interrupted her thoughts and handed over a blue silk shawl.

'Wow.' Ashley placed her beer on the table and stared open-mouthed at the locally-crafted garment; allowing it to open fully in her hands, revealing several shades of blue and a delicate silver thread that sparkled, even in the low light. 'It's beautiful. Thank you.'

'It's from Iman too,' he added, lowering his eyes to observe the gift. 'I'm glad you like it.'

Ashley flushed. 'I do, very much.' Her voice faded, her fingers appreciating the lightly textured material. 'Thank you,' she said, holding his light-brown smiling eyes. She reached for the engineer and pulled him in for a hug. He resisted the close contact and pulled back. 'Sorry,' she said, her cheeks flaring at her spontaneous reaction to being given the gift. Even though she had been working with Tarek for over a year, the fact that they were on opposite shifts meant she saw very little of him. She scanned the room urgently.

'It's okay, Dad's not here,' Tarek said with a coy smile.

Ashley released the breath she hadn't even realised she had been holding, and nodded, smiling apologetically for her public display of affection. Tarek and Iman's father, Muhammad al Maghout, had worked at the base for over thirty years and was very familiar with expat living and the exploits of engineers a long way from home. That didn't mean he necessarily approved, though he had always treated Ashley with kindness and respect.

Ashley's attention wavered from the shawl, and she turned. Iman was standing behind a table loaded with food, smiling directly at her. The leftover cake was perched on the end, surrounded by a seductive display of freshly baked sweet treats.

Iman nodded towards the sumptuous feast.

'Thanks, Tarek.' Ashley rubbed the silk between her fingers. 'I think your sister's calling me to eat,' she said.

Tarek's eyes shone as he glanced across at his sister. 'She is an excellent cook. She'll make a good wife one day.'

Ashley's eyes widened, and she cleared her throat, holding back the speech she might have liked to give him. She

22

moved towards the table before the rising heat hit her cheeks, holding up the shawl in her hand. 'Thank you. I...'

'Happy birthday, again,' Iman interrupted before Ashley could present any form of complaint about the extravagant gift. It had been Tarek's idea after all, but she had chosen the blue shawl intentionally. 'I'm glad you like it.'

'It's beautiful, thank you.'

'Here, try some Shawarma and bread.' Iman filled a small baguette style bread with sliced marinated lamb and held it out. 'Take it.' She pointed at the bowls filled with thinly sliced sweet onions, salad, pickles, and hummus. 'It goes well with those,' she added.

Ashley wrapped the shawl loosely around her neck, followed Iman's instructions, and groaned as the spicy, salty flavours blended with the crisp, fresh salad on her tongue. 'Wow, this is amazing.' She swallowed and took another large bite of the baguette. Iman's smile, revealing bright white teeth against her naturally tanned skin, left Ashley with partly chewed food stuck, refusing to budge no matter how hard she tried to swallow. She started to splutter and raised the back of her hand to her mouth. Taking the glass of water Iman offered, she sipped and swallowed until the lump had squeezed its way down her throat. 'Thanks,' she said, in a broken voice, her face flushed.

'It matches your eyes,' Iman said, with a warm smile.

Ashley glanced down at the shawl and smiled. 'Yes, it does.' When she looked up, Iman was busy filling another small baguette and handing it to one of Tarek's crew. Another local. She held the same warm smile and used the same words, and the man added the garnishes to his meat sandwich, just as she had done. There was something about his presence though, his demeanour; the way he talked too casually, with Iman. She couldn't put a label to it, but the tingling sensation riding her spine didn't excite her. She dismissed the feeling and headed into the kitchen, for the fridge. She pulled out a beer, rested the top against the black-marble work surface and hammered her hand down on the metal cap, flicking the lid off and sending it across the floor. Worked every time!

'Hey!' Craig slurred. He must have started on the beer straight after they got back from the base. She smiled at his rosy cheeks and the mismatch with his otherwise unshaven and rugged appearance. 'How ya doin'?' He slugged at the bottle in his hand.

'Good.' Ashley raised her bottle, and he clinked it with his own, downing the last dregs and throwing the bottle into an open bin. He nodded towards the fridge, and she pulled out another beer, flicked off the cap, and handed it to him. Knowingly, they stepped out the back door and onto the patio set back from the house swimming pool.

Craig reached into his pocket, pulled out a pack of Camel cigarettes, and offered one to Ashley. 'So, ya havin' fun?' he asked, holding his lighter at its tip.

Ashley dragged the smoke into her lungs and released it slowly, gazing into the clear night sky at the thousands of bright lights flickering back at her.

'It's an amazing place you know.'

He followed her eyes, swigging from his bottle, blinking, unable to register one star from its neighbour through the alcoholic fog in his mind. 'If ya say so.' He shrugged and beamed a weak smile.

She slapped him on the arm. 'Arse.' She stood in silence, staring up at the stars, the loud chirping of crickets singing in her ears. Strange day. 'Thanks for...'

'Is that Uranus?' he asked, interrupting and pointing into the air somewhere, laughing.

'Funny! In fact, I don't think you could see Uranus right now even if your head was on the other way round.' She threw the cigarette to the ground, elbowed him in the ribs, and walked off. She was still chuckling to herself when she entered the living room.

'Hey boss, happy birthday.' Dan held out a wrapped present with a handcrafted red bow on its top. 'It's from the lads,' he added, his cheeks flushing as he spoke.

Ashley took the gift and smiled at the junior field-technician, who was swiping his long blonde fringe from his face and exposing his baby-blue eyes. 'Thanks Dan.' He nodded his head, smiled, and stared at his feet. Carefully she removed the paper, revealing a hand carved and painted sculpture of an oil rig set in the desert. It could be any one of the rigs she had worked on in Syria.

'That's incredible,' she said, her index finger studying the fine details.

'A guy at the souk did it for us,' he said, with a proud smile.

'It's awesome, thanks.' Ash held up the statue, turning it, watching the colours shift as they reflected in the dim light.

'Happy birthday,' Dan reiterated. He bobbed his head again, turned sharply, and scuttled off to the group of men in the corner of the room. Increasingly-raised voices, jeers and challenges, filled the room, as alcohol fuelled the multi-national group's passionate debate over the on-going football World Cup, in Paris. With a strong contingent of French and English expats, that debate would continue deep into the night.

Ashley placed the gift on the low table and she glanced around the room, her eyes settling on Iman clearing away the food table. When Iman looked up and smiled, she couldn't stop the fire that instantly infused her cheeks. She hadn't realised she had been staring. She brushed her hands down her white t-shirt for want of something better to do with them. 'Can I help?' Ash mouthed the words across the short space, her eyes tracking the food table to add clarity to the unspoken message.

The word no and a shaking head came back at her, so she squeezed her hands into her pockets and stood, rocking on her feet. She sighed. She couldn't let Iman do all the work. She stepped across to the table, picked up a triangular cake and popped it into her mouth, groaning at the sweet, nutty taste, grabbing a napkin and wiping her lips. 'Mmm, these are delicious,' she said.

'I'm glad you like them,' Iman said with a warm smile, though her soft voice sounded tired. She had considered becoming a trained chef a while ago, but something had stopped her. Maybe one day.

'Can I help you? I can't let you do all this on your own.'

'No, it's your birthday, and anyway, that wouldn't be right.' The forthright tone gave the impression that for Ash to help would be an insult.

Ash picked up another sweet cake and started to nibble. If she wasn't allowed to help, then the least she could do was show her appreciation for the food and eat it. 'Did you make all of these?' she asked, her arm sweeping across the display.

Iman's eyes lowered while her hands worked, piling up plates and emptying the serving trays. 'Yes,' she said, picking up the large stack of used dishes, and carrying them effortlessly through to the kitchen.

Ash swallowed another delightful sweet and wiped her hands on a napkin. She didn't want to offend Iman but was feeling deeply uncomfortable at watching and doing nothing. 'It's excellent,' she said, as Iman returned. 'There's going to be a very lucky man out there.' The words were out before she considered censoring them and she winced.

Iman held her gaze, but something subtle, intangible, reflected through the light dancing in her eyes. Hurt?

'Sorry, I didn't mean to... Your brother said...' Ash cringed as she continued to dig a deep hole in which she wanted to bury herself. Why the fuck was she having this conversation anyway? Well, it wasn't a conversation because it was currently one way. She was only repeating Tarek's words, trying to fill the space her discomfort had created. Words that had infuriated her just a couple of hours earlier: words that now flowed uncensored from her mouth. *What the fuck!* The idea that Iman, or any other Syrian woman, could only marry a man, and often an arranged union at that, was beyond her comprehension, so why the fuck was she repeating a proposition she would violently oppose?

'I love cooking. It's my passion,' Iman responded. The smile that formed, and the soft focus in her eyes, went some way to easing Ash's apparent awkwardness.

Ash stared, captivated by the warmth in Iman's light-brown irises.

'You're very good at it,' she said, the words broken, and her mouth dry.

'Maybe.' Iman continued to hold Ash with curiosity.

Ash broke away from the intense gaze and stared at her fingers, picking at her nails. 'Right, I'd better be off. Early start tomorrow,' she said.

'Yes, of course.' Iman lowered her eyes to the table her hands were resting on. She would be preparing breakfast in less than four hours from now.

'Right... see you tomorrow then.' Ash was already staring at the door she was about to dive through.

'Yes. I hope you had a lovely birthday Ash.'

The words halted her. There was something in the tone. 'I did, thanks.'

Dashing out the door, she almost fell into the street, her heart racing. She'd only taken two beers and hadn't even finished the first one. The balmy night air was doing nothing to help her to breathe. She stood for a while, trying to settle the jittery feeling, heightened by the burning sensation low in her belly.

Approaching her house, she frowned. She didn't remember leaving on the ground floor light. The door squeaked when she pushed it open, but its voice was nowhere near as loud as the scream that came from the redhead standing at the kitchen sink, followed by the sound of glass smashing on the stone-tiled floor.

'Kate!' Ashley shrieked, joining the cacophony gripping the small space. Goose bumps prickled her skin, and her knees momentarily refused to hold her body up. Her jaw opened, but no other words came out. She gulped in the air instead, and her head shook from side-to-side. No, no, no!

'Jesus Ashley, you scared the shit out of me.'

'I… um…' Ashley would have helped to pick up the glass but her hands were shaking, and she couldn't move.

Kate was standing taller and smiling now. 'Sorry, I'm sure I must have freaked you out too. Is there a dustpan and brush anywhere?' she asked, softly.

Ashley pointed to the cupboard under the sink and stood rooted to the spot, stunned by the frantic clearing up that was now taking place in front of her.

'There, no harm done.' Kate tipped the glass into the bin and returned both pan and brush to their place under the sink. 'I was just getting a drink,' she explained, stating the obvious. 'I found the spare room. I hope you don't mind. I'm meant to be living at number one, but there's a problem with the water and… and Lars sends his apologies … I hope you don't mind… It shouldn't be for long.' Her eyes scanned the ceiling as she rambled apologetically.

Ashley removed her thumb and finger from the bridge of her nose and stopped shaking her head. 'What are you doing here Kate?' Her glare seemed to escape Kate's notice.

'I took a job, Ash.'

Kate's smile caught her off guard. It wasn't the smug, conceited smile of one person getting something over on another. It was more compassionate, vulnerable even. Ashley let out a deep sigh. The anxious jittering of moments ago had turned into a full-scale war, and she felt close to throwing up. 'It's late. I need to get to bed.' She turned swiftly and started to climb the stairs, stopped momentarily by the words that followed her.

'Happy birthday, by the way.'

She had no control of the moan that escaped. She took another two steps and stopped again. 'Thanks.' The word came out wearily, edged in defeat.

4.

Ashley walked swiftly down the food counter, grabbed a pastry and a coffee, and stepped straight out the back door of the restaurant. At 5.30am, it would be another half-hour or so before the place started to fill with hungry expats, and if she timed it right, she could get through breakfast without having to face, or interact with, Kate.

She rested the pastry on a napkin on the window ledge and stood with her back to the wall, closing her puffy eyes into the sun. The warmth helped. She leaned her head forward, opened her eyes, and sipped at the hot drink, wincing as the bitterness hit the back of her tongue. The view from the building was technically the same as yesterday; only she wasn't. She spied through the dust-coated window back into the restaurant. Still empty. She spotted an army of ants hastily heading for the pastry, picked it up quickly and took a large bite, finding it hard to swallow. No matter how she might be feeling, she needed to eat, or she wouldn't last five minutes at the base. Her work was too physically demanding to punish herself by abstaining from food. A slug of coffee softened the pastry, and its sweetness made the bitterness more tolerable. Perfect.

Movement caught her eye, and she froze. As her brain registered who it was, she released the breath that had stopped mid-flow and leaned back into the wall. The door behind her opened and Craig stepped out, coffee in one hand and a cigarette hanging from his lips. He had it lit within half a second of being on the outside.

'Mornin',' he grunted, his tone thick with the after-effects of excessive drinking and cigarettes. He sucked on the cigarette between his lips and started coughing. 'That's better,' he jested, as he pulled it from his mouth and sipped at his hot drink.

'Late one then?' Ashley said grinning at the state of her friend.

'Looked in the mirror this mornin', have we?' he chuckled, nodding towards Ashley's face. The dark rings supporting her puffy eyes could easily compete with his bloodshot-eyes and grey skin-tone. She'd win hands down.

'Should've stayed til the end eh?' She wasn't joking.

'Can't handle it now yer old,' he teased.

'Fuck off,' she laughed, swallowing the last piece of pastry, and finishing her coffee. Pointing her hand in his direction, she wiggled her fingers at him. He reached into his pocket and handed over the packet. Placing the end against the red tip, she drew off Craig's cigarette to light her own. 'Thanks.'

'So, what ya doin' eatin' out here?' he asked.

'Getting some fresh air.' She inhaled the smoke and blew it up into the sky above her head, coughing at the irony. 'Can we get going early today?' she asked.

'Yup, I'm ready t' go.'

'You not eating then?'

'Already eaten.'

Ashley's eyes widened. She hadn't been aware of Craig eating in the restaurant, and if she hadn't noticed him, she could easily have missed seeing the woman she was trying to avoid. Kate! She peeked through the window, her eyes darting around the room. 'Right, let's go,' she said. She stomped the barely touched cigarette into the ground and pushed Craig through the door. 'I'll get us another coffee for the road.'

Craig couldn't resist grabbing a handful of pastries as he passed the counter and had started chomping on them before he got to the car door. Munching on the last bite, he turned the ignition and revved the engine.

Ashley placed the drinks in the cup-holders and belted up. 'Let's go.'

He slammed his right foot down on the accelerator, and the 4x4 lumbered out of the car park and into the relatively quiet city street. 'Hey, that reminds me.'

'What does?'

'I meant t' ask yesterday, but with yer birthday 'n' all.'

'What?'

'When we fixin' t' build our raft? We ain't got long.'

Ashley curled up her nose and hummed. 'This weekend?' she offered.

Craig nodded, keeping his eyes on the road. 'You reckon we'll be called to the rig soon?' she asked.

'Well, unless they fuck somethin' up, kit'll be mobilised early to mid-week.'

'Good.' The word came out more assertively than she had intended, drawing Craig's eyes.

'Yeah, can't wait, eh?' he responded in a tone lacking sincerity. He slammed his hand on the car horn, cursing at a battered yellow taxi that threatened to move out in front of them, and Ashley glared at him questioningly. He ignored her. 'So, ya thought of a design?' he asked, with enthusiasm.

'Barrels and planks,' she offered, with a grin that spanned her face, breaking into a chuckle.

'Well ain't ya the genius. How 'bout somethin' more sophisticated? We're gonna win this year.'

'Barrels and planks won last year.' She shrugged, studying the blue water of the Euphrates as they crossed the bridge. Her eyes settled on a specific spot in the river, and she started laughing. 'You were going to win last year, right before we sank... over there.'

Craig glanced across, his face alight, beaming with excitement. 'Fuckin' good effort though,' he laughed.

'Without the barrels you mean?' He slapped her on the arm, and they were still laughing about the dire state of their barrel-less raft when he pulled the vehicle into the base. 'We'll do it properly this year,' she said with a wink, skipping out of the vehicle and heading for the workshop.

*

'Can I help you?'

Katherine had stood observing the food for some time, and already passed by several hungry workers. She looked up, her breath hitching at the light-brown eyes smiling softly from across the counter. 'Umm, it all looks so delicious,' she said.

'What flavours are you looking for?'

Interesting! Katherine held Iman's gaze, assessing her, entranced by something that passed between them. The cook's hair sat tied at the back of her head, but she figured it probably relaxed below her shoulders: flowing, light auburn, and slightly wavy. Her tanned skin wasn't the dark colour of Middle-eastern or even South American skin, nor was it the rugged, suntanned, southern European look. Its tone was subtle, and her skin the texture of fine porcelain, delicate, but not fragile. She seemed a lot taller than most other Syrian women at about five-feet-six-inches and carried herself well. She certainly didn't look as though she belonged in a kitchen.

'Sweet, or savoury?' Iman asked.

The soft smile, seemed to be directed at her, and the woman's full lips, were captivating. Katherine faltered, gave her attention to the question and the food options in front of her, and hastily selected the familiar fried eggs, pita bread and what looked like a stew of some sort.

'That's eggplant,' Iman said, noticing the frown on Katherine's face as she picked up the dish. 'And I can recommend this... for after your meal.' She handed over a saucer with two small biscuits coated in icing sugar. 'I'm Iman by the way.'

'Umm, thank you. Katherine, or sometimes Kate,' she added, smiling hesitantly.

'And which do you prefer?' Iman asked. Katherine looked from the eggs to the biscuits. Iman started to chuckle. 'Which name?'

'Oh, umm, Kate is fine. Thanks for the recommendation,' she said, indicating to the food.

'You're welcome. Enjoy your day, Kate.'

'You too.' Katherine slid her tray down the rails to the coffee machine. The after effects of her interaction adding to the natural heat that already had her breaking into a sweat. She filled a mug and sat at the now familiar table behind the pillar, bit into a biscuit and groaned. *Wow!* The sweet almond melted on her tongue and the intense flavour lingered in the back of her throat, teasing her senses with ecstasy. She groaned again, unaware that pairs of eyes watched quizzically from around the room. She flushed, picked up her coffee, and sipped repeatedly. 'Food's excellent here,' she said, to no one in particular.

Iman's smile deepened as she observed the new woman enjoying breakfast. She turned away and stepped back into the kitchen, empty serving dishes in hand.

*

Ashley waved her arm, guiding the choke manifold into position. 'You got it!' she shouted, giving a thumbs-up to the forklift driver. He lowered the equipment to the floor watched by Ashley's keen eye.

Craig approached from the other side of the bay and scrutinised the metal structure, paperwork in one hand and a bottle of water in the other. 'How's it lookin'?'

'All good,' Ashley responded, but her attention was still with the equipment.

It was Lars Eriksen's voice projecting, as the man himself did at six-feet tall, above the drilling and grinding of metal ringing out around the workshop that took her attention from the task at hand. But, it was the intensity in the bottle-green eyes of the redhead by his side, staring directly at her, that caused her stomach to flip and her attention to wander.

In an instant, Katherine looked away. 'Hello Craig, how are you?' She held out her hand, stepping towards the Texan who towered above her.

'Katherine,' he said, in a cheery tone, taking the offered hand but also moving in and kissing her affectionately on the cheek.

Katherine flinched at the touch of his rugged face on her soft skin but continued to smile.

Ashley slunk behind the control panel, snuck to the left, and made her way to the workshop where she could remain out of sight.

'I'll leave you to it then,' Lars interjected, wiping at the sweat that was sliding down the side of his face. He turned and strode off in the direction of the air-conditioned offices. The base offices were a far cry from his office in Damascus, but even they were luxury compared to the oppressive heat inside the workshop.

Spying through a small gap in the rack of steel-pipes, Ashley pondered what might have attracted Craig and Kate to each other. To all intents and purposes, they were complete opposites, and not just regarding their height differences. Katherine was far too prim and proper for his rugged, and rough, character. Maybe that was it. Perhaps that's why it worked. Craig was laughing, and Katherine kept touching his arm as she spoke. She'd never seen Craig look so enamoured by anyone.

She sighed, stepped back from her vantage point, and leaned against the workbench. Tarek's tight smile held questions she had no intention of answering. She recoiled, pushed away from the bench, and raced out the nearest door. Skulking across the site to the base canteen, she removed the safety hat that was pressing too hard against her skull and wiped the cuff of her sleeve at the sweat on her cheeks. She stepped through the door and grabbed a cup of water, downing it in one long gulp. She poured another, sat directly under the air conditioning unit, and closed her eyes. Perhaps the cold air would bring her to her senses. Kate was history. Kate was...

'Can I get you anything?'

Ashley jumped, opened her eyes, and sat bolt upright. Squinting to focus, she rose to stand. She had at least two inches on the cook, but Iman's stature made her appear taller.

'It's okay you don't need to get up. I can get you something.'

The soft tone did nothing to slow Ashley's racing heart. 'I'm fine, thanks,' she said.

Iman smiled. 'I have another hour before I go back to the hotel,' she said. 'A cup of tea?'

'Sure, thanks.' Ashley never drank tea, but it hadn't occurred to her to refuse. Her eyes lingered on Iman's back as she floated into the kitchen.

Moments later Iman returned with a white china pot and two cups. 'It's my break time too,' she said.

'I don't want to take up your time,' Ashley blurted, starting to stand again.

'Sit, please,' Iman said, taking the seat across the table from Ashley and starting to pour.

Hesitantly, Ashley sat back down. She took the drink and sipped. 'Mint!' she exclaimed.

'Yes.' Iman started to laugh. 'You don't like mint?' she asked.

'Yes, I do. I...' Ashley stopped, spellbound. 'I just hadn't expected...'

'Would you like to go to the souk one day?' Iman interrupted. Heat rose to her cheeks instantly, and she opened her mouth as if to speak again.

'The Deir ez-Zor market?' Ashley asked before Iman could retract the offer.

'Yes. I thought you might like to see the shawl shop... and the other stalls of course.' Iman flustered, puzzled by her physiological response to the offer that had just popped out of her mouth.

Ashley paused and smiled. 'Umm.' She had been to the souk many times with her work colleagues, but the idea of going with Iman; that would be a very different experience.

'It's okay if you don't want to,' Iman offered. She sipped her tea and refilled their cups.

'No. I'd like to. Maybe, when we get back from the rig?' Ashley lowered her eyes to the drink and raised the cup to her lips.

Iman cleared her throat. 'When do you go?'

'I don't know, late next week maybe.' Iman nodded. 'We're building a raft tomorrow... for the annual raft race next month,' she added, unsure why she was telling Iman, but enthused by the act of sharing the details with her.

Iman's irises had shifted to a light golden-brown, and she studied Ashley carefully. 'You're excited about the race.' It was a statement rather than a question.

Ashley could feel the heat rising and colouring her cheeks. 'It's great fun,' she said. 'All the oil companies here take part,' she added.

'Yes, we usually cater for it, apparently.'

Ashley lowered her head. 'Maybe you could be on our team this year,' she said. She sat back in her seat, confused by the ease with which she was talking and suddenly including Iman in their race plans.

'Maybe,' Iman said, but her smile said no.

Ashley's stomach lurched, and she gulped down the last of her tea. 'Right, I'd better get back to work, or I'll get fired,' she said with a half-grin, trying to recover from the disappointment of the slight rejection.

Iman rose effortlessly to her feet, stared at Ashley intently for a moment, and then smiled softly. 'Ah, you're teasing me about being fired.'

Ashley winced and stuffed her hands into her coveralls' pockets. 'I didn't mean to offend you,' she said, the desire to fidget pricking her conscience.'

'None taken.'

Ashley's eyes were drawn to the light shimmering on Iman's face, highlighting her delicate bone structure and elegant features. She swallowed past the lump in her throat. 'Thanks for the tea,' she said, her voice slightly broken.

'Will you be in for dinner later?'

Ashley opened the door, allowing a rush of heat to suck the cooler air out of the large dining hall. 'Yes, I'll be starving,' she said, smiling.

Iman's cheeks flushed and when she grinned her eyes shone. She picked up the cups and stepped into the kitchen.

Ashley watched until she could no longer see the cook's back, turned to face the yard, and released the breath she had been holding. She found herself striding to the smoking area. A cigarette would ease the pressure in her chest. A warm feeling infused the beaming smile that she landed on Craig, as he approached.

'Uh huh, where d' you skulk off to?' he asked, opening his pack of cigarettes. He placed two of them between his lips and lit them together, handing one to Ashley.

'So, all good in there?' she asked, taking the cigarette, ignoring the question. 'Got a happy boss?'

'Seems so.' He sucked in the smoke and breathed out slowly. 'They're mobilisin' mid-week, so, we'll be out Thursday. Better get that raft built darn quick. I got a plan.'

Ashley laughed, releasing the tension that had accumulated. 'Right, I look forward to seeing that then.' Her sarcastic wit didn't go unnoticed, and he thumped her on the arm.

'It's in my head,' he defended.

'It's easy.' She drew down on the cigarette. 'Empty sealed barrels and planks across the top,' she said, through the smoke clearing her lungs.

Craig frowned. 'Wasn't there one like that last year?' He drew on his cigarette, tilted his head, puffed out small rings, and blew them into the blue sky.

'Yeah… it won.' Ashley laughed.

'Can we have a flag?' he asked, after a moment's contemplation.

'Good idea, you design that.'

He stomped his cigarette into the dirt. 'What's wrong with my raft designs anyway?' he asked.

'They don't work,' she said, with a shrug.

He pushed her through the door into the workshop. 'Get that separator checked 'n' the lab cabin restacked,' he teased. He could never assert his authority with her.

'Aye, aye captain.' She saluted, still laughing.

Craig was chuckling too.

*

Ashley tilted her head, allowing the citrus-scented suds to sweep away the sweat and grime that had clung to her body all day. Even though she wasn't on the rig, which was hotter than hell, there was always the aroma of petroleum and grease: locked into the equipment, clothing, and even her skin. It wasn't particularly offensive; it just seemed to be omnipresent no matter how hard she scrubbed. Stepping out of the shower, she tried to suppress a yawn but failed, her legs and arms still heavy from the day's work. She rubbed the towel over her hair and held the soft pile against her tired eyes.

Tap tap tap. She groaned at the disturbance, wrapped the towel tightly around her body, and half-opened the door.

Kate's dark green eyes widened, and she tried to avert her gaze. 'Sorry, I...' She stopped speaking. 'I... umm...'

Ashley shivered. 'You, what?' Her tone was curt.

Kate blinked, forcing the words to come. 'I wondered if you wanted to talk; to catch up.' She lowered her eyes from Ashley's bare shoulders, only to have them settle on the athletic legs exposed by the small towel. She tried to swallow, but her throat wouldn't comply.

'Why?' The response landed with a thud.

Kate held her gaze. *Had she hurt her so badly?* Ashley's eyes were as dark as her face was pale. The flat stone-features seemed to create an impenetrable barrier that ripped into Kate's heart. She looked away, seeking something upon which her eyes could be distracted; something that would stop the tears from flowing. She turned to face Ash again, her dark green irises lightened by the sheen of water on their surface. 'Please?'

Ashley sighed, started to roll her eyes, and then stopped. 'Fine, I'll be down in five.'

Kate nodded slowly, turned, and started down the stairs.

Ashley closed the door and released a deep breath. With her heart thumping in her chest, she hurried into her jeans and pulled on a t-shirt. Looking into the mirror, ruffling her hair, the inverted words, Fuck me, reflected back at her. Fuck no! She ripped the t-shirt off and pulled out a red shirt. Not her favourite but the only one in her wardrobe that didn't need ironing. By the time she stepped out of her room, her cheeks had a healthy glow and beads of sweat lingered at her temples. She stood momentarily, allowing her pulse to settle, before slowly making her way down the stairs.

'Coffee?' Kate asked, facing the sink, her back to Ashley's footsteps.

'Sure.' Ashley stood in the doorway leaning against the frame her mind telling her to steer clear, her body screaming for something far more dangerous. She pocketed her shaking hands and dropped her eyes to the floor. 'Sorry. I didn't mean to be...'

Kate turned slowly, her eyes puffy, her lips swollen. 'I guess I deserve it,' she said, her voice heavy with the tears she had shed. It had been years ago. Yes, their time together had been intense, and yes she had ended it suddenly, and without explanation when Ash finished Uni. But when she accepted this assignment knowing Ash would be one of her engineers, she had done so expecting the past to be long since dead and buried. How wrong could she be?

Ashley couldn't stop herself. Compelled to stop the pain in Kate's eyes and driven by the fire in her belly, she crossed the space between them and pulled Kate into her arms. She squeezed her, held her tightly, and lightly kissed the top of her head. 'I'm sorry,' she whispered.

Kate clung on to Ash's narrow waist and rested her cheek into the firm breasts behind the crisp cotton shirt. 'You smell good,' she said, sniffling.

'Must be the Envy for Men.' The light drawl had both women jumping apart. Craig looked from one to the other. 'I take it ya two know each other then,' he said, addressing Ashley. He wasn't smiling, and his frown looked distant, betrayal reflecting through his eyes.

Ashley brushed at the damp patch on her shirt and cleared her throat. She tried to hold his gaze. 'Long story,' she said, with a strained smile.

His head sat at a tilt as he mused. 'Ah huh,' he said, in a sombre tone. He ruffled his hair then scratched at his stubble. 'Anyway, I was wonderin' if ya wanna get t' fixin' that raft tonight, but I'm guessin' not.' His eyes skipped around the room, not stopping on either woman until eventually, they locked onto the door he'd just walked through.

'I'm knackered bud.' Ashley spoke softly, drawing his eyes to her. 'Tomorrow first thing,' she offered, her smile widening.

Katherine watched the interaction between the two engineers in silence.

'Ah huh,' he responded, pulling himself up to his full height and putting on a brave smile. 'Y'all have a good night,' he said, turning and heading out the door.

Ash turned back to see Kate standing open-mouthed, her hand resting over her heart. 'You'll get stuck in that pose,' she said, trying to lighten the tone.

'There's something I need to explain,' Kate said.

'I think there's a lot you need to explain.' Ash responded. 'Beer?'

'Do you have gin?'

Ash nodded. In silence, she pulled out two tumbler glasses and made them both a long drink. 'Garden?'

Kate flushed at the strong shoulders, the platinum blonde bob sitting on the red collar, and the woody scent that seemed to make even the red shirt seem alluring.

*

Iman stood in the kitchen, peeking through the porthole out into the restaurant. Niomi was leaning over the food station, one leg firmly grounded, the other bent at the knee, toe to the ground, swaying back and forth. Zack's white teeth gleamed, and his deep sky-blue eyes sparkled. He looked transfixed. Niomi's head and shoulders bobbed up and down when he laughed, and she tilted her head as he spoke. After the fifth worker asked him to move so they could reach the food that his body obscured, he shifted along the counter, his cheeks rosy, and his eyes never leaving Niomi.

Niomi turned, coming face-to-face with Iman's wide eyes on the other side of the glass. She pushed open the door and entered the kitchen, forcing Iman to step back. 'What?' Her tone was sharp, and her posture stiffened as she pushed past Iman's questioning gaze.

Iman studied her friend carefully. Niomi, flushed cheeks, was busying herself, and deliberately avoiding eye contact. 'You like him.' It was a statement of fact.

Niomi's shaking hand released the knife onto the chopping board, and she raised her damp eyes. 'You can't tell anyone,' she pleaded.

'What about Joram?'

Niomi's eyes skittered around the kitchen, the absence of a smile conveying the weight in her heart.

'You're not in love with Joram are you?' Iman said softly, stepping closer, taking Niomi's hands and squeezing them tenderly.

Niomi couldn't stop the tears from sliding down her cheeks. 'No,' she sniffled.

'Sshhh.' Iman cupped her face close to her own. 'No one must find out,' she whispered. Her eyes were stern, and

43

her voice determined, but the tenderness in her hands reflected the compassion she truly felt. She brushed her thumbs softly under Niomi's eyes, sweeping away the tears, and released her. 'Let's work,' she said.

'Thank you,' Niomi said sheepishly.

Iman sighed, but her gut was twisting uncomfortably. She cleared her throat, put on a smile, and carried a dish of fresh salad and basket of flatbreads out to the counter. Her heart stopped at the sight of Ash and Kate entering the restaurant. Her knees weakened, and she instinctively grabbed at the countertop for support. Turning swiftly, she dived back into the kitchen and leaned against the door panting for breath. *What is wrong with me?* She flapped a hand frantically in front of her flaming face.

'Everything okay?' Niomi asked, her eyes wide with concern.

Iman cleared her throat, brushed her clammy hands down the front of her uniform, and then brought them up to her face. 'Yes, I'm fine,' she lied, releasing her hands from her temples and rubbing furiously at her cheeks.

There was no way she could explain to Niomi. Niomi wouldn't understand. She didn't even comprehend it herself. She'd had to work so hard to control the overwhelming feelings that had emerged as she and Ash had sat and drank tea together at the base earlier. It was like nothing she had ever experienced before, ever. The light-headedness had sent her dizzy and unable to think straight. The butterflies doing somersaults in her stomach had also made it difficult to concentrate on anything but the intense blue eyes staring back at her. And, the burning low in her private parts, that had caused her to want to reach out and touch the engineer, had been close to unbearable. None of it had made any sense. She couldn't stop herself from staring at Ash. She didn't want to stop. Ash's dark-blue eyes seemed to speak to her in a language she didn't have words to express.

Just now though, seeing Ash with Kate, an entirely different emotional response had emerged, and a not altogether comfortable one at that. Her heart pounded in her chest, and her hands were shaking. She rubbed them together, trying to gain her composure. 'Are you okay?' she asked Niomi, with a forced smile, needing a distraction from the bewilderment.

Niomi nodded vacantly, too entranced by her worries to notice the depth of Iman's anguish.

'Let's make some biscuits,' Iman said.

5.

Soft melodic voices eased Ashley into wakefulness, but her lids refused to open. She listened; captivated by the chanting that brought the sunlight with it every day and broadened the smile on her face. Eventually, the sounds died away, and she stretched out on the bed, groaning as she eased the tightness in her legs and shoulders. *We've got a raft to build.* She jumped out of bed, into the bathroom, and stood briefly under the cool shower. The smile suddenly dropped from her face as an image of Craig standing in her kitchen doorway the previous evening appeared in her mind's eye. She would have to talk to him about her and Kate, but she hadn't given any thought as to how she would approach that particular conversation.

She searched through her clothes, picked out a plain black t-shirt and threw it over her wet hair, then pulled on her jeans and work-boots. She'd change into her coveralls at the base. At least the base would be abandoned today so they could relax protocols a bit and, more importantly, take a cool-box of beer with them.

Opening the front door, she was struck by the heat and by the time she reached the restaurant she was wiping beads of sweat from her hairline.

'It's going to be hot today.' Iman said, with a welcoming smile.

'Yep, and we'll be out there building a raft.' Ash responded, her eyes rising in her head at the insanity of it, while sporting a broad grin that conveyed the excitement of a child about to explore.

'What can I get you?' Iman asked, hoping to entice Ash to stay for breakfast.

'Umm.' Ash pondered briefly and then shook her head. 'Just coffee for now,' she said, moving swiftly down the counter.

Iman watched Ash pour a large mug, stride across the restaurant, and take the exit to the rear. Her heart sank at the emotional distance she sensed between them, rooting her feet to the spot.

'Mornin'!' The chirpy drawl interrupted her thoughts.

'Morning Craig, what can I get you?' she asked, staring at the tall man, her irises darker than usual and her tone lacking the jovial resonance of just moments earlier.

'Ya good?' he asked, scanning the counter, licking his lips.

'Yes. Thank you,' she said, swiftly shaking the disappointment from her mind, clearing her throat, and concentrating on the food in front of her.

'How 'bout some o' special eggs o' yours?' he asked, putting on his best doe-eyed grin.

His cheery disposition went some way to break the spell binding her, and she smiled warmly. 'Yes of course. I'll bring them out to you.'

'Thanks.' He was already filling a mug of coffee and adding three sugars. He took the drink and stepped out the back door.

'Hi,' Ashley said, trying to sound normal but failing as the short word came out with a slight croak. She drew down on the roll-up.

'Mornin!' He pulled out a cigarette and was quickly engrossed in his first smoke of the day.

'So, you ready to build?' she asked. He seemed to be behaving like his usual cheery self, thankfully! Perhaps she wouldn't need to talk about Kate after all. She sipped at her drink.

'Hell yeah,' he said, his face beaming with excitement.

Ashley smiled. 'Great.'

'I got a real good plan,' he said, raising his index finger to his temple.

She rolled her eyes. 'That's us fucked then,' she said, with a half-laugh.

He slapped her on the arm. 'You eatin'?' he asked, tilting his head towards the restaurant.

Ashley stomped on the cigarette butt and blew out the smoke. 'Sure, I'm starving,' she said, following closely behind the tall Texan.

Craig's eyes widened at the large plate of eggs waiting for him on their usual table. He had the fork in his hand and had shovelled a giant heap of the breakfast into his mouth before his bottom hit the seat.

'Smells good,' she said, approaching the counter and filling a plate. She poured another two mugs of coffee and placed them on her tray. By the time she returned his plate was empty. 'Tell me your plan then,' she said, slipping a forkful of food into her mouth. Her hearing stopped suddenly. Savouring the sensations dancing on her tongue, she groaned with pleasure. 'So good.'

47

'Thanks,' he responded, pleased with himself.

'The eggs,' she clarified, chewing on another mouthful.

He tried to look deflated but failed, a crooked smile appearing.

*

'So!'

The simple word stopped Ashley's hand from reaching for the angle-grinder on the bench. She had managed to avoid any conversation en-route to the workshop, sticking instead to mulling over technical aspects of the raft plan, and Craig hadn't given any signs of interest in the previous evening either.

'What?' she said, feigning ignorant.

'Ya gonna spill?'

He continued dragging the heavy barrels into position, but his eyes drilling through her back seemed to drown out the rumbling of metal on the concrete floor. She pulled in a deep breath, released it, and turned to face him. At least the empty workshop meant they could speak freely. His eyes were questioning yet there was warmth there too, and his smile offered more reassurance than criticism. She pulled the angle-grinder from the bench and approached him, resting the machine on the barrel. 'It was a long time ago,' she started.

He nodded, but his eyes remained fixed on hers.

'We met when she was in her first year at Imperial, and I was in my final.'

'Y'all were lovers?'

Ashley held his stare. 'Yes.' The word came out softly, and she lowered her eyes a fraction.

He sucked in through his teeth. 'I fuckin' knew ya fancied her,' he said, wagging his finger in her direction, seemingly more pleased with his accurate assessment than the fact that they had shared the same love interest.

She stared up at him, biting down on her bottom lip. 'So, it doesn't bother you?' she asked, intrigued.

The grin on his face widened, and he flicked his eyebrows up and down. 'Kinda hot,' he responded, starting to laugh.

She balked and frowned, and he winked at her. 'Fuck off,' she said with a broad grin, the penny dropping with a thud. He was teasing.

'You gals,' he said, with a shake of his head. He lifted the grinder off the barrel and plugged it into the electric socket. She could see him still smiling through the protective shield across his face as he flicked the switch. At least it looked like a smile. The grinding noise drowned out any further conversation and sparks flew as metal-cut-through-metal.

Nothing disturbed the silence between them, as Craig shaped the metal strips and welded the barrels together, while Ashley constructed the wooden slats for the top platform of the raft. Standing, she rubbed her lower back. Even though she had dropped the top half of her coveralls to hang freely from her waist, her t-shirt was soaked, and a continuous trail of sweat ran down her temples. She stood back and admired her work. 'Beer?' she shouted, above the drilling, indicating with her hand tipping to her mouth.

Craig gave a thumbs-up with one hand, the other continuing to work the metal pins into position. Turning her back, she started towards the cool-box on the bench, wiping the sweat from her face.

'Ahhhhhhhhh!'

She froze at the piercing-scream that bounced off every wall in the workshop and shot straight through her chest. She turned quickly to assess the damage, knowing before she looked that it wasn't going to be pleasant. Craig didn't shout out like that. He was as tough as they come. 'Fuck! Hang on bud!' she shouted, sprinting to the first aid box and back to

Craig's side. She pulled open the lid with controlled urgency. 'It's okay bud, I got you,' she said, her focused efforts providing the reassurance he needed.

Craig was kneeling, looking up at the workshop roof, his face taut, and his teeth clenched through thin lips. Sweating profusely, puffing hard, and groaning sporadically, he was holding the wrist of his gloved right hand. Through the centre of his palm was a shard of glinting metal. Blood seeping into the heavy fabric, the glove was fast assuming a tighter fit on his hand than it would under normal circumstances.

'It's okay, we got it,' she said, in an authoritative tone. 'It's okay bud, deep breathing... slowly now.' The calming words kept coming in spite of her racing heart. She lifted his hand, steadily cut the glove free and applied soft padding around the exposed metal, taking care not to cause any further pain. Craig screamed out anyway and puffed hard, his jaw tensing with the pressure of his clamped teeth. With the padding in place, she applied a bandage.

Craig paled. 'Thanks,' he said, his body shaking.

'Hold your arm up bud.' She directed his arm across his chest and approached the cool-box. She pulled out a bottle of beer, and water, handing him the water. 'Small sips,' she said. Cracking open the bottle on the side of the bench, she took a long swig of the beer. 'Right, let's get you to hospital,' she said, helping him to his feet.

Craig took two sips of the water then dumped the bottle on the top of a barrel. 'Jeez, open me a beer will ya?' he asked, wincing as a sharp pain shot through his hand. 'Shoot!'

'You shouldn't.'

'Fuck that. I need a beer.'

Ashley frowned, reluctantly opening a bottle and handing it to him. One wouldn't hurt. 'Take it easy bud,' she said, heading out to the 4x4.

Craig swigged hard at the drink and followed her, panting with every step. He eased himself into the passenger seat complaining bitterly, silenced only by his mouth pressing against the bottle and the glugging that followed. 'That's better,' he said, settling into the seat.

Ashley keyed up the engine and eased the vehicle forward, briefly glancing to the side to check the status of her patient. Craig screamed out at the first bump in the road, and she winced. This journey was going to hurt!

He leaned back in the seat, bracing himself against the terrain, moaning at every undulation, the colour steadily draining from his ordinarily ruddy complexion. As they pulled up outside the Deir ez-Zor hospital, he opened the door and almost fell out, immediately vomiting the liquid diet into the gutter. 'Ahhh,' he cried out as his body wretched, sending bolts of lightning through his throbbing hand.

Ashley dashed through the main doors, her wide eyes scanning the space. Spotting what looked like the reception area, she approached the desk. Craig followed her, with an uncharacteristically short stride, holding his arm close to his chest.

The clean-shaven, blue-eyed man, sitting behind the desk tapping on the keyboard, eventually looked up, his eyes bypassing Ashley and stopping at Craig. His unhurried manner, and the fact that he had ignored her, had her blood hitting boiling point. 'We need a doctor,' she insisted, holding back the fire that would have had her jump over the desk and pin him against the wall had she not needed his help.

'Yes, I can see that,' he said, a kind smile appearing probably because some instruction manual had told him he should, though still not looking in her direction. 'Name?' he asked, staring at his screen.

Ashley stiffened.

'It's okay, I got it,' Craig said, softly. He placed his good arm on her shoulder, and she softened.

When she turned away from the irritating man she noticed the other patients in the waiting room, and the medical aroma filling the space. Craig's neatly bandaged injury would most likely put him further down the queue. She sighed.

'Go find us a coffee,' he said. 'I'll sort this out 'n' grab us a seat.' His eyes scanned the room. 'Somewhere,' he added, his face still tense, smiling stiffly.

'Okay.' Ashley looked in all directions for some signage that would indicate which corridor she should take.

'The cafeteria is down that corridor, turn right, and it's on the right.' The administrator was pointing in the direction he referred to with one hand and typing with the other.

'Thanks,' she responded, gruffly.

By the time she returned Craig was ensconced in a chair in the corner of the room, his arm resting across his chest, his long limbs sticking out in front of him. He moved to sit up as she approached and winced. He looked tired. Drained. She handed him the drink and took the only available seat, opposite him.

'Thanks.'

She nodded, craning her neck to check out the status of the other patients and sipping her coffee. 'God this is grim,' she said.

Craig's eyes scanned the room. 'It's not so bad,' he responded.

'The coffee,' she said, pulling a face.

He started to laugh. 'Beer would be better.'

She smiled weakly and nodded.

'Craig Johnson,' a nurse called, drawing the eyes in the room.

'That was quick,' he said, rising carefully to his feet.

Ashley jumped up and followed him to the woman in the white gown.

'Craig Johnson,' she confirmed, studying her clipboard.

'Yup,' they both responded in unison.

She looked up at Craig, across to Ashley and back again, and smiled warmly. 'Follow me please.' Her soft shoes padded on the industrial linoleum and she continued to consult the notes in her hand. Entering a large room containing two rows of cubicles, each booth separated by a thin curtain, she stopped at the third bay on the right and pointed to the single chair. 'Take a seat, please. The doctor will be with you shortly.' She smiled again, turned smartly, and padded out of the room.

Craig sat, moaning.

Ashley lingered in front of him; her hands thrust deeply into her coveralls pockets. They waited, no words passing between them. Entertained only by the conversations taking place around them in a language they didn't understand, the ripping of paper, and the clinking of lightweight metal instruments. Not like the heavy, gross, yet more comforting sounds that spilt out around the workshop. Ashley sighed and fidgeted her feet.

Craig closed his eyes.

Another woman entered the cubical, studying the clipboard in her hand. She pulled the curtain closed behind her. Ashley met her dark assessing gaze and her mousy-brown short hair, momentarily struck by a subtle sense of something familiar.

'You must be Craig,' she said, glancing at the bandaged hand, with a kind smile.

Ashley couldn't place the accent, but she certainly wasn't Syrian.

'I'm Giselle Benoit, one of the doctors here today,' she confirmed. Craig nodded, and she turned her attention to

Ashley. 'I'm sorry we don't allow friends in here while the patient is being treated.' Her chocolate brown eyes held Ashley's with curiosity, but it was the delicate lines that revealed themselves when the doctor smiled that touched something in Ashley.

Ashley's neck started to flush. Doctor Giselle Benoit was a lesbian; of that, she was convinced. A coy smile appeared on her face. 'Okay,' she said, her eyes diverting to Craig. 'I'll see you out there when you're done, bud,' she said.

'I can come and get you when he's patched up,' Giselle offered.

'Thanks doc,' Craig said, breaking the intensity between the two women.

Ashley nodded, winked at Craig, and strode out to the waiting room. *Looks like you're in safe hands bud.*

6.

Katherine paced around the kitchen, taking small sips from the tumbler of water she had just poured. They should have been back just after lunchtime at the latest, and it was fast approaching six-thirty. The idea that something might have happened to them caused her knees to weaken and her breathing to shallow. An image of Ashley lying hurt somewhere in the desert played out in her mind. She chastised herself for agonising over the ridiculous and massaged her forehead with her index finger and thumb. Of course, they would be fine; Ash would be okay. Both engineers were competent and knew this territory better than she did. Why then was her stomach churning? Why hadn't she been able to settle her mind to the work she had planned to finish? Why hadn't they answered the phone when she called to check on them? Even swimming hadn't relaxed her. She walked through to the living room window and searched the road that separated the short distance between the expat houses and the hotel. Pacing again, she sipped the water, keeping vigil.

When the 4x4 eventually pulled up outside Craig's house, Kate ran frantically towards the opening car doors. Flustering and floundering, she tried to approach the last few steps with some semblance composure, but her feet were moving too quickly, and she tripped, throwing herself into Ash's path. Her heart raced and she struggled for breath. Scrambling to retrieve her full height of five-feet-six inches, she stared at the two frowning faces gazing back at her.

'Jesus Kate, are you okay?' Ash asked, scanning the flushing redhead for injuries. Reaching out, she placed an arm on her shoulder.

'What's happened?'

Kate was shaking, fighting the tears welling in her eyes, and challenged by a mouth refusing to comply with her mind's instructions. 'You're late,' she blurted.

Ash recoiled from the contact. She hadn't realised they were on a stopwatch, and it hadn't been her choice to spend the best part of her day in the emergency department of the local hospital. An image of the kind doctor brought a smile to her face, and her shoulders relaxed. At least there had been one benefit.

'Sorry, that came out badly. I was worried about you both. And judging by that.' Her eyes locked onto Craig's bandaged hand, housed in a sling around his neck. 'I'd say, my concern was justified,' she complained, shaking her head back and forth as she spoke. 'What on earth have you done?' she asked.

Craig cowered. Staring at his hand in the sling, he wiggled each finger, one after the other. 'See, works just fine,' he said, looking up, a beaming smile plastered across his face.

'You're supposed to be on the rig in a few days. How's that going to happen?' Katherine's eyes flared light green, and she tussled with her hair. She started to pace and huff.

Craig locked eyes with Ashley, and neither could stop the jiggling in their chest from escaping. They started to laugh then stopped instantly. Katherine was glaring at them both.

'I'll be fine,' Craig interjected before the redhead exploded. 'Doc said I gotta keep it raised for the rest of the day. I got strong painkillers, nothin' broken, and no nerve damage. So,' he said, moving towards Katherine, encasing her under his good arm and pulling her into his chest. 'Everythin' 'll be fine, Katherine.'

'I need a beer,' Ash said, observing Kate as she regained her composure under Craig's natural masculine strength and effortless dominance. Craig was squeezing Kate tightly and rubbing his hand comfortingly up and down her arm. Ashley smiled at the Texan's protective stance.

'Good idea,' he said.

'No,' both women retorted simultaneously.

'You're on pain-killers,' Katherine admonished, pulling out of his grip and glaring at him.

'Fuck that,' Craig grinned. He was already high as a kite on the hospital drugs, and his hand was feeling great. 'Yer place or mine?' he asked, addressing Ashley.

'Mine,' she said, striding down the street and leaving the other two standing.

Craig's good arm still hung around Katherine's shoulder, and he pulled her close again and squeezed. 'I'll be fine,' he said softly.

'You'd better be,' Katherine responded, suddenly dragged along by his long gait as he marched them down the road.

*

Ashley left the front door open and took the stairs two at a time. She stepped into her bathroom, dropped her clothes, and slipped into her bikini. She needed a swim more than she needed a beer. She threw the towel over her shoulder as she descended the stairs and stepped into the kitchen.

Kate's eyes widened. She held out an open bottle of beer but couldn't speak. *Wow!* She slugged at her beer, acutely aware of the growing grin spanning Craig's face. His eyes were fixed firmly on her; more particularly, her reaction to Ash's near naked body. The heat that had caused Kate's skin to wet increased tenfold and she still couldn't find her voice.

'Swim?' Ash asked, taking the beer.

Kate took another slug. The descending liquid collided with her need to breathe, and she coughed violently. Craig moved to help, but she raised her hand and composed herself. 'I've... I...already,' she stuttered.

Craig raised his wounded arm. 'Nu-uh,' he said, swigging from the bottle in his good hand. 'I'll come 'n' watch though,' he said, with a cheeky grin.

Ash stepped into the back garden. Kate followed her, her eyes refusing to budge from the tight butt cheeks that moved seductively with every pace. Craig chuckled to himself, sauntering behind the two women. Ash placed her bottle on the low table, dumped her towel on the lounger next to it, and ran the four paces before taking off and diving into the pool. Kate, and Craig, took a seat at the round plastic table, under the shade of the expansive canopy.

Kate watched Ash swim the full length of the pool underwater. When she emerged, her hair was darker and hanging a little further down the back of her neck. Kate swallowed hard, and her skin flamed.

'Ya like her,' Craig said. 'A lot.'

Kate gulped. 'Is it that obvious?' she asked, her voice yielding to the truth.

Craig held her gaze, and she studied him. His dark-brown eyes seemed lighter than she had remembered them, softer even, revealing tenderness, and concern.

'It's 's clear as the nose on ya face; ya got it bad Kate.' He responded. He swigged from his beer and turned his attention to the movement in the water. 'I can see the attraction,' he admitted with a tilt of his head.

'You like her too?' Kate asked, sitting straighter in the hard plastic seat.

He locked onto her questioning eyes and smiled warmly. 'Not like that no. But she's the best friend I ever had,' he said, suddenly standing. 'There's somethin' 'bout her, a kinda innocence... and that fiery determination. And she's loyal,' he added, heading back to the kitchen.

Kate watched Ash's strong arms cut through the water effortlessly, her lithe body gliding across its surface. Light vibrations warmed her stomach, and she couldn't deny that the lower parts of her body were starting to scream at her. It had been a long time since she had felt this way.

Craig returned; two beers poised between the fingers of his good hand. He pointed one at Kate, and she took it. He plonked the other on the table and sat.

'Ya got married,' he said, matter-of-factly.

Kate looked into Craig's eyes. 'Yes,' she said. 'I got divorced too,' she added quickly, turning her attention back to the pool.

'Ah huh!' he said, softly, noticing Kate's mouth twitch involuntarily. The move was barely noticeable to the naked eye, but something was endearing about the display of vulnerability. He tilted his head to the side and assessed her from a different angle.

'He was the son of my employer,' she continued, her eyes never leaving the body in the water.

Craig slouched into the back of the plastic seat, wriggled trying to get comfortable and grimaced, before sitting back up.

'Rumour had it that I married him to get ahead,' she said. There was more than bitterness in her tone.

Craig's eyebrows rose.

'I married him because I thought it was the right thing to do. It was expected of me.' She rubbed her fingers across her tired eyes and emptied the first beer with a long gulp. 'Turns out I was wrong,' she said, with detachment.

'Did ya love him?' Craig asked tentatively, disorientated by the tightness cutting across his chest. There was something else too, but he couldn't put a word to it.

'I thought I did at the time, but...' She turned to face him, suddenly acutely aware, her eyes dark and distant.

'Didn't mean t' pry,' he said, sensing the discomfort between them.

Her focus switched, her eyes lightened, and a smile started to appear. 'I loved you once too,' she said, in a softer tone. He smiled, but something said he didn't quite believe her.

'Ya's still in love with Ash though,' he said, taking a swig from his beer.

Kate lowered her gaze. 'Aaahhh,' she screamed, leaping up from the seat, swiping at the water that had caught her square in the face.

Ash was laughing, and Craig started chuckling.

Kate brushed frantically at her clothes. 'You...' she yelled, but the tears that were trickling down her cheeks had little to do with the laughter enticed out of her in the moment.

Ashley sprayed the water gun again targeting, firstly Kate, and then Craig.

'Watch the arm,' he pleaded, his eyes scanning the area for something with which to retaliate. A wicked grin appeared on his face as he jumped up and leapt for the high-power water pistol at the side of the pool. 'Shoot!' he cursed as he tried to fill it with one hand.

Ash continued to spray his back. 'Call yourself a cowboy?' she heckled.

He spun around, pointed the automatic weapon, and pulled the trigger. The jet smacked Ash squarely between the eyes before she could duck under the water. She came up spluttering and giggling and got shot again.

A sudden splash caught both their attention. Kate had dived into the pool fully clothed and was heading towards Ash. Ash tried to run, held back by the water's resistance. Kate grabbed Ash's legs, upending her and pulling her under the water.

Craig stood, gun poised, waiting for the two women to emerge, holding back the rumbling in his chest. He released the trigger at the top of the redhead beginning to surface, firing the last of his water, and threw the empty weapon into the pool.

Two heads bobbed up sporting wide grins. Ash pulled her pistol out of the water and fired, firstly catching Craig on the back of the legs, then targeting Kate, who submerged before the water reached her.

'Right, enough,' he shouted, staggering towards the kitchen.

Ashley stood up, suddenly serious. 'You okay bud?'

'Yup,' he said, turning to face her. 'Just the beer chasin' the pills 'round my head,' he said. 'And my hand's throbbin' like fuck,' he added, but he was grinning like a Cheshire cat.

Ash watched until his back had disappeared. When she turned around, Kate's eyes were locked onto her, undressing her skimpily dressed body.

Ash's lips parted, and a surge of energy zipped down her spine, settling low in her belly. She crossed her arms and held onto her shoulders, covering her exposed body. It didn't help. Kate's red hair was hanging loosely down her face; the intensity in her gaze; their history, all calling to her. The desire was running through her, like their first time together, and causing her sex to throb. God, she hadn't felt this strongly in a long time. The sensations intensified with every step Kate took towards her. Ash wanted to move away, but couldn't. Her eyes must have closed because the heat of Kate's breath burning her right cheek caused them to flash open. Any objection she might have presented died before it aired itself, with the touch of Kate's lips pressing firmly against hers.

Kate's heart was pounding in her chest as she wrestled with why this was such a bad idea. Driven by something more profound; something over which she had no control, she had made the contact she had been craving since she had set eyes on Ash that first morning in the restaurant. Her cheek was never going to be enough. She needed the warmth, the familiarity, and the intensity of the kiss. Oh god yes, the fire through her veins was lighting up more than the passionate past they had shared together. Such tender lips: soft and wet. So fucking inviting. Her tongue delved, searched, danced, toyed.

Ash's arms held their position firmly across the front of her body in a vain attempt to claim some semblance of control. Only the water surrounding her was keeping her upright. Kate's hands were cupping her face, tenderly pulling her deeper into the kiss, and she was succumbing to the surges of passion firing in every cell in her body. The groan she elicited was the only invitation Kate needed.

Kate groaned in response. She had missed this. Missed Ash; missed them.

Ash pulled out of the kiss suddenly, her eyes darker than the night sky. She stared, into Kate's dark-green irises, but she wasn't smiling. She backed off, increasing the space between them, clinging to her shoulders, lowering her eyes to the water.

'You okay?' Kate asked, in a tone slightly deeper than her normal resonance. A dark feeling had settled instantly in her gut, and her eyes were burning. 'Sorry,' I shouldn't have kissed you,' she offered, hoping it wasn't what Ash wanted to hear.

'No, it's me. I'm sorry. It's just…'

'I know it was a long time ago. And we can't recreate the past but…'

'No. That's not it. I'm just not sure I'm ready for this,' she indicated between them. 'At least, not yet,' she added, unsure as to why she was leaving the door half open, knowing her body craved release from the sensations Kate had stimulated... but not from Kate.

Kate held out her hand. 'Sorry,' she said. 'Can we be friends?' she asked. She could work with that; give Ash the space she needed. She couldn't cope with losing her, not again! Craig was right; there was something extraordinary about Ashley Roberts. She'd known it at the time they were together too, but she was so much younger then, and frankly, the strength of her feelings had freaked her out. *Fuck!* Those feelings scared her now too, but for an entirely different reason.

Ash took the offered hand and held it firmly. 'Friends,' she agreed, aware that something had shifted between them. Kate's vulnerability was perplexing. She would never have backed down so quickly in the past. The Kate she had known back then, always so vibrant, confident, and so alluring, where was that Kate; the one with whom she had fallen head over heels in love? Yes, the way those green eyes looked at her now still sent her body wild with desire. Hell, she was an easy target for that right now! But beyond those sexual urges, what did they share? She couldn't find the answer. She freed herself from Kate's grasp. 'I'm going to get dressed and then eat. I'd rather do that on my own please.'

Katherine took a step back in the water and glanced towards the pool steps. She had been foolish and taken it too far. 'Sure,' she said, flicking her hands through her hair. She made her way out of the pool, leaving Ash where she stood.

Ash slowly lowered her arms and dangled her fingers in the warm water, gathering her thoughts. She wasn't quite sure what had happened between them, but the last few days suddenly hit her. *It's thirty-five degrees for Christ's sake, why am I shivering?*

7.

Iman placed the finishing touches to the round tin and rested it delicately on the kitchen surface. She peeked through the porthole into the restaurant. Zack was the only worker in the place and even he was in a lot earlier than usual. Breakfast didn't start for another hour. She smiled at the tin, rubbed her fingers across its textured surface, and basked in the warmth that settled lightly in her chest.

'That's beautiful, what's it for?' Niomi asked, reaching across and touching the textured material.

'It's for Ash,' she said, in a dreamy tone, suddenly forgetting herself.

Niomi withdrew her hand, huffed, and looked out the porthole window. She started giggling. 'Zack's such a handsome man, don't you think?' She turned to Iman, her eyes reflecting the vibrancy resonating in her cheeks. The contrast with her response to the tin for Ash couldn't have been more obvious.

An image of Ash appeared in Iman's mind. She instinctively looked over her shoulder and around the kitchen, even though there wasn't anyone else in the room. 'Shhh.'

Niomi's features flattened, and her eyes dulled over.

'You know you can't say those things about him. It's forbidden.'

Niomi's eyes widened, and she glared unrelentingly. 'And...' she flared, unable to hold back. 'What about Ash? I know you've got a thing for her,' she asserted. 'That's forbidden!'

Iman gulped in the humid kitchen air, her hand rushed to cover her mouth, and a surge of blood targeted her cheeks.

'Don't try and deny it. I've seen you looking at her, and all the things you do for her. That is definitely forbidden, Iman.

And, it's unnatural.' She was shaking her head back and forth as she moved to her station in the kitchen. Eyes lowered, she continued preparing breakfast. She had thrown the accusation out of anger, but Iman's response had confirmed what she had hoped wasn't true. She looked up at Iman with dark eyes, unable to bridge the gulf that now sat between them.

The deadly glare from across the room floored Iman. Bells were ringing loudly in her ears, competing with the voices arguing in her head. Her heart pounded, causing her legs to try to fold, and she couldn't move her feet. She reached for the surface and waited to gain her composure. Glancing at the tin, wrapped in the handcrafted patterned cloth, a well of sadness opened in her chest and tears slid down her face. The joy she had experienced seconds ago at the thought of the gift she would give to Ash, had collapsed catastrophically, forming the darkest of all realities. She could never have what her heart desired.

'How could you?' Niomi spat. 'How could you commit such a sin?'

Iman looked up. The water from her eyes had darkened the lashes that housed the hollowness she now felt. She took one careful step and then another, passing Niomi in silence and heading for the restroom.

Niomi shuddered. She'd never seen Iman react in such an emotional way. The kind, gentle, and compassionate Iman, with whom she had been a friend long before Iman had started at the restaurant. Iman, who had supported her, looked out for her, and even helped her learn to cook all those years ago. Whatever the sin, and the pain on her friend's face; she didn't deserve that, surely? Niomi's twenty-four-year-old mind tried to reason with the lessons her parents had taught her, and she started to backtrack. 'I mean...' But, the door had long since closed, and the words didn't reach Iman's ears.

Iman sat on the toilet seat, head in hands, tears streaming down her face. What was she thinking? She wasn't. She hadn't even considered what her feelings meant: the lightness in her heart baking the birthday cake, or her delight making the treats for the party. Not to mention how time seemed to fly-by when she made the cloth wrap for the tin, for Ash to take to the rig. She had started the day filled with excitement at the idea of making all the sweets to go inside it.

It's what friends did for each other, wasn't it?

She hadn't thought of Ash as a lover. Or had she? The sensations flooding her body since she'd first seen Ash at the breakfast counter, on her first day working at the hotel? The heat and the featherlike fluttering that seemed to dance in her belly continually? Secretly, she had dreamed of holding her, sweeping her fingers through the short, sometimes unruly hair, and kissing those soft lips. And, the pounding in her chest as her heart raced when she considered Ash in that way; in a sensual way, surely such love couldn't be a sin?

Niomi punched the dough hard enough that she winced, flipped it over, slammed it onto the table, and punched it hard again. She had heard of women liking women, but she had never thought of Iman being like that. She'd been told that such affections were a disgrace. Iman's parents had always been too liberal, even with Tarek, she'd heard her mother say. Perhaps this is what happens when parents allow too much? What would her parents say about Iman? They would ban her from working at the base and blame the expats, and that would mean she'd never get to see Zack again. What would happen to Iman? She might not agree with her, being that way. Her hands trembled. But Iman was still her friend. Those were her mother's words she had spat at Iman, and for that, she felt ashamed. The thought of Iman being harmed, or even killed flashed through her mind. No. That wasn't right either. She sighed deeply, moulding the bread with a firm hand, trying to think of other people she knew. Other people like Iman. *It is 1998 after all, not the 1800's. Yes, but it is Syria!* She could only think of two: Sami, who did the driving and admin for the base, but his parents had died a long time ago, and Aimar, who had fled the country to work in Fashion somewhere in Europe. Her mind wandered to the women she knew. No one like that came to mind, not even Ashley! *Poor Iman.*

*

Soft knuckles wrapping gently on the toilet door drew Iman away from her sombre thoughts. Disoriented, she opened her eyes and stood from the seat. 'What?'

'I'm sorry,' Niomi whispered from the other side of the door. 'Please come out.' Iman opened the door slowly and presented her puffy eyes and face, but she didn't speak. She looked defeated, the life drained out of her in such a short space of time. Niomi opened her arms, and Iman fell into them, Niomi unconsciously tensing before relaxing and comforting her friend. 'I'm sorry. I didn't realise. You really are... you really do feel something for her.'

Iman remained silent, eased out of the embrace, and moved to the sink. 'Yes, I think I do,' she whispered. She splashed water over her face and patted it dry with a paper hand towel. Her light-brown irises had taken on an entirely different hue, picking up the red from her sore eyes.

'Is she?' Niomi faltered with the words she was trying to say. 'Is she, umm, like that too?'

'Is she into girls? That's what you're asking.' Iman held onto the rising fire that wanted to lash out at the assertion there was something wrong with her, or Ash. She took in a deep breath and held back the tears that were starting to form again. 'I don't know,' she admitted. What were Ash's blue eyes trying to say? The intensity of the look that passed between them, on occasion, what did it mean? The burning in her chest and that other sensation that wouldn't relent; did Ash feel those things too?

'I thought she and Craig were together,' Niomi said, more bluntly than she intended.

The thought sent Iman's stomach into spasm, and her mind whirled with despair. She had hoped the rumour wasn't true and even denied it in her mind. Had she fallen for someone who wouldn't, or couldn't, love her back? Was she just deceiving herself, making a fool of herself? No! She had felt it; of that, she was sure. She took in a deep breath and released it slowly, swallowing back the tears. No! Surely, Ash felt something for her.

Niomi studied Iman for a few moments, touched by the honesty and the raw emotion that exposed her friend. 'Well, if she is, I don't think the red-eyed vampire look will work for her,' she said, trying to be more upbeat. With a coy smile, she broke into a nervous giggle.

Iman turned to face the mirror. Her jaw opened and closed, and she too smiled weakly at her reflection. Her heart felt heavy though, as images of Ash and Craig played out in her mind. Please don't let that be true!

'What will you do?' Niomi asked.

Iman sighed and shrugged. 'Make the sweets and give her the tin,' she said, sighing deeply again. 'Then there's nothing else I can do,' she said, her tone despondent.

'Maybe the feelings will change,' Niomi offered, trying and failing to be of help.

'Do you think your feelings will change towards Zack or any other man you fall in love with?' she asked. There was no malice, just resignation.

Niomi lowered her gaze to her feet and mumbled, 'No.'

Iman puffed out a breath and brushed vigorously at her sore eyes, willing them back to normal. 'Come on. Let's get to work.'

Niomi followed her into the kitchen. Occupying their workstation in silence, they continued to prepare food until the dishes in front of them were piled high. They each grabbed a serving tray and stepped into the restaurant.

Zack stood at the food counter filling another plate of food, grinning. His sky-blue eyes sparkled as he locked onto Niomi's coffee-brown irises. 'Morning,' he said, struggling for the simple word.

'Morning Zack.'

Iman watched the couple. Niomi had responded in a silky, seductive tone that she had never heard before. She studied them as they held each other's gaze with adoration, mirroring each other's movements effortlessly, dancing in tune together. Uplifted by the display of affection, her mind drifted to her interactions with Ash. Had Ash looked at her like that or was she just polite, kind, and considerate? Whatever it was passing between Niomi and Zack, that was something special. And she didn't like the dull ache sitting in her chest and making her world look grey. A well of sadness overcame her and tears sprang into her eyes. She hastily left the serving tray on the counter and returned to the kitchen.

*

'Morning.' Kate's tone was tentative, her eyes searching Ash for any repercussions from the kiss. The kiss that had occupied her thoughts kept her awake for the best part of the night, and sexually frustrated.

'Morning.' Ash refused to look up. What had happened; the kiss, the sensations that had burned long into the night, was all too confusing. She had no intention of

69

bridging the gap that Kate had created by kissing her, and yet, what if she dared to? What if she opened her heart again and followed her desires?

'What?' Kate asked.

Ash looked up, frowning.

'You were shaking your head,' she clarified.

'Oh! Just thinking; it's nothing.'

'Right.' Kate gazed at the ceiling and released a long breath that brought her eyes down on Ash's slightly scruffy hair. 'I'm sorry,' she offered, with a kind smile

'It's okay; I'm sorry too.' Ash looked up, unable to stop her eyes locking onto the green pools holding her gaze. She tried to smile, but it was tight. Forced.

'So, what are you up to today?' Kate asked, changing the focus.

Ash pondered. 'Not sure! You?'

'Well, while you're swanning around here waiting for the client to mobilise the gear, some of us have work to do.' She was trying to be jovial. 'I have a briefing in Damascus. You could come with me. We can do some sightseeing after my meeting, and maybe have lunch?' she said, with enthusiasm.

'I guess...'

'Well, I would appreciate the company. It's four hours each way, and I don't know these roads either.'

Ash assessed her. She seemed genuinely concerned about taking the trip on her own, and probably rightly so. 'Okay.'

Kate beamed. 'Thank you.'

'Breakfast?' Ash asked, turning towards the door. Kate nodded.

'Bloody hell it's hot here.' Kate remarked, wiping at her brow before they had taken two paces outside the front door.

'It's only going to get hotter,' Ash said, staring into the clear sky, the white sun sitting on the hotel roof. 'Wind will pick up later,' she said, pointing to the dust swirling innocuously on the street.

'What makes you say that?' Kate asked, furrowing her brows.

'The dust does this strange thing around here just before the wind gets up.' She perused the skyline. 'And the reddish streaks low on the ground over there.' She pointed towards the open desert to the south.

'Right.' Kate's eyes widened. Syria wasn't anything like Russia.

*

'Mornin' ladies,' Craig chirped, easing his tray along the rails with his good hand, wincing as he moved. At least his arm was out of a sling, but the hospital injection had worn off, and the painkillers were only just taking the edge off the throbbing pain in his hand.

Iman's breath hitched at Ash and Kate's presence, and she turned her attention instantly to Craig's fumbling movements. 'Let me help you.' She put down the serving dish and reached for the plates Craig was trying to pick up, placing them on his tray. 'What happened?' she asked, aware that three pairs of eyes were on her.

'Fought with a piece o' metal,' Craig said.

Iman frowned. 'Looks painful.'

'Nu-uh, the Texan always wins,' he said with a crooked smile that said otherwise.

Iman smiled graciously. 'Eggs anyone? she asked, her heart pounding in her chest as she glanced fleetingly at Ash, before settling uneasily on Kate.

'Yes please,' Ash said.

'Me too,' Kate confirmed.

Craig nodded his affirmation.

'I'll bring them out to you.' Iman had to concentrate hard not to run through to the kitchen, instead, taking her usual pace and stride. Out of view of the restaurant, she breathed deeply until her heart had settled. She couldn't even face Ash without burning up and flustering.

'You gonna need help packing?' Ashley asked, nodding towards Craig's wounded hand.

'Nu-uh, I'm good t' go,' he responded, precariously resting his tray on the table as he stooped, and spilling his mug of coffee. 'Shoot!' he cursed. Ashley threw a napkin at him. 'Four o' everythin',' he continued as he sat and mopped at the tray.

'Four?' Katherine balked.

'One for each week,' he said, nonchalantly. Katherine's nose turned up, and her eyes seemed to move backwards in her head as she scrunched her brows. Craig rolled his eyes, his face twitching with the grin he was holding back.

'Yer so easy,' he teased. 'Anyway, we're not goin' yet. What's the rush?'

Katherine tutted, and then huffed, turning her attention to Ash. She sipped at her coffee, pleasantly distracted by the deep-blue eyes and blonde bob.

'Eggs are coming,' Ashley said, hastily making a space on the table, watching Iman glide across the room, balancing the tray effortlessly.

Iman landed the tray and placed a plate in front of each of them. 'I hope you enjoy your breakfast,' she said, with an honest smile, her eyes skittishly trying to avoid Ash, failing, and holding her gaze.

Kate watched, from Ash to Iman and back again. There was something different about the smile that passed from Iman to Ash, and especially the way Iman's eyes lingered with fondness on her. 'Thank you,' she said, drawing Iman's attention to her. The subtle shift in the cook's demeanour didn't go unnoticed.

'My pleasure,' Iman said.

Kate's concerns disappeared as the delicate aroma merged with the taste sensation that exploded on her tongue. Finely grated zucchini, fresh parsley, chopped onions, and a hint of something she couldn't place. 'This is fabulous.' Something about the cook was indeed, also, very intriguing.

Craig's plate was already empty. 'She sure 's a brilliant cook,' he said, his eyes following his thought processes and gazing towards the kitchen. 'Wasted here,' he added.

Kate followed his gaze. 'Seems so,' she said, the two words drifting with her musings. *She's certainly alluring, in an untouchable kind of way.* 'Interesting!' She hadn't realised she had spoken the word.

'What is?' Ash asked, placing her knife and fork on the empty plate in front of her.

'Oh, umm, the food.' Kate mumbled, placing another forkful of the omelette into her mouth.

Ash flicked her tongue at a piece of parsley stuck in her teeth and took a glug of her coffee. She glanced at Kate, her eyes drawn to her soft lips as they moved with the food. Reminded of the kiss, parts of her started to ache - yet studying the woman further those sexual feelings abated. She couldn't articulate the doubt, but it was present none-the-less. And, where Kate was the subject of that doubt, she would be wise to err on the side of her rational mind, not her sensual body. 'I'm going for a smoke,' she said, suddenly rising from the table.

'Good idea,' Craig said, standing up and stretching out his legs.

Katherine's nose twitched. 'I'll see you outside,' she said, addressing Ash. Another forkful of eggs softened her features again, but Craig and Ash were already out of sight.

73

'What's that 'bout?' Craig asked.

'She wants me to go with her to Damascus today,' she said, not looking up from the paper in her hand, struggling to get it to sit right.

'Want one a these?' Craig offered.

'No thanks.' Something about the process of rolling her-own was reassuring, comforting, distracting even. She scrunched up the paper and pulled out another one, which automatically complied with her fingers. Holding the paper out flat by one end, she dropped a thin row of tobacco down its centre. A twisting motion brought the two sides together before she licked lightly down the sticky strip and sealed the roll-up in place. Inhaling, she stared at the cloudless sky. 'It's gonna be hot.'

'You want me to go with her?' he asked. She looked up at him. The way he was staring at her was giving her an easy way out. 'I'm pinned down with this.'

He waved his bandaged hand at her.

'You sure?' she asked.

'Yup. We can talk managerial bollocks for eight hours.' He was chuckling, leaning against the wall drawing down on his cigarette, his eyes set on her. 'Everythin' okay?' he asked.

She inhaled again, pulled the cigarette from her lips, and reached to her mouth, trying to pick out a strand of tobacco that didn't exist. She picked at the nail bed of her thumb. 'I kissed Kate,' she said eventually.

Craig tilted his head in response and continued with his smoke.

'Well, she kissed me actually,' she corrected, pulling her fingers through her hair then tucking it behind her ear.

'Ah huh!'

The chirping of crickets filled the silence, with the occasional horn beeping in the distance. 'How'd 'at go?' he asked.

Ashley turned and faced him, her eyes vacant. 'Honestly, I don't know.'

He stood away from the wall and slapped her on the arm. 'Well look at it this way, at least yer getting some now,' he teased, but it didn't raise a smile. 'Okay, we'll all be 'way soon so none of us'll be gettin' any,' he added, hoping to hit the mark with something funny.

'Yup,' she said, mimicking his drawl, but her tone lacked humour. She stamped out the last of the roll-up and wiped away the beaded sweat on her forehead. 'Remember your suntan lotion,' she said. 'It's gonna be fucking hot out there today.'

'Yup, ain't that the truth.' He threw his cigarette butt to the floor, stepped on it and started back through the dining hall. 'I'll let Katherine know the good lookin' one's goin' with her,' he said, with a mischievous smile.

Ash slapped him on the arm then stopped. 'Wait.' She sucked through her teeth and looked skyward. 'I'll go. Maybe it'll give us time to talk about stuff.' She put her hand on his arm and squeezed. 'And,' she started, placing a light kiss on his cheek and wrapping her arms around his neck for a hug, 'I reckon your hand could do without a day trip to Damascus.'

He looked down, wriggled his fingers, his features tightening with the sharp pain. 'Yeah... still hurts like a sonuvabitch!'

Iman lowered her eyes to the floor, unable to watch the apparent display of affection between Ash and Craig. Her gut tugged with the anxiety that had flared up in an instant. She removed the apron from around her waist, folded it carefully, and set it down on the side, next to the tin. *I need some air. Think, think, think!* 'I'm just going outside,' she said, fighting the spinning in her head, and nausea that had just hit the pit of her stomach with a thud.

8.

Ash pulled out the tobacco pouch from her jeans' pocket, one hand guiding the steering wheel.

'Please don't smoke in the car,' Kate objected, not leaving any room for challenge.

Ash huffed. 'When did you stop smoking?' She threw the pouch onto the dashboard, her arm resting lazily on the armrest between them.

'Just after Uni.' Kate stared out the side window, her mind lost in the thought.

Ash nodded. The sand was starting to whip up, swirl, and sweep across the road, making its way north. Two hours on the road already, it was going to be a very long day.

'Were you in love with him?'

Kate stiffened. 'Who?'

'Alan, your husband! Unless you don't want to talk about it,' Ash added hastily, suddenly worried she was pushing too hard. 'The other night, I just got the impression you were, I dunno, holding back a bit. You didn't say much about him.'

Kate's eyes rose in her head, and she released a slow breath. She had deliberately avoided the details about that part of her life, hoping instead to reconnect through their shared past and get Ash's forgiveness for abandoning her. Kate clamped her arms around her body. 'I...' She paused. 'I thought I was.

But I think I was in love with the illusion.'

'Which one?' Ash asked, with more than a hint of cynicism.

'You're right.' She scoffed. 'The illusion that he would protect me as per our vows,' she added. There was anger in her tone, but something else too. Disappointment? Betrayal?

'He let you down?' Ash asked.

Kate turned her eyes to the front. 'He assaulted me,' she said, with more calmness than she felt, though she had practised the line sufficiently over the years.

Ash turned, wide-eyed, and stared briefly before turning her attention back to the road. 'Shit, Kate!'

'Yes. He was, a shit, actually.'

'What happened?' Ash asked, reflexively. She flushed instantly. 'Sorry, it's none of my business.'

Kate turned her head and studied the side of Ash's soft face for a moment.

Ash turned too, catching the depth of Kate's green eyes, suddenly feeling uncomfortable.

'It's okay. I don't mind telling you.' Kate said.

Both pairs of eyes settled back to the road. 'He raped me.' Kate continued, her voice uncharacteristically quiet.

Ash felt the knife enter her gut and twist sharply. Her mouth moved, twitched, tried, and failed to form any words. I'm sorry, just didn't cut it. It wasn't enough, but it was the only thing that had the strength to be heard. 'I'm sorry,' she said. Her voice was timid, her eyes burned, and she was finding it hard to swallow. She glanced sideways, taking stock of Kate.

'Everyone looks at me like that when they find out.' Ash froze. 'Wondering what to say to me? How to make things better? Pity, that's the worst of it. Apparently, I was asking for it,' she said, cynically. 'Who asks to be raped, Ash?' she asked, the question a rhetorical one.

Ash remained silent, waiting for her to continue.

'No, I didn't take it to court. I couldn't bare my soul in that way. Too humiliating. But I made them pay. Him, and his bloody family.'

A gust of wind caused the car to sway, but it was the wrong moment to comment on the deteriorating weather.

'It never leaves you.' Kate continued. 'The pain, yes, that eases a little. But it's the realisation of your weakness, how fragile you are, and the hollow, empty feeling that isolates you from the rest of the world. That doesn't seem to lift. Even with all the highs, the alcohol and the drugs. I get to escape in the moment, and in the next, I'm feeling lower and more alone than I ever was before.'

'I can imagine,' Ash said, softly.

'No you can't, Ash. No one can unless they've been there.' The words came out abrasively, but it was the undeniable truth that caused Ash's eyes to drop a fraction.

'You're right.'

'So, you see. When you add it all up and slap a large dose of pity in the mix, it's ugly. I'm ugly. I'm tainted goods unworthy of love. And certainly not the good wife I was supposed to be; the one that took it all and bowed graciously, thankful for the big home, the fast cars, and social engagements. What price the high life, eh?' She snorted. 'And all to please Ma and Pa,' she added, with resentment.

'Shit.'

'Yes, shit! I got caught in the trap, Ash.'

'I'm sorry, but we're going to need to pull over.' Ash said, searching for the horizon in all directions. The sand was swirling faster and higher than it had been a short distance back. 'I can't see well enough,' she said.

'It doesn't look too bad,' Kate said, pulling herself up in her seat, and peering through the windscreen.

'I could push it a bit further, but it's deteriorating quickly,' Ash said, pulling the car to the side of the road and switching off the engine, and with it the air conditioning. 'If we get sand in the engine we won't be going anywhere!' she said.

'What do we do now?'

'Wait it out.'

They sat in silence, the car rocking, bracing them from the wind and sand, the heat steadily rising inside the car. Kate slumped back into her seat, her eyes locked on the front windscreen.

'Does Craig know what happened?' Ash asked.

'No.'

'He cares about you, you know.'

'He's kind but he's still a man, and that is...'

'Difficult?'

'Raw,' she corrected. 'It's still early days for me. Sadly, my...' She struggled to find the right words. 'My experiences with that man have affected my relationship with all men. I... struggle.'

'I'm not surprised.'

'Seeing you though.' She turned to face Ash, raised her hand and brushed the bob behind Ash's ear. 'You make me feel something again.'

Ash went to speak, but nothing came out.

'My biggest mistake was breaking up with you,' Kate continued, her eyes watering.

Ash swallowed the lump in her throat.

'I knew it then too. I had no choice though. Ma and Pa were going to withdraw their support for my education unless I 'changed my ways'.' The wind buffeted the car suddenly, and she gasped, stared out the side window, her hand holding her chest.

'It's okay; we'll be safe here. It should blow through soon enough,' Ash said, reassuringly. She studied the sand filled sky around the car and winced.

Kate relaxed her hand. 'I don't think I ever stopped loving you,' she continued.

'It was a long time ago,' Ash responded, with a hint of remorse.

Kate leaned towards her, a sense of urgency in her voice. 'I feel something with you, Ash. Something I've never felt with anyone else. I thought I was over you.' She ruffled her hair as she spoke. 'And then I turn up here and bam!' She pulled back; she'd already said too much.

'I know,' Ash mumbled picking at her fingers. 'It's been tough for me too, seeing you again.' She wanted to reach across and pull Kate into her arms, comfort her, and take away the pain. But she couldn't, something stopped her. She took a deep breath and blew it out towards her hairline. 'It's fucking stifling in here,' she said, acutely aware of the rising heat and lack of airflow.

'Please don't say anything to Craig.'

Ash raised her eyes and held Kate's pleading gaze. 'Of course not,' she said softly, noticing Kate's irises shift in colour. 'How long ago was the rape,' she asked in a whisper.

'Just over two years and my divorce came through six months ago. We were in Russia. His father owned the company, so he got me the job out there.' She leaned back in the seat staring out the front window, ignoring the passing sand. 'We were isolated, and marriage happened very quickly. It was after that he changed, became aggressive, and expected me to do things. I did what he asked at first, but when it didn't feel right anymore and I wanted to stop, he didn't. He just wanted more and didn't take 'no' too well.' She turned and focused on Ash's deep blue eyes. 'It cost them a lot of money to buy my silence.'

Ash nodded, not needing the details.

'Does that make me a prostitute, Ash?'

Ash flinched. She held Kate's eyes with sincerity. 'I guess that depends how you feel about it,' she said. 'It's his punishment for hurting you,' she said, shrugging.

'Thank you.' Kate smiled.

'For what?'

'For not thinking badly of me,' she said.

'I could never...'

'It's okay; you don't need to justify.' She raised a hand in Ash's direction. She leaned forward and pressed a light kiss on Ash's cheek.

Heat rushed to the spot instantly. 'I think it's clearing,' Ash croaked. Sand still blasted across the front of the car.

'Maybe.'

Silence filled the space, both women glancing at the sun trying to peek through the airborne sand.

'What about you?' Kate asked.

'What about me?' Ash repeated.

'Anyone special? I mean I assume not, or you wouldn't have kissed me,' she added.

'You kissed me.' The words came out sharply.

'Sorry, you're right, I kissed you, and I don't regret it.' Kate started to smile. 'And you did kiss me back.'

'There isn't anyone,' Ash said, drawing the conversation away from the kiss.

'Iman?'

Ash jolted. 'Iman?'

'It's clear she likes you a lot.'

'She's Syrian, and she's kind to everyone.' Ash's eyes widened, and her heart raced.

'And, she likes you. You seriously haven't noticed how she looks at you?'

'Err, no.' A sudden burst of heat flushed Ash's cheeks with the white lie.

'Well, she does. And, it makes me very jealous,' Kate added, crossing her arms in front of her chest.

Ash stared at the sweeping sand. She'd never seriously considered Iman as a love interest because of her being Syrian, but there was something about the intensity in the young cook's light-brown eyes that hooked her in every time. And more... She was gracious, helpful, and a great chef, and yes, if she thought about it, she was hot too! But? 'There's nothing to be jealous about,' she said, though not entirely convincing in her tone, and her body's response also seeming to counter the words from her mouth.

'Fuck, it's hot in here,' Kate complained.

'I can try starting the car now,' Ash said. The wind was dying down and the road ahead more visible.

Kate looked tense and started to blow out hard, staring vacantly. 'It's suffocating.' She was beginning to hyperventilate.

'Are you okay?' Ash asked, urgently assessing her. Kate's eyes lacked focus, and her breathing was fast and shallow. 'Kate,' she shouted, grabbing her attention. 'Breathe with me, slowly. Watch me. In, slowly, out.' Ash demonstrated; Kate's stricken gaze fixated on her mouth. 'Come on, in, and out,' she repeated until Kate's breathing was close to normal.

Kate slumped back in the seat, grey, sweating profusely, and breathing deeply. 'Sorry,' she said.

'Hey, it's okay,' Ash said, sweeping the damp, red hair from her eyes and thumbing the sweat from her cheeks.

The tenderness in Ash's touch was comforting, reassuring. 'Thank you.'

Kate averted her gaze to the front windscreen, unable to bear the intense compassion in Ash's dark-blue eyes.

'You'll get used to it,' Ash offered with a warm smile. 'I'd rather have the heat than freezing my arse off in Russia,' she added, grimacing instantly, regretting mentioning the place.

'It's okay Ash. I hated the cold too,' Kate said.

*

Amena ambled into the garden, wholly engrossed in the large hardback book in her hands. She looked up, spotted Iman on the bench-seat under the shade of the canopy, and slapped the tome shut. She strolled over and sat next to her. 'Glad that wind has stopped,' she said, looking towards the clear-blue sky.

Iman looked up but didn't respond.

'Is everything okay Immy?'

She nodded, but the truth, revealed in the dullness in her eyes, told a different story.

'Is it work?' she asked. 'You're too good for that place,' she added, protective of her older sister.

'Work's fine.' Iman turned to Amena's bright, dark-brown eyes and her fingers stroked tenderly down the side of her happy face. 'How was school?' she asked, deflecting the conversation.

'It's not school, it's University,' Amena retorted lightly, opening her book and half-studying the page of philosophical words. She rested her hand on the face of the book and looked up. 'You sure you're okay?' She stared straight into Iman's light-brown gaze. 'You're not, are you?'

Suppressed tears were finding their way into Iman's eyes and starting their journey down her cheeks. Amena inched closer, put an arm around her shoulder, and pulled her close. Iman swatted at the tears that had let her down.

'I'm fine,' she said.

'What's happened?' Amena asked.

Iman started to sob.

'Sshhh... It's okay; you can talk to me you know.'

Iman shifted to snuffling and tried to speak through the soft wailing sounds that she couldn't suppress. 'I'm fine,' she spluttered.

'No you're not. And now I'm worried about you.' Amena released her sister and stared into the damp, puffy eyes. Something unspoken passed between them, and Amena started nodding, almost imperceptibly. 'Is it about a girl?' she asked.

Iman startled and pulled back, her eyes widening, confused, and wanting to lie. 'It's…'

'I know how you feel about girls,' Amena interrupted. 'It's fine with me.'

Iman's jaw sat open. The tears stopped suddenly, and her mind seemed to be throwing thought after thought at her, too fast for her to process. Her lips moved, but no words came.

Amena grinned. 'Is she cute?' she asked. 'And hot?'

'Amena!' Iman exclaimed, her body tensing and her eyes scanning around them.

'Relax. There's no one in and anyway, who cares what they all think?'

If only it were that simple. 'It's complicated, and not to mention a disgrace,' Iman reminded her.

'No it's not. It's love. And who are they,' her arms flung wildly and circled the outside world, 'to say who you can and cannot love? Who is she?' she asked, excitedly.

Amena's passion caused a coy smile to appear among the tears tracing Iman's face, as she watched her sister's passionate display. 'That's all well and good, but it's not what most people think. And anyway, it's Ash. She's an engineer at the base, and I'm not sure she's into girls,' she added. 'I think she's with Craig.'

'I bet she's into girls,' Amena retorted with a chuckle. 'Ask Tarek; he works with her.'

'I'm not asking him.' She grabbed her chest. There was no way she could speak to her brother about this. He wouldn't understand.

'Ash, eh?' Amena said, drifting into a fantasy world with a beaming grin.

'Stop it,' Iman pleaded.

Amena continued to tease. 'When can I meet her?' she asked, suddenly serious.

Iman studied her. 'How did you know?' she asked, ignoring the question.

'I've known about you for a long time. You've never been into guys, and especially not that, Rifat.' She made a gagging motion, and Iman slapped her on the arm.

'Don't be unkind.'

'Well, even if you were into guys, you wouldn't be into him. He's too dull,' she continued. 'You've never looked at guys the way you look at women.'

Iman's hand covered her mouth. 'Really?' she asked.

'Well it's obvious to me, and now you've confirmed it anyway.' She shrugged, turning her eyes to the pages beneath her hand.

'What will Mum and Dad say?'

'Uhh?' Amena looked up, adjusting to the question. 'I think Dad knows and I'm sure he's spoken to Mum too.'

'What!'

'You're twenty-six and have never shown any interest in men. They're not that blind, and Dad has travelled. He's not like the others.'

'Oh my, no.' Iman jumped to her feet and started pacing the well-manicured lawn in front of the bench, disturbed only by the hissing of water as the sprinklers kicked off and damped down the surrounding flowerbeds. 'Oh my, no,' she muttered again.

'They're fine Immy. Tarek knows too.'

'Holy heavens.' Iman stopped pacing the lawn and started frantically rubbing her clammy hands down her dress.

'He's cool about it.' Amena raised her eyes and scrunched her face.

'What was that face for?' Iman asked.

'Well, they're worried about you of course. What it will mean for you, and, well, a little concerned as to what people might say, or do...'

Iman's jaw widened as Amena reeled off the list of concerns. What had she done? 'Well, no one needs to worry. There's nothing I can do about it no matter how I feel.' Her words conveyed with certainty the decision her mind had decreed, her eyes, on the other hand, revealed the empty soul, whose heart lay broken and bleeding.

Amena stared at the pain that was cutting her sister into small pieces and gripping at her own heart. 'Don't say that Immy. Please don't say that. The world is changing.'

'Maybe out there,' Iman indicated towards the horizon. 'But here.' She was shaking her head. 'Here, Syria, if anything it's getting worse.'

'I love you,' Amena said, standing and pulling Iman into her arms.

Iman fell into the embrace with a deep sigh. 'I love you too; all of you,' she added, allowing the tears to fall.

*

'I've asked the company to book us a room,' Kate shouted above the cacophony in the busy city street, stepping into the waiting car.

Ash frowned.

'To stay overnight! One each,' she qualified. 'We shouldn't travel back tonight. You know where the Sheraton is, I assume?'

Ash squeezed a smile. 'Sure. It's not far.'

'It's too late, and it'll be dark soon, so I made an executive decision,' Kate added.

Ash mumbled and nodded, her eyes fixed on the chaotic evening traffic. It wouldn't be dark for another two hours, and the sandstorm had already died away, but feeling tired she wasn't about to argue. She pulled up outside the grand hotel - the suited doorman contrasting with her faded jeans causing her to fidget. He held out his hand with a pleasant smile, and she gave him the keys to the car. Kate joined her, linked arms, and dragged her towards the reception desk.

'No, no luggage, and we'll find our way thank you,' Kate stated to the concierge. 'We need to go and shop,' she added, at his bemused glare. Ash grinned sheepishly.

Kate turned the key in the lock and stepped into the large suite with adjoining bedrooms. She threw herself onto the double king-size bed, landing on her back, and stared at the ceiling. 'Oh that feels so good,' she said, patting the space beside her.

Ash moved slowly to the edge of the bed, sat, and then flopped onto her back, her legs still dangling to the floor. The soft quilt and mattress cushioned her body, and she released a long sigh. She lay, staring into space for a few moments. 'We need to get some clothes for tomorrow,' she said.

Kate turned on her side, resting on her elbow, head in hand. 'Or, we could just get naked and let the concierge sort it for the morning,' she said, a wicked twinkle lighting up her green eyes.

Ash sat bolt upright. 'Ummm.'

Kate laughed. 'There are robes,' she said. 'And we could spend some time in the spa. I wonder how long it will take them to turn our clothes around,' she pondered aloud.

Ash stood. 'I'll get changed then,' she said, stepping through to her room.

Kate jumped to her feet and picked up the phone. The bellboy was on his way. Within two minutes both women stood in a white gown and slippers, and a small pile of clothes tucked into a white plastic bag sat waiting.

Ash answered the door to Kate's room and was politely ushered out of the way by the incoming trolley hosting a bottle of champagne and a plate of hors-d'oeuvres. 'I don't think…' she started.

'It's okay I ordered them,' Kate interrupted, directing the trolley and handing over the washing bag. 'Thank you,' she said, smiling sweetly and handing over a Syrian ten-pound note.

The young man's eyes bulged, his grin widened, and he swiftly exited the room.

Ash looked at her quizzically. 'They'll turn our things around in ninety minutes, so I took the liberty of ordering us a drink. Then, I thought we'd get dressed and maybe go out to dinner.'

'What happened to the spa?' Ash asked.

'I thought dinner might feel… more comfortable for you,' she responded, lowering her eyes a fraction.

Ash tilted her head and studied the wavy red hair. 'Thank you.'

'Would you like a glass of champagne?' Kate asked.

'Sure.' Ash approached the trolley, her arms wrapped around her body, releasing one hand to take the offered drink. 'Cheers,' she said, raising the glass in a toast. Sipping the drink, she recoiled at the bubbles. She would never get used to Champagne and much preferred a beer, but she appreciated the gesture and persevered with the drink. 'So, how did the meeting go?' she asked, breaking her gaze from Kate's intense stare.

Kate frowned. 'That's boring. Tell me more about what you've been up to the last ten years.' She placed the bottle into the ice bucket and moved across the room, easing herself into the lounger and relaxing her head back.

Ash followed and sat on the couch opposite her. 'There's nothing to say,' she said, knowing Kate wasn't going to back down that easily. But, there really was nothing to tell.

9.

Iman slid the last small piece of decorated paper in front of her, placed an almond-topped sweet inside, and wrapped the paper round, twisting each end, and put the sweet into the tin. Her fingers traced the layer of candies with the lightest of touch. I hope she likes them. The thought sent a flush of heat to the butterflies dancing in her stomach.

'Excuse me!'

The unexpected voice caused her to jump, her hand tumbling sweets onto the surface. She scrabbled for a cloth to cover the gift then turned like a scolded child.

'Sorry, I didn't mean to scare you.'

Ash's blue eyes caught Iman's breath, and she was finding it hard to think let alone behave normally. Blood stormed her cheeks.

Ash watched and started to smile. She'd never seen Iman as edgy. 'I'm sorry, I really did make you jump,' she stated.

'Ash.' Iman's eyes darted around the room. Ash had never entered the kitchen before, ever. 'Can I get you anything?' she asked, stepping away from the covered tin and errant sweets. It was still early, and she hadn't started on breakfast, instead, taking the time to make and wrap the special gift.

Ash leaned over, trying to take a peek, and Iman moved subtly to block her view. She smiled at the cook's slightly defensive posture. 'Umm, yes. Sorry. I know I'm early,' she apologised, lowering her eyes to her hands. 'Could I get some coffee please?' she asked.

Iman's hand covered her mouth. There was always a pot of coffee ready. It was the first thing they did when they arrived at work, and she had forgotten. Her cheeks burned, and her heart pounded. 'Oh… yes. Sorry, I'll just…' she flustered.

Ash held her hands out, palm down. 'Hey, it's okay. I can do it if you point me in the right direction,' she offered.

'No, no,' Iman insisted. She glanced down, ensuring the sweets were covered, before seeking out the ground coffee. 'It's my job,' she stated.

Ash frowned. Iman seemed unsettled. 'Hey, it's okay, there's no rush,' she said, putting a hand on her arm.

Iman froze at the burning sensation shooting up into her shoulder and down her spine. Her breathing stopped, and her eyes opened, consuming the sight in front of her, challenging every muscle in her body to hold her upright.

Ash removed her hand quickly. 'Sorry, I err.' She took a step back, thrown by the electric connection that had hit her in the chest and caused her throat to clamp.

Iman fought the sinking feeling in her gut as a result of the absence, and smiled, grabbing the coffee. 'It's fine. I'm fine. Honestly, I should have sorted the coffee already.'

'Right,' Ash said, slowly backing out of the kitchen. 'Thanks.' Lingering at the counter, watching through the porthole window into the kitchen, she couldn't wipe the soft smile from her face or stop the pounding in her chest. Well, that was weird.

Iman spun through the door at a pace; her eyes firmly fixed on the coffee machine. She lifted the pot and shot back into the kitchen, returning with it filled with the cold water. Within moments the machine started to gurgle, and coffee began to drip through the filter. She glanced at Ash. 'Can I get you some breakfast?' she asked.

'I'll wait til it's ready,' Ash said, pausing, still staring into the captivating light-brown irises. 'I was wondering…' she paused again.

Iman's heart thumped, and the shaking in her stomach was fast approaching her hands. She cleared her throat, waiting for Ash to continue.

Ash glanced around the room. 'Um, you know you said about going to the souk?' she began.

Iman released the breath that had lodged in her throat. 'Yes,' she said, quietly.

Ash's fingers twitched, and she tried to hold Iman's worried gaze. 'I was wondering if you wanted to go tomorrow? I mean...'

'Yes, I'd love to,' Iman blurted, the beaming smile, lighting up her face, instantly replacing the tension of moments ago.

Ash smiled, relieved. 'Good.' She stood just grinning and staring, unwilling to make the first move away.

Iman stood, paralysed, smiling, her heart still pounding.

'Right, I'll get that coffee,' Ash said eventually, breaking the trance, and indicating with a tilt of her head in the direction of the machine as it huffed the hot water through its filter.

'Of course.' Iman rubbed her hands on her apron. 'I'd better get breakfast prepared,' she said, glancing briefly towards the kitchen.

The awkwardness shifted when Ash took a step towards the coffee machine. 'Tomorrow,' she confirmed.

Iman couldn't pull her gaze away. Suddenly she flushed, turned into the kitchen, and continued straight through to the restroom.

*

Ash leaned against the wall, absorbing the gentle heat from the rising sun, listening to the familiar chirping of crickets.

She sipped at the hot drink - the sudden hit of caffeine meeting with the heady, floating, sensation in her mind, drifting into a beautiful dream. She groaned outwardly.

'Aww, hell, fess up, Ash! You jes gotta share that thought,' Craig said. Squinting his eyes, he studied Ashley carefully. 'Didn't realise the trip was that good,' he added.

Ash frowned and slapped him on the arm. She and Kate had been back two days, and she hadn't had cause to groan, at least not in that way!

'We gonna get t' fixin' this raft?' he asked.

'Yep,' she responded, taking the offered cigarette and drawing down to catch the flame. 'You're going to have to follow instructions,' she teased, eyeing his bandaged hand.

He splayed his fingers wide in a demonstration of his improved movement. 'See, better already,' he said, dismissing any implication that he might still be in pain, though the tension in his face said, it hurt.

She sipped her coffee. 'Yeah right,' she said.

'Anyway, how come ya's up so early?' he asked, wiping at the beads of sweat that had already started to form on his forehead.

'Couldn't sleep,' she said, a wry smile appearing.

'Wouldn't have anythin' t' do with that groan, would it?'

'Fuck off,' she responded, teasingly, slapping him on the arm. 'C'mon, let's get breakfast and get out of here.'

He draped his arm over her shoulder and she steadied herself with an arm around his waist, and they squeezed through the door laughing. He placed a friendly kiss on the top of her head as they approached the counter.

Iman placed the dishes of fruit on the shelf, the chilled air filtering across their surface. She was aware of Ash's presence before the movement of the two engineers caught her eye. Her stomach lurched, a wave of anxiety burned in her chest, and her mind went blank. She hesitated to look up, turned, and ran into the kitchen, barely able to breathe. She couldn't bring herself to watch the two of them laughing together and holding each other. *Amena was wrong.* The mantra repeated itself in her head, her shaking hands working frantically to load the pastries onto a tray, her heart aching.

'Morning.' Niomi's chirpy voice and vivacious energy jolted her out of her gloomy reflections, and she locked eyes with her.

'Morning,' she said, in an upbeat a tone as she could muster, missing the mark by a million light years.

Niomi didn't notice; bounded across to Iman's side, picked up a pastry and placed it between her swollen lips. 'Yum,' she said. 'Shall I take them out?' she added, putting on her apron.

'Thanks,' Iman responded flatly, her eyes fixed on Niomi's vibrant, flushed state. She'd never seen her in such high spirits this early in the morning. She stepped into the pantry as Niomi picked up the tray. When she returned with a bowl of eggs, Niomi was in the restaurant; her attention entirely focused on the dark-haired field-technician, whose sky blue eyes were notably darker than usual.

Iman cracked the eggs and whisked them, added the chopped parsley, onions, and her special-spice-mix, and stood the bowl by the hotplate, waiting for the oil to heat. The dark shadow in her mind wouldn't lift. The sizzling sound and lightly spiced aroma lifted her slightly, as she stirred the mixture in the heavy metal pan. She could never let her passion for food to die, no matter how low she felt.

Niomi bounced back through the door and grabbed the cooked eggs, her desire to be front-of-house outweighing the tasks she needed to perform inside the kitchen.

Iman sighed and started on the long list of things to prepare for lunch.

*

'You're…' She couldn't find the right word. 'Happy,' Iman said, staring quizzically at Niomi, who had spent the best part of the morning hopping and skipping around the kitchen, and even humming to herself, and looking as if she were glowing.

'I am,' Niomi responded, holding Iman's gaze across the kitchen. 'We did it,' she said, unable to contain her excitement any longer.

'Did what?' Iman asked, her eyes searching Niomi's sparkling gaze. The penny dropped. 'Oh no!' Her hands covered her mouth, and her eyes nearly popped out of her head.

'What? You should be pleased for me.' Niomi defended.

'You… slept with Zack,' she whispered, her tone held tension not joy.

'Yes I did, and it was…' Niomi tried to continue, standing taller and beginning to strut.

'What if you…' Iman let out. She stopped, calmed herself, and started again. 'What if you get pregnant?' she whispered, with no less intensity in her voice.

'I won't.' Niomi responded, sticking her chin out dismissively.

'How do you know?'

'Zack said he'd be careful.'

'Please, tell me he used protection! Iman begged.

Niomi's eyes dropped to the floor.

'Oh no!' Iman gasped. She ran across to Niomi and held her shoulders firmly, bringing them face-to-face. 'Look at me.'

Niomi's head lowered but she held Iman's gaze. Defiance, replaced by fear, she looked like the child that she was.

Iman lifted her chin a little. 'Listen, I'm going to ask you some questions, and you need to answer them honestly, okay?'

Niomi blinked.

'Did he use any protection?'

Niomi's head slowly rocked back and forth, in response.

'Did he...' Iman breathed in deeply. This wasn't a conversation she was used to having, or had any desire to have, but she needed to know what had happened. 'Did he... you know...' she was gesturing with her eyes towards Niomi's crotch, 'inside you?' she asked, trying to give Niomi her full attention. The tears filling Niomi's eyes spoke for themselves.

The quivering turned into a full-on quake and Niomi sobbed. Her knees buckled, and Iman caught her. The ecstasy of the morning had shattered into the spinning reality that now consumed her mind.

'What was she thinking? Zack had promised. Her wide-eyes stared up at Iman, pleading for a solution.

'We'll sort something out,' Iman promised, with as much authority as she could muster. There was no way Niomi could see a local doctor. 'Wait here,' she said, darting into the dining room, scanning the familiar table and finding it empty. She shot back through the kitchen, out the back door and across to Ash's house.

'Hey, is everything okay?' Ash asked, staring at a wide-eyed, rosy-cheeked and panting cook. Their previous interaction had been a little odd, but something else had changed since then. 'What's up?' she asked again, waiting for Iman to catch her breath.

'Can you help me?' Iman begged.

Ash's heart raced. 'Is everything okay? Are you okay?' Her blood was beginning to burn her skin, as she considered the possibilities. 'Come in,' she said.

'I'm okay. It's Niomi. She needs your help.'

Ash's eyes locked onto Iman. The sense of relief smacked her in the face, and she released a long breath. Thank god. 'Come through. What's happened?' The raft would have to wait.

10.

Ash poured a glass of water and handed it to Iman. Her breathing had calmed, but a slight twitch persisted at the corner of her right eye. Ash studied the movement with curiosity, momentarily distracted from her thoughts as to how to solve the problem. Niomi couldn't risk the possibility of pregnancy, no matter how slight.

'Please, can you help her?' Iman begged.

Ash admonished herself. Iman's stunning eyes and display of vulnerability was having a strange effect on her ability to concentrate. She licked her lips, trying to quench the dry feeling in her throat. It persisted. 'She can't go to the expat doctors,' she said. 'They're locals.' She rubbed at her temples, urging the solution to come to her. She'd been fortunate never to have needed the attention of the medics on base, but they too were locals, and also men. Giselle! 'The doctor at the hospital,' she blurted.

'The hospital!' Iman repeated, two fine lines appearing between her eyes.

'Yes. The doctor who treated Craig, she's French.'

Iman twitched at the mention of the engineer's name. 'How can Niomi see her?' She was shaking her head, unable to see a way to get to the hospital doctor. This situation wasn't technically an emergency.

'I'll go. I'll find a way to be seen by her and say it's me that needs the help. Maybe she can give me something.'

Iman's eyes widened, and her lips parted. Just the thought of Ash having had sex with a man filled her with an uncomfortable feeling that caused her to shudder. Her eyes dropped to the floor; this wasn't about Ash and Craig. Niomi needed this help and Ash was willing to expose herself to save her friend. Her watering eyes lifted and locked onto Ash. Ash was staring straight at her; through her, and she froze. Could she tell? Had Ash seen the truth? Her breath caught, and her heart thumped.

Ash took a step forward, placed a hand on Iman's shoulder and encouraged her to lean into her chest. Ignoring the disconcerting sensations radiating through her, she held Iman's rocking body until she calmed. 'It's okay. I'll get it sorted Iman. Please don't worry,' she said softly. The intensity of the burning sensation in her chest and throat had consumed her entirely before Iman eased out of the embrace, and she moved away swiftly, scalded, almost throwing Iman off her. Her pupils conveyed the fire that fuelled the temptation of something far more alluring and she couldn't breathe. 'I need to get over to the hospital,' she said, averting Iman's gaze.

The feel of Ash's warm chest, against her face, had dried the tears and comforted her. The delicate-woody-scent though, flooding her senses, and causing unimaginable discomfort. Worry? She couldn't even think! Niomi's problem had faded, in that short embrace. Her heart was racing, and it was making it difficult to focus on anything but the woman holding her. And then, Ash had abruptly moved away, leaving her bare and exposed. She shivered at the chill created by the lack of contact. Ash was walking, talking, and wouldn't look at her. 'Sorry?' she asked.

Ash turned to face her and coughed to clear her throat. 'I need to get over to the hospital,' she repeated.

'Yes, yes, of course,' Iman stuttered, brushing her hands down the front of her uniform and turning towards the door.

'I'll be back as soon as possible,' Ash added, but Iman had already darted out the front door. Ash blew out the air that had lodged itself in her chest and stopped her mind from working. *Hospital!* She rubbed her hands up and down her cheeks and her fingers into and around her eyes. *Focus!* She puffed out again and headed for the door. Craig!

*

'What?' Craig grumped.

'I need you to come to the hospital with me,' Ash repeated. 'I need to speak to Giselle, the doctor that treated you,' she added with urgency.

Craig's eyebrows rose in his head and a slight chuckle formed on his lips.

'Uh huh,' he responded, his grin widening by the second.

She slapped him on the arm. 'Fuck off,' she teased. 'Niomi needs help,' she said, more seriously.

'Why can't she go then?' he asked, shrugging his shoulders. 'We've got a raft t' be fixin'.'

'Not right now we haven't. Niomi could be pregnant.'

'Shoot!'

'I know. And, worse still.' Her brows rose.

Craig rolled his eyes. 'Fuckin' Zack, dumber than a box of hammers.'

'Yeah, not the smartest move.' She tilted her head back and forth. 'But, in fairness, they do seem pretty into each other.'

'Clearly.' Craig sucked hard on the cigarette in his hand. 'He's still a dick.'

'Clearly,' Ashley repeated, with a wry smile.

'We ain't all dicks,' he defended.

She slapped him on the arm. 'Come on bud let's go. You need to be in a lot of pain, got it? You think you can do that?'

'I did actin' at school,' he said with a wink, heading out the door.

Ashley climbed into the driver's seat and took the offered cigarette. 'Right, start groaning,' she said.

Craig laughed.

'Not very convincing,' she teased, putting her foot down hard on the accelerator.

'Ahhhh!' he groaned, his body shifting unexpectedly with the movement of the vehicle.

'That's better,' she chuckled.

The route through the city centre was slower than usual, the horns louder, and the heat hotter. Ashley wound her window up, switched on the air conditioning, and eased back into the seat, her eyes locking onto the souk as they passed. The bright coloured garments caused an involuntary twinge between her legs and a soft groan escaped her lips.

Craig looked across at her. 'Ya okay?' he asked.

'Umm,' she mumbled. 'Yeah, sorry, just thinking aloud?'

Craig frowned, stared out the window, then focused back on her. 'Ya keep doin' that a lot.'

'What?'

'Groaning.' He smiled. 'It's new,' he added. 'Cute as a Possum,' he chuckled.

She rolled her eyes and wriggled in her seat. The pulsing sensations were pleasantly distracting, but if they continued she would need to do something about them, and there was only one person she could get that type of satisfaction from. Kate! An altogether different feeling diffused from her stomach, and she grunted. 'Fucking traffic,' she retorted.

Craig hobbled out the car door, moaning. 'There's nothing wrong with your leg,' Ashley remarked, frowning at his random display of inappropriate pain.

'Ahhhh, it hurts!' he groaned more loudly, holding his arm out in front of him. Even his eyes were half shut and his face contorted perfectly.

'Well done,' she whispered, pulling open the doors and heading to the reception desk. She puffed out a loud sigh as the same dark-haired man, with the same dark eyes, and the same insolent attitude looked up from behind the computer, ignored her, and focused his eyes on Craig.

'Name,' he asked.

Craig motioned to Ashley to sit, but she hovered by the junction to the corridor monitoring the doctors and nurses as they worked. 'Go 'n' sit,' he insisted.

'I'll wait for you,' she retorted, her attention with the movement around the treatment room.

He tapped her on the shoulder. 'I've asked t' see Dr Benoit,' he said. 'He wasn't happy,' he said, nodding towards the administrator, '"n' it means we might need t' wait a bit longer.' He pulled her towards a waiting room seat. 'So, wanna get some coffee?'

'Sure,' she said. 'Save that one for me.' She pointed at the seat with a view down the corridor to the treatment room.

'Ahhh,' Craig moaned again for all to hear, taking his seat.

'I'll be right back,' she said, heading to the cafeteria.

*

He was resting his arm on his chest when she returned, his long legs sticking out in front of him, his good arm resting on the empty seat next to him. His eyes remained shut, and he was snuffling through his nose. She sat softly, avoiding his

101

hand, perching on the end of the seat, and sipped at the coffee.

'Where's mine,' he said, without opening his eyes.

Ashley jolted, just barely avoiding a spillage, the hot drink splashing from her cup to the floor. 'Thanks,' she said, sarcastically.

He slid up in the chair, stretched out his good arm and took the offered drink. The waiting room was still full. Ashley finished her coffee, slouched back in the chair and started picking at her fingers. She sighed and began to fidget, sat up, then slumped again. If the clock made a noise, it couldn't be heard over the din and general clanging sounds emanating from the clinical rooms lining the corridor. She watched the second hand click its way around the Roman numerals on its face. How slowly time moved! She sighed and tried focusing on something else, but her eyes kept drawing back to the clock. Ten minutes turned into an hour, and an hour into four.

'Fucking hell,' she mumbled, for Craig's ears. 'You hungry?'

'Could do with a smoke,' he said, pulling his eyes from the Arabic newspaper he'd been studying. There weren't enough pictures to keep him entertained for very long. He huffed.

'You can't, just in case we get called,' she said. 'I'll go and get us a snack.' Craig huffed again and folded the paper. Ashley stood and stretched.

'Craig Johnson please.' The name caused them both to come to attention.

Craig stood enthusiastically, then remembering himself, groaned out in pain. Pairs of eyes locked onto him from around the room and he hobbled down the corridor, following the nurse into a treatment bay. Ashley held her head in her hand and walked a pace behind him, trying not to smile.

'I didn't expect to see you again.' Giselle's chirpy voice broke the silence between them, as she closed the curtain behind her and eyed Craig carefully. 'So, what seems to be the problem?' she asked. She followed Craig's gaze and turned her attention to Ashley.

Ashley fiddled her hands in her pockets, her eyes failing to focus. She hadn't thought through the plan any further than getting to see the doctor. She hesitated. 'Umm.'

Giselle frowned, looked at the notes in her hand and shrugged her shoulders. 'Is there something I'm missing?' she asked, with genuine concern.

'I need to ask a favour,' Ashley said, through a shaky voice.

Giselle recoiled a fraction, her brows rising as she processed Ashley's words. 'A favour,' she repeated. 'This is an emergency department,' she said.

'What are you doing here?' She eyed Craig again, puzzled by his treated hand and smiling face.

'I might be pregnant,' Ashley said.

Craig's eyes popped out of his head, and his jaw dropped.

'Oh!' Giselle assessed her momentarily then lowered her gaze to the notes in her hand, but she wasn't reading them. 'You could see your local doctor for that,' she said, looking up, her eyes probing further.

'Well, it's complicated,' Ashley continued, many thoughts rushing through her mind and none of them helpful.

Giselle frowned and tilted her head. 'I'm sure it is,' she said in a softer, quizzical tone. She studied Ashley again, settling on her shifty eyes. 'Who exactly is pregnant?' she asked.

Ashley's mouth opened, but nothing came out. Craig buried his head in his hands, stifling a laugh, and Ashley closed her mouth.

Giselle's smile broadened. 'Whom are we talking about here?' she asked, putting down the clipboard. She perched on the window ledge and crossed her arms, waiting for a response.

'A friend of a friend,' Ashley answered, her eyes slowly meeting Giselle's gaze. 'She's a local, and she slept with one of our technicians.' She faltered. 'Unprotected,' she added with a cough. 'I was hoping we could help them.'

Giselle held Ashley's eyes. 'When did intercourse take place?' she asked.

Ash flushed. 'This morning, I think. Or maybe last night.' She cursed to herself. It hadn't even occurred to her to ask the question.

Giselle nodded. 'I can organise a prescription for the morning after pill,' she offered. 'I'll need to use your details though,' she said, staring at Ashley

Ashley shrugged and nodded, a smile forming as the words registered. 'Thank you so much.'

Giselle took down the details, pulled back the curtain and exited the cubicle, returning moments later with a piece of paper in her hand. 'Here, take this to the pharmacy. Your friend needs to take it immediately. The medication will bring on a bleed, so she needs to be prepared for that. If you have any concerns, please bring her here and ask to see me.'

Ashley nodded at the instructions. 'I can't tell you...'

'It's okay, I understand,' Giselle said, her dark-brown eyes holding a pain of their own.

Craig set off, hobbling his way back through the reception.

Ashley stopped, turned, and faced the gaze that had fixed on her back. 'Can I take you out for a drink sometime. To say thank you?' she asked.

Giselle smiled. 'Maybe. If you call the hospital, my extension is 3467,' she said. Her smile was kind and reassuring.

'Thank you,' Ashley said again, holding out her hand.
Giselle shook it firmly. 'You're welcome.'

*

Ashley stepped out of the 4x4 and walked around the back of the hotel to the kitchen's main entrance. She stopped on the step, the slight aroma of food waste emanating from the industrial size bins causing her nose to twitch. She knocked on the door, opened it, entered, and halted. The long wavy brown hair caused her breath to hitch and the pleasant aroma of spices, almond and cinnamon instantly seduced her senses. 'Hi,' she said, reaching into her pocket for the small paper bag. She held out the drug, her hand shaking.

'Ash!' Iman stood still. She stared at the small bag, a wave of relief relaxing the tension she had carried all afternoon, and smiled warmly.

Ash traced the long pale dress sweeping down to just short of her exposed ankles. She swallowed hard. 'You look... nice,' she said, cringing. Nice sounded so lame and didn't represent what she wanted to say, but that was the word that had popped out. She lowered her eyes.

'Thank you.' Iman didn't move.

Ash stepped towards her and placed the drug on the worktop. 'Hmm, Niomi needs to take this straight away,' she said. 'It's going to make her have a bleed, like a period,' she continued. 'How is she?' she asked.

Iman raised her chin a little and breathed in deeply. 'Distraught.' Ash nodded, fiddling with her fingers. Iman closed the gap between them and reached out her arms, pulling Ash into a full embrace. 'Thank you so much,' she said. When she eased back, an errant tear had slipped onto her cheek.

Ash reached up and wiped it away, the feel Iman's soft skin drying her mouth, stealing her words. 'I'm glad I could help,' she said eventually, releasing the cook and taking a pace backwards. She turned before the door. 'I'm guessing she'll be needing you tomorrow,' she said.

Iman nodded, her eyes failing to connect fully with Ash's.

'That's okay. We've got a raft to finish building, and we can always go when I get back from the rig,' she offered, trying to sound upbeat and feeling quite the opposite.

'I'd like that,' Iman responded, confused by the burning in her heart and the wet, throbbing sensation between her legs.

'See you at breakfast then.' Ash said. She stopped her hand on the handle and looked over her shoulder. 'There's a leaving party tonight at Craig's house. You're more than welcome to come along; Niomi too if she's up to it,' she added.

Iman's face remained tense at the mention of Craig, and the smile wouldn't come. 'Thanks,' she said. 'I'll let her know.'

Stepping out into the heat, the smell of the bins hit the back of Ashley's nostrils and clung to her throat. She moved swiftly crossed the road and stepped through her front door, her heart racing. She needed a cold shower.

Iman stood staring at the small bag; her head swimming with ideological possibilities, wanting to believe her feelings meant something, that Ash felt something for her, and that Craig was just a friend. Sighing deeply, she glanced around the room. Maybe she should think more seriously about training to be a chef. She could go away for a bit. Another country, meet other women; women like her! Surely the pain of not seeing Ash couldn't be as punishing as the turmoil she was experiencing right now. Is that what this was? A heart breaking! One minute feeling elated at the thought that Ash was attracted to her, the next fighting the misery, loneliness and desolation at the idea of Ash and Craig being intimate together. She clung to her waist, squeezing at the ache gripping her gut, screaming silently until the tears had stopped falling. She wiped at her damp eyes and picked up the medication; closed the door behind her and climbed into her car.

11.

Craig put his foot on the barrel to brace the row of six, even though they were welded together and unlikely to move, his good hand fully occupied by the beer in his hand. 'So, party tonight.' he said.

His excitement didn't lift Ashley, her thoughts consumed by the shift in Iman's interaction with her. Iman had seemed distant, evasive, in a way that was out of character for her. Maybe it was to do with Niomi. 'Sure,' she said, pulling herself from her thoughts and heaving the wooden slatted structure into place on top of the barrels, her tone lacking in enthusiasm. 'I've invited Niomi,' she added.

Craig flinched. 'What for?' He threw his bandaged hand into the air for dramatic effect.

She landed the planks into place and stood up straight, puffing in the stifling air, sweat trickling down her brow, wiping her arm across her face before the salty liquid burned her eyes. 'I figured if they want to be a couple we should at least give them the chance to have time together, without doing something stupid.' She shrugged her shoulders.

'Her parents won't let her near the place on her own,' he said, drawing down on his cigarette and puffing out small rings.

'That's why I asked Iman to come with her, and I'm guessing Tarek will come too,' she continued before he could comment.

'Ah huh,' he said, but Ash's features remained unmoved. He continued to stare, assessing her.

In the absence of any further comment from him, she reached for the bolts and started to connect the planks to the barrels.

'Here, I'll do that,' he said, wiping at his brow. 'Ya 'll need to screw the nuts on though 'n' I'll tighten 'em when we get back from the rig,'

'Fuck off,' she said, digging him in the ribs. There wouldn't be any turn in those nuts by the time she'd finished with them. 'Go get me a beer,' she said, indicating to the cool-box on the bench.

The cold bottle in her hand, Ash followed Craig outside and slumped onto a makeshift bench-seat at the back of the workshop. Taking advantage of the shade and uncharacteristic quiet in a place that was usually humming with noise and activity, she sipped at the cold beer and stretched her legs out in front of her. 'How's the hand?' she asked.

'Good,' he said, offering her a cigarette.

She shook her head and pulled the pouch from her coveralls pocket. 'You want one of these?' she asked, taking out a paper.

'Sure,' he said.

They slumped. Tomorrow would be the start of hell, on the rig. Tomorrow was another day. Tomorrow could wait.

'Come hell or high water we're gonna win that race,' he said, staring into the clear-blue sky.

'Ah huh,' she said, with a slight twang, her mind distracted.

*

Ashley jumped out of the shower and threw on her faded jeans and white shirt. The oversized top hung too low for her liking, but it was cool, airy, and comfortable. She flicked her fingers through her lightly dried hair allowing the wet to shape it behind her ears while brushing her teeth with her free hand. The call to prayer had woken her. She'd fallen asleep on the bed after a late afternoon swim. She looked at her watch.

9.15 already. *Fuck!* She slammed the door behind her and sprinted the short distance in the direction of the rumbling music. Opening the door, she bumped straight into Kate.

'Hi. I was beginning to think you weren't coming,' Kate said.

Ash looked at her with a sideways glance. She was slurring her words and the glassy, bright-green eyes were sliding up and down her body. Ash gulped. 'I fell asleep,' she said, searching over Kate's shoulder to locate Craig.

'You should have called me,' Kate said, seductively. The innuendo missed Ash, and she excused herself, heading for the fridge.

'You made it then?' Craig held out the open bottle, cigarette hanging out of his mouth. 'Here!' he chuckled.

She swigged from the bottle, sinking nearly half its contents in one go. 'Thanks.'

'Someone's thirsty,' he said with a broad grin, the sound of a loud splash diverting his attention. 'Fuck, they're startin' early,' he said, peeking out the kitchen door towards the pool.

Ashley followed his gaze. Zack and Dan's heads popped out of the water to the cheering audience of local workers sat around the pool. She swigged again, put the empty bottle on the table and pulled another from the fridge. 'You coming?' she asked.

'Nu-uh, gotta pee,' he said, staggering in the opposite direction.

She wandered into the garden and leaned against the wall, maintaining her distance from the party. The crickets were managing to chirp into her right ear from the heavily planted garden, drawing her attention from the loud voices and squealing noises coming from the frivolities. Staring into the star-filled sky, she took a long slug of beer, and then another, enjoying the subtle shift from the heightened emotions and confused thoughts that had tormented her all day.

Although, Iman was nowhere in sight, and that left a hole that needed to be filled.

Niomi was stood by the pool, laughing. Zack pulled himself out of the water and stepped towards her, his gaze never faltering, his smile broadening with every pace. He shook himself down in front of her, a light shower spraying her, causing her to laugh and wave him away. They looked happy. Ashley smiled, warmed by the obvious of affection they held for each other.

'Here you are.' Kate said, holding out her hand, interrupting Ash's reverie.

'Thanks,' Ash said, taking the offered beer, locking onto the green-eyes momentarily. Kate still had the power to stimulate the tingling sensation in her core, and maybe she always would. She sighed and finished the last of the old beer.

'Set for tomorrow?' Kate asked, sipping the long drink in her hand.

'Yep.' Ashley put down the empty bottle and slugged at the new one.

Looking back to the pool, only Zack and Niomi remained. His hand was dancing with hers, their fingers lightly interlocking and releasing as they spoke. There was tenderness between them, but something else. Zack wiped his thumb softly under her left eye, his other hand lifting her chin. She couldn't hear what he was saying, but the solemnness between them tugged at her heart. The two lovers were oblivious to her watching them, but he took Niomi's hand and led her around the corner of the house and into the privacy of darkness.

Ash wiped at her eyes, willing the dampness away. 'You okay?' Kate asked, placing a comforting arm around her shoulder.

'Yeah,' Ash said, unconsciously leaning into the physical contact she craved. The tender kiss warming her temple wasn't entirely unpleasant either, but she moved away out of respect for the local worker's culture, even though there wasn't anyone in sight.

Iman's eyes widened, and her irises darkened. The smile she had held in place all evening waiting to see Ash, disappeared instantly. She continued to watch the two women, obscured by the olive tree that sat between the pool and the rear entrance to the lounge. The large room was being turned into a temporary sacred place, the local men preparing for the last call to prayer of the day. She dived through the door, through the living room and out the front door.

Slamming her car door just as the chanting filled the night sky, she sat in silence, her body convulsing uncontrollably. Her thumping heart drowned out the melodic tones and her vision narrowed to a fine point. There was no light, just a well of darkness: and the pain, more excruciating than any thoughts of Ash with Craig. She hadn't even considered Kate! She tugged at her chest, fighting for breath. There were no tears, just a red rage sweeping through her mind. She slammed her hands down repeatedly on the steering wheel. No, no, no. She wrestled with the high dress-collar that threatened to choke her, ripping it away from throat. Pulling at her hair, wanting to scream, unable to release the energy that was consuming her, she felt trapped. She pushed her back into the car seat, flung her head back; tensed her legs and then her body. *Nooooooo!* She screamed silently.

Suddenly sitting bolt upright, and wide-eyed, she stared through the windscreen. Her heart raced, but the thumping in her chest had shifted to her head, and the streetlights were bouncing in front of her eyes. She blinked to clear her view. Another wave of rage voiced itself through a high-pitched scream that got lost in the chanting reverberating around the city and through the expat compound. She turned the ignition. She needed to escape. She would drive, calm herself, and then return to collect her brother and Niomi. She sat, trying to compose herself, unable to focus on the road in front of her glassy eyes.

*

The night sky quieted, and the garden remained deserted. 'I love the call to prayer,' Ash said.

'Mmm.' Kate lifted her head. She hadn't taken any notice of the chanting, distracted by Ash's woody scent filling her with a different kind of visceral response. 'It's quaint,' she responded.

Ash pulled away from the warm shoulder and tutted. 'It's more than quaint. 'It's ethereal. There's something, I don't know, haunting, yet also reassuring about it.'

Kate's eyes were locked onto Ash's mouth as she spoke, the words though never made it to her ears.

Ash swallowed hard, unable to pull away from the dark-green stare; the pulsing in her clit dominating her senses, and the alcohol blinding any sense of reason or will she might have otherwise applied. She groaned at the all too brief, soft, wet touch to her lips.

The warm sensation flooding Kate was urging her hands to explore, but this wasn't the place. Restraining, she pulled back and rested her forehead on Ash's, her fingers tracing lightly down the blonde hairline. She fixed the bob around Ash's ear. 'Shall we go?'

Ash moved away and turned towards the door to the kitchen, her glazed eyes studying the route intently, finding it hard to focus. *Fuck it!* She took Kate's hand and led her urgently, releasing it as they passed through the house and back down the street.

Iman observed the two women in the rear-view mirror. She couldn't hold back anymore, and the tears flowed down her cheeks in waves. Ash was grabbing Kate's hand and pulling her through the front door of the house. She slammed her foot down on the accelerator; driven by the burning heat and pounding in her chest.

*

Ash leaned into Kate, forcing her back and pinning her against the closed door. Taking her mouth fiercely and biting down on her lip, she dived into the explosive kiss.

Kate groaned at the hungry lips on hers, sending waves of fire down to her core. 'Fuck me, Ash, please,' she whispered.

Ash lowered Kate's jeans zip and her fingers teased across the soft skin beneath. Compelled by Kate's musky scent, driving her senses wild, she eased inside the jeans and slipped her hand down to the familiar smooth bare flesh. Ash moaned at the warm silky sensation on her fingertips. She relaxed into an effortless rhythm, delicately sliding along Kate's throbbing lips, her mouth pressed firmly against Kate's. She stopped kissing suddenly and eased away, watching, assessing.

Kate's eyes fluttered but remained closed.

Ash continued to observe the impact of her fingers, playing out on Kate's face, staring at her; reading her.

Kate bit down on her bottom lip, unable to control her ragged breathing, or her hips from moving with the rhythm of Ash's touch, and fighting the urge to scream out.

Ash pulled her hand out of the restricted space causing Kate's eyes to bolt open. Placing a hand either side of Kate's hips, with an unwavering gaze, she pulled the jeans sharply down to the floor.

Kate quivered. With legs that were already struggling to hold her upright, she staggered out of the jeans and stood, swaying, biting down, her eyes only half open.

Ash eased her against the door, her hand cupping the point between her legs. 'Open for me,' she whispered.

Kate groaned at the hot breath on her ear and gasped as Ash's fingers slipped into the space, and then gently inside her. 'Fuuuuccccckkkk.'

Ash's hand didn't move, but her fingers tenderly explored the silky depths, seeking the spot she knew so well. She continued to assess Kate's reaction to every shift in her touch.

'Yes.' Kate cried out.

Ash moved from the spot. It was too soon!

'Back, back, back,' Kate pleaded, her face contorted with the shuddering sensations through her centre.

Ash moved again, her thumb slowly beginning to take control of the bundle of nerves sitting at its tip.

Kate started to spasm, again and again, her knees giving way.

Ash pressed against Kate's body, more firmly pinning her in place and moving her fingers, sliding them in and out: slowly, then pausing, her thumb softly toying, and repeating the cycle. The intoxicating rhythm sensitising her own pulsing core, she eased against Kate's exposed thigh. Leaning into the firm muscle, she moved, groaning at the intense burning at the crotch of her jeans. The fire coursing through her veins quickened her fingers. She delved deeper, feeling Kate widen with every thrust. Lost in wild frenzy, absent of all thought, she dropped to her knees and drove deeply into Kate. With the slightest of movements, she teased her, her tongue caressing her exposed clit.

'Ahhhh. Fuck... fuck... fuck... I'm coming.' The words screamed into the silence, and Kate's legs collapsed.

Ash withdrew slowly, eased her to the floor, and stared at the closed eyes of the woman she had fallen in love with all those years ago. She wiped tenderly at the beads of sweat that clung to Kate's face and kissed her softly on the lips.

Kate opened her eyes, fixed her arms tightly around Ash's neck, and wept.

Ash held her until the tears stopped.

*

Amena turned over in her bed to face the sobbing noises that had roused her from a deep sleep and forced her eyes to open. 'Immy, are you okay?' She pulled herself up and blinked at the crumpled heap rocking in the corner of her room; arms wrapped tightly around her middle. 'Immy, what's wrong?' Leaping out of bed, she crouched beside her sister and pulled her into her arms. 'It's okay Immy, talk to me.'

Iman continued to sob, unable to speak.

'Do you want some water?'

Iman shook her head, her eyes closed.

Amena pulled her closer and kissed the top of her head. 'What's happened?' she asked, calmly.

'I think she likes girls,' Iman cried through the sniffling, easing out of the embrace and willing her eyes open.

'Surely that's good news,' Amena said, her high-spirited tone failing to impact her sister's distress. She swept the errant hair out of Iman's face and cupped her cheeks. 'How is that not good news Immy?' she asked, holding her gaze with tenderness, trying to reconcile the positive words with the distressed state. They didn't match!

Iman averted her gaze. 'She's with Katherine,' she sobbed, even louder, her hands clinging to the fire trying to escape from her chest.

Amena sat, motionless. 'How do you know that?'

'I just saw them together.'

'And what if you didn't see what you thought you did?'

Iman shrugged off her sister. 'I know what I saw,' she said, her tone angry, confusion in her eyes at the obviously immature statement. There was no mistaking what she had seen.

'Maybe.' Amena said, softly. She couldn't think of anything else to say, but she would think of something, maybe tomorrow, maybe the next day. There had to be a way. There was always hope.

'I need to speak to Mum and Dad,' Iman said, moving to stand.

Amena looked at her watch. 'It's late now,' she said, rising to her feet.

'Tomorrow.'

'What will you say to them?'

'I don't know. I think I need to get away.'

Amena's heart sank, and she gasped at the resignation in Iman's voice. She reached out, pulled Iman to her feet and hugged her, squeezing the tense frame tightly. Nothing came back. 'Please don't leave. I love you,' she said, her stomach churning as she spoke.

'I just need to think,' Iman said. 'Sorry. I need to...' she ran down the corridor fighting the next wave of tears.

Amena slumped onto her bed, her head in her hands, tears rolling down her cheeks. *She can't leave!*

Iman leant against the closed door of her room, her head throbbing from the constant pressure behind her eyes, her thoughts chasing each other around her mind, her heart aching and heavy. *What if she had misread the situation as Ammy had suggested? No! She definitely saw something more than the comforting hug of close friends. Yes, Ash likes women, and so it seems does Kate.* Uugggghhh! She screamed silently. At least Ash was going to the rig tomorrow. She would give her the gift, be respectful, and maybe the distance would help her adjust. She would wish Kate well because that was the right thing to do.

She pulled off her clothes and allowed them to drop to the floor. Lying on her bed, she waited for sleep to come to her. Her heart burned so painfully she didn't think she would get through the night, and part of her didn't want to! Her eyes were still open as the chanting echoed through the city, before the first light of day. With heavy lids, she dressed, determined to be professional in her dealings with both women.

12.

'Fuck,' Ash mumbled as she tried to lift her head. She checked herself, suddenly reminded of the fact that she wasn't alone in the bed. She opened her eyes slowly, thankful that it was still dark. The snuffle emanating from the other side of the mattress caused her gut to twist. She raised her hands to her head and squeezed at her temples. *What the fuck was she doing?* She felt sick, but it wasn't from the hangover that was now trying to break out of her skull. It was a painful bubbling pressure that cut into her chest, a finger that poked and poked. Unremitting. It was harsh, a combination of profound grief and self-loathing.

An image of Iman appeared in her mind's eye; in her flowing creamy white dress, with her long wavy hair hanging freely, and a tear slid silently onto her cheek. She turned away from the body lying next to her and glanced at her watch. She couldn't face Iman, even though she would suffer later for not eating, and anyway it was still too early for breakfast. Sliding out of bed, she crept out of the room and into her bedroom. She would shower, dress and go and wait in the car.

She loaded her travel bag onto the back of the 4x4 and climbed into the driver's seat. She pulled out a thin paper and started filling it with tobacco. It would be a long wait, but she couldn't stay in the house. She couldn't face Kate, not right now. She hoped they would be on the rig before Kate hit the base. She might even be able to avoid her for the time on the rig, though somehow she doubted that would be possible. *Fuck. Fuck!* She drew down slowly on the roll-up and closed her eyes. A vision of Iman appeared, and they flashed open again. She sat bolt upright, finished the cigarette, and threw it out the window. Resting her head back, her attention piqued by the approaching car lights, she skulked down in the seat and averted her eyes.

Iman stepped out of her car and walked around to the kitchen's entrance. She unlocked the door, flicked the lights on, and placed her bag in the restroom. Rubbing at her temples, she glanced in the mirror. Puffy red eyes stared back at her. She hadn't slept. The raw pain and the gaping hole in her heart didn't seem to budge, and her thoughts were turning her stomach inside out, but she was determined to treat Ash and Katherine as she always had done. She wrapped her apron around her waist and set to work.

*

Craig was late! Ash fiddled with the paper in her hands, the fourth of the day already.

'Hello Ash.'

The soft voice made her hands jump, spilling tobacco down her jeans. 'Fuck,' she cursed, flapping the bits off her shirt before looking up. 'Sorry. Iman.' The words stuck in her throat, and she could barely look into the gorgeous soft brown eyes. The aching in her heart was swelling and pressing against the back of her ribs.

'You didn't come in for breakfast.'

'No.'

Iman's heart raced, adding to the conflict raging inside her chest. She looked at the sky. 'It's hot.' She winced at the words coming out of her mouth, and her eyes darted around for something other than Ash to focus on, inescapably drawn to the blue-black rings under her dark-blue eyes. She looks rough. Another fissure opened in her heart. Just the thought of holding her; taking in her scent, feeling her warmth. Her hands were beginning to shake.

'Yes.' Ash admonished herself for her clipped responses. It wasn't Iman's fault she had fucked up. It wasn't Iman's fault she'd drunk herself into a stupor. 'It's going to be hell on the rig,' she added, planting a forced smile. Her eyes softened with sadness, and her heart thumped hard, envisaging her time alone in the desert and away from Iman.

'I often wonder what it might be like.' Iman said, offering a slight smile. She made daily trips to the base to provide the workers with their lunch; the rig itself though wasn't a part of their catering remit. 'It sounds tough. Tarek always complains about the heat... and gets excited about the dangers.' She shrugged at his bravado. 'My father thinks if he experiences a blow-out he wouldn't feel quite as thrilled about it,' she continued. 'Is it really that dangerous?' she asked, suddenly curious to know Ash's perspective.

Ash sensed Iman's irises darken as she spoke and another wave of something - guilt, remorse - hit her, as last night's memories came flooding back. Muhammad al Maghout was well respected among the expats. His experience, knowledge and wisdom had, saved more than one rookie supervisor over the years. 'It can be,' she said. 'I guess, that's why we're there, knowing what we're doing, training, preparation, it all helps make the rig safe.'

'Are you ever scared?' she asked, the intensity of her gaze confirming the genuine sincerity in her question.

'Sometimes, maybe.' She screwed up the paper in her hand and let it fall into the footwell. 'But I think I'd be in more danger working an oven,' she added light-heartedly. Iman's laugh had a quality of openness to it that made Ash's heart dance with joy, and she couldn't help but be drawn in. Its resonance coloured her cheeks, and she smiled warmly.

Iman shifted suddenly. Holding the cloth-covered tin through the car window, 'I made this for you,' she said. 'I hope you don't mind. I know you like sweet things, and these will last you… While you're on the rig I mean. I can make some more when you get back.' She was babbling and couldn't seem to stop, all thoughts of Ash with Kate temporarily resigned to a distant memory.

'Wow, thanks. Food's awful out there.'

Iman laughed heartily, folded her arms around her body, and took a short step backwards, placing her hand over her mouth.

Ash's fingers delicately traced the textured material around the tin, fighting the twisting in her gut. 'It's beautiful. Thank you.' She didn't need to ask its provenance. Everything about the tin had Iman's touch written all over it. A touch that felt so… beautiful. *Fuck!*

'Stay safe, Ash.'

The passenger door thundered open, and a paper bag landed in the middle seat. Craig climbed into the passenger seat, juggling two steaming mugs. As he landed, the 4x4 tilted and the hot drinks sloshed.

The aroma of sweet pastries and coffee enlivened Ash's senses, and she licked her lips. 'I will,' she said, through the pressure in her chest and the gripping pain in her gut. 'And I'll look after twinkle toes here too,' she added, with a mischievous grin. She placed the tin in the middle seat next to the pastries and revved the engine.

'Bye!' Iman waved. 'Bye Craig.'

'I'm gonna miss yer food,' Craig said, with a coy smile.

'Me too,' Ash remarked, but she was going to miss much more than that.

Iman turned and made her way back to the kitchen and Ash continued to watch her until she was out of sight. 'What's that?' Craig asked, housing the drinks in the cup holders and pulling out a packet of Camels, throwing one between his lips.

122

'That, my friend, is mine.' She put her arm around the tin and pulled it closer, shifted the gear stick and eased her foot on the accelerator, mindful of not spilling their drinks.

'Gonna be like that is it?' He teased, trying to peek into the tin. She slapped his hand and flicked her fingers at him. He passed her his lit cigarette and lit himself another one. 'I am seriously jealous,' he said, after a few hundred yards. 'She sure 's the best cook I've come across, and she's a looker!'

'Yes, she is,' Ash said, screaming inside with the sharp pain of regret preying on her mind.

*

Iman stepped into the kitchen's restroom and leaned against the wall. She breathed in and out deeply, allowing her heart to settle. *Well done!* She'd managed to give Ash the tin, and maintain her dignity. God that hurt! She looked down at her shaking hands and lowered herself into the seat, waiting until the trembling had eased. Standing abruptly, she forced a smile, walked back into the kitchen, and started gathering ingredients. The distraction of preparing lunch would help, she hoped.

Niomi looked up from her workstation, a sad smile on her face, her eyes glassy. Holding Iman's gaze, she nodded.

'Thank god,' Iman said, breathing a sigh of relief. The medication worked. With increasing vigour, she rubbed the flour and butter together. 'Let's cook,' she said.

The white elephant in the room, the absence of Zack and Ash that neither of them wanted to speak of, resulted in silence. Iman's hands moved diligently, her passion for food lifting her spirits sufficiently.

Niomi's hands worked slowly, every movement effortful. 'Do you think they'll be okay?' she asked eventually.

Iman looked up and smiled kindly at the worried expression on Niomi's face. She was in love with Zack. 'I'm sure they will,' she said. She rolled out the dough. Niomi was still staring at her, vacantly. 'You okay?' Iman asked.

'Not really. You?'

Iman held her gaze intently. 'Not really,' she whispered.

*

Kate turned in the bed, Ash's scent hitting her senses and setting off the throbbing between her legs. Pleasantly tender; she moaned at the intoxicating memories of Ash's sensitivity that had brought her quickly to climax. How much she had missed the intimacy between them. Nothing, no one, had come close since the year they had shared at Uni. But something niggled at the back of her mind. She groaned at the thumping in her head, distracting her from her concerns, and eased out of bed. Heading straight for the Aspirin in the kitchen cupboard, she gripped at her temples.

She played with her tongue; it's rough surface clinging to the roof of her mouth; the taste causing her to dry retch. Yuk. She filled a glass of water and gulped hungrily, emptying the glass in one go. She refilled it and swallowed the two tablets. Finishing the second glass of water, she headed for the bathroom and put on her swimsuit. She would hear from them if there were a problem. But for now they would be on the road, and she needed to do something to alleviate the raging hangover and the other dull feeling sitting in her gut, before heading out to the base.

*

Iman sat on the garden seat, entranced by the intermittent hissing from the sprinklers, the chirping of crickets, and the sweet aroma drifting from the flowered borders to the lawn. She poured the tea and sipped from the cup, savouring the delicate mint flavour on her tongue. She glanced around at the broad reach of the olive tree, shades of red and lilac, interspersed with white, dotted around the garden beds, and the dark green, manicured lawn that seemed to frame the picture. So beautiful, yet her heart felt empty and hollow. Her mind was made up.

'Immy, you want to speak?' Muhammad approached with a broad, soft smile, and she poured him a cup of tea.

'Yes, I need to talk... about something.'

His light-brown eyes settled on the cup in his steady hand, and he sat slowly. He sipped unhurriedly and placed the cup back on the tray. She set her empty cup next to his. Turning to face her, he spoke softly. 'Whatever you have to say, it will all be fine you know.'

His compassionate tone did very little to stem the anxiety sitting just below her ribs and beginning to spill into her stomach. 'I...' she started.

He reached out, delicately taking her shaking hand with his warm touch. His large palms enveloped her with tenderness, comforting her, drawing her attention to him. 'I understand,' he said.

She nodded, aware of the physical strength lying beneath the rough, calloused skin, squeezing lightly, providing the support she needed. The tears started to slip down her cheeks, and she didn't sweep them away. 'I'm sorry,' she said.

He released her hand and pulled her into his arms. 'Immy, you have nothing to be sorry for. Love does not know the boundaries we create through our insecurities, religious beliefs or dictated rules.'

125

He ruffled her hair, reminding her of when she was a child. He hadn't done that in as many years as she could remember.

'I worry about you, that's all. I've always wanted you to think freely; maybe I'm to blame.'

'No.' Iman pulled back and held his eyes with her own. Studying him closely, she cupped his bearded cheeks. 'No, you did nothing to create me this way. Mum did nothing. You cannot blame yourselves.'

He kissed the inside of the palm of her hand. 'I hope so,' he said.

The vulnerability in his tone didn't escape her, and she pulled him into her arms, holding him tightly. Releasing him, tracking his eyes, 'I want to go to Paris,' she said.

His gaze lowered to their joined hands. 'I don't want that for you,' he said. 'I don't want you to feel that you have to run away from your home and those you love to be who you are.' Looking up at her, he failed to smile.

Iman's heart shattered at the tears forming in his eyes. She had never seen him cry. She took in a deep breath. 'I'm not running away,' she said.

'But you will be Immy, like the others before you.'

'No. I've decided, I want to train to be a proper chef.'

He released her hands, placed his palms into his eyes and rubbed. The tears stopped, the lines that had been evident before receding. 'Oh,' he said, tilting his head back and forth. 'I didn't know…'

'I didn't know either until I thought about it,' she said, with renewed enthusiasm. 'I've been doing some research at the Embassy, and I'd like to train properly, in Paris. I'm a good cook, Dad.'

'You are the best,' he said, starting to smile. 'Paris eh?'

'Yes, or maybe London.'

126

He released the air from his lungs and studied the grounds around them.

'We will all miss you,' he said.

She lowered her gaze, rubbing her clammy hands together. I'll miss you too. 'I will come back regularly,' she offered. She couldn't admit to herself how much she would miss them all, and especially Ash, or she would never leave.

'I'll see what I can do,' he offered. 'We have friends; maybe we can help you find somewhere to work.'

Iman leapt into his arms, nearly throwing him off the seat. 'Thank you, thank you, thank you,' she said, squeezing him with all her strength.

'Is there anyone special?' he asked as they walked back to the house.

Iman stalled. Her voice was soft, tender. 'Sort of.' Her eyes dropped.

'Ah...'

'I... there was' Iman struggled to speak. She couldn't say what she didn't want to believe.

'Is she, Syrian?' he asked tentatively.

Iman looked up, holding his concerned gaze. 'No.' She stared directly into his pain and couldn't lie. 'It's Ash,' she said, feeling the swell of hope in her heart, followed by the dark cloud of truth.

His eyes held firm, and his smile was genuine. 'She's a good engineer,' he said, approvingly.

Iman nodded. 'She's with someone else,' she said, her lashes darkening with the water forming on their surface.

'Oh!' He brushed the tears that were spilling onto her cheeks. 'I'm sorry Immy.'

She smiled through the sniffles, kissed him on the cheek and tucked her arm around his back. 'I'll bake some ma'mul,' she said.

He smiled, but his eyes remained distant. Patting his flat stomach, 'You make great cookies Immy,' he said. 'But now you want to go and make them for the French,' he teased, shaking his head and beginning to chuckle.

She laughed past the sadness that was trying to drown her.

'Let's go and talk with your mother,' he said.

13.

'You need a hand with the rig up?' Craig asked with a wry smile, watching Ashley strain connecting the heavy metal pipes.

'Fuck off,' she said, standing, raising her middle finger, with a broad grin. Tarek was laughing. She pulled up from the sand, sweat dripping from her face. 'Do something fucking useful and pass me that crossover,' she said.

Craig pulled the metal linking joint out of the basket and handed it over.

Levering the threaded end to the pipe, she started turning. 'Urrgghh, fucking thread's knackered.' She dropped it to the floor and kicked it. Craig dipped into the basket for another joint. 'We already used the spare,' she said.

'Fuckin' piece a shit,' he said, picking up the broken joint and assessing the crushed thread. I'll see if we can get it filed down, or another one sent out.'

'Jeez it's fucking hot,' she moaned, shaking her head to avoid the sweat running into her eyes. She groaned with the physical exertion of standing. 'Right, at least the choke manifold's connected.'

Craig nodded, assessing the metal in his hand. 'Tarek, get this piece a crap to the workshop 'n' see what we can do with it?

'I'm on it.'

'You okay?' he asked, eyeing Ash suspiciously. She'd been on edge since heading out to the rig, and that was out of character.

She grimaced and squinted into the sun. 'I'm fine.' She fixed her eyes on his and forced a smile. 'I'm starving,' she said, fiddling with her safety hat.

'Right y'all, let's take a break.' Craig waved across to Dan and Zack, fitting the piping for the oil line. Dan nodded and raised a thumb.

'Thank fuck!' Zack said, wiping across his brow. 'It must be nearly forty-fucking-five degrees out here.' Dan slapped him on the back, and they made their way to the canteen.

Ash removed her protective gear, stepped into the air-conditioned cabin, and stood under the cold flow of air. 'Ahhh.'

Craig grabbed a glass of water and slumped into the chair, his eyes firmly fixed on the paperwork in his hand. 'Should be rigged up by mornin',' he said. 'Assumin' we get that crossover fixed by lunchtime.' He slapped the paperwork on the table, stood, and approached the food counter.

Ash had already stacked a plate of stew and a mug of coffee onto her tray and was heading for the table he had vacated. 'Looks shit,' she said, as he passed her and reached for a tray.

'Uh huh,' he said, with a smile that revealed his crooked teeth, loading his plate anyway.

Ash leaned back in her seat watching Zack and Dan as they scarfed their large plates of stew. They looked fresher than she felt. The strain of nearly two days rigging up was testing her muscles to the limit of their thirty-two years. She rubbed her lower back and moaned.

'So, how is it?' Craig asked, noting Ash's half-empty plate.

'As predicted,' she said, picking at something stuck in her lower teeth. She gazed out the cabin window towards the tall metal structure reaching into the clear blue sky. An image of Iman's beautiful smile and soft light-brown yet intense eyes interrupted her, and a wave of electric heat shot through her body, settling low in her gut.

'Uh huh,' Craig commented, shovelling the stew into his already full mouth, his grin widening.

Ash glared at him, but couldn't stop the gleam in her eyes. She hadn't spoken about Iman or Kate. She hadn't wanted to talk about Kate, and he hadn't asked about either of them.

'How 'r' those sweets?' he asked, his skin wrinkling at his eyes with the depth of the smile on his face. Ashley flushed. 'Ya gonna share?' he asked, directing his attention to his food and filling his mouth again.

'No,' she said. 'I might trade some,' she added.

'I'm in,' he said, and he was serious. The best he could get otherwise would be a chocolate bar from the small shop run by the catering company, and that didn't come close to the standard of Iman's handmade sweets. 'How's Kate?' he asked, his smile retracting.

Ashley crossed her arms over her chest and slouched into the hard plastic chair. A deep sigh released from her chest and her eyes scanned the ceiling, searching for the words she needed to say. She pulled herself up in the seat, placed her elbows on the table and rested her chin in her hands, rubbing her fingers across her eyes.

'Thought that might be it.'

'What?'

'Ya's been distracted, 's all.' He rubbed his hand across his mouth and sipped at his drink.

She sighed. 'It's complicated.'

'She's into ya, yer know. Big time.'

'That's not fucking helpful bud.'

'I know. Just sayin'.' He shrugged his shoulders and shovelled more food. 'Ya...' He was tilting his head and looking up at her through the top of his eyes. 'Ya slept with her.' It was a statement. He observed Ashley's response.

Ashley raised her hand to cover her eyes and pressed her fingers to her temples. The conversation they had avoided since leaving for the rig was about to happen, and she didn't much feel like contributing. 'Yep,' she said, through tight lips.

'Yer in a mess o' deep shit then,' he stated. 'Shoot! I thought us guys had the market cornered in that department, but you ladies are just as fucked, darlin',' he said, with a slight smirk.

'Fuck off,' she teased. 'What the fuck am I going to do?' she asked in a whisper, leaning across the table.

'Y'all looked good together,' he said, sipping his coffee. 'I thought ya was reeal into her,' he added. His eyes had withdrawn in thought.

Ashley shuddered. Looks could be so deceptive. 'Right,' she said. Kate's face, contorted in ecstasy appearing in her mind's eye, a surge of anxiety firing into her stomach. 'It's complicated,' she repeated.

'You don't love her?' he asked.

'No, I do,' she responded. 'Just...' she paused. 'It's not like it was when we were in Uni. I thought I was in love with her, but now, so much has changed.'

Craig frowned.

'I do love her, and I care about her, but I'm not in love with her,' she said. Expressing the words aloud seemed to settle the feeling of apprehension that had occupied her thoughts since the night before leaving for the rig. The slight relief felt good and strengthened her resolve. 'I just need to find a way to tell her,' she added.

'Yup,' Craig responded, staring at her.

She released a long breath.

'Anyone else?' he asked, knowing the answer. He scratched at his rugged cheeks and lounged back into the seat, placing his arms across his chest.

She released another long breath. 'No,' she said, her eyes lowering to the table, Iman's reflection staring back at her. 'That's complicated too,' she added, with a deep sigh.

'Ah huh. Ya's gotta lotta complicated goin' on,' he said, shaking his head and standing. He slapped her affectionately on the arm. 'Ya wanna smoke?' he asked, heading towards the kitchen clearing-hatch and placing his empty mug on the shelf.

'Yup.'

'Jeez,' he said, as the blast of heat hit them and sweat beaded on his forehead instantly.

'Yep, hotter than hell,' she said, heading straight for the perimeter boundary. She pulled out the pouch as she walked, fiddled with the sheet of paper to open it, and strung out the thin line of tobacco. She had the roll-up between her lips and lit one pace short of the boundary.

'I'll card ya for that,' Craig teased.

'Fuck off,' she joked, knowing he wouldn't report her for smoking one step before the perimeter. Inhaling and breathing out the smoke, fixated on the image of Iman in her flowing dress and the intensity behind her light-brown eyes, she moaned. She inhaled again, staring into the vast expanse and the waves of sand that stretched into infinity. Only the persistent pounding and grinding of metal on metal interrupted the desert's natural beauty. 'Look,' she said, pointing to the movement in the sand. A scorpion darted in front of them; its tail poised.

Craig scanned the sand by his feet and started hopping from one foot to the other. 'Long as there's no fuckin' spiders,' he said. 'Hate 'em critters.'

'You wuss,' she teased, slapping him on the arm. She stamped out the last of the roll-up and blew out the smoke from her lungs. 'Come on darlin',' she teased. 'I want to get that separator connected tonight. Can you go see if they can get that crossover fixed? If not, we'll need one first thing!'

'Uh huh', he said, heading towards the workshop. 'Tarek's on it.'

*

Ashley groaned. The hot water was too hot. It was always too hot! She eased under the shower resting her hands against the cubicle wall. Slowly adjusting to the temperature, she leaned her head into the spray and allowed it to flow down over her aching body. She moved her feet, and they found the gritty water in the shower bowl. She raised her foot and washed the underside, massaging its arch. Standing tall, she pressed her thumb and fingers into her right shoulder, trying to relieve the tension that had built there.

'Ya gonna be long?' Craig hollered.

'Yep,' she shouted back, starting to laugh. She took the shower gel in her hand and rubbed it into her cheeks, progressing down her body and down her legs, her senses invigorated by the fresh citrus and spicy tones of juniper and rosemary; the detoxifying effect helping to ease her tired muscles. She rinsed the suds slowly, finally appreciating the heat of the water. Stepping out of the shower, she rubbed the small towel roughly through her hair and then loosely down her body. Still damp, she threw on her t-shirt and shorts and stepped into the room. 'All yours,' she said. Craig dived in and shut the door.

She pulled back the curtain separating her bunk from his and lay on the thin mattress, resting her hands under the back of her head. Drifting with the running water from the shower cubical and Craig's tenor voice through the thin wall, her eyes wandered to the cloth-covered tin on the low table next to her bed. She pulled herself up, reached for the tin, and wrestled off its stiff lid. The sweet-nutty aroma assaulted her senses, and she swallowed. She toyed with the differently wrapped sweets, her eyes selecting one, her fingers unwrapping it.

'Ya fixin' t' give me one?' Craig interrupted, the sweet poised at Ashley's lips.

She popped the dark chocolate into her mouth and groaned. 'Nope,' she moaned, closing the lid on the tin before Craig's hand reached it.

'Come on, fess up; ya know ya wanna share.' He put on his best doe-eyed look, and she started laughing.

She wiped at the corner of her mouth, trying to contain the melting chocolate that had caused her jaw to ache with ecstasy. 'They're soo good,' she said, teasing him.

He stood; towel wrapped around his waist, a wicked grin spanning his face. He made a move to unwrap the towel and started to expose his leg, threatening to reveal more.

Ashley's brows rose, and she started to splutter. She opened the tin and presented it to him. 'Fuck, bud, put it away and take one,' she said, still choking on the crushed nuts, hidden inside the chocolate shell.

Craig tucked the towel back in place, unwrapped a purple-covered sweet and popped it into his mouth. 'I'll be damned,' he said, throwing himself onto his bed, chuckling. 'These are reeal good!' He sneaked his arm across the space, seeking out the tin.

She slapped the lid on and pulled it out of reach. 'Tomorrow,' she said.

'I'll trade ya,' he said.

'Yep. Tomorrow.' She closed the curtain and turned towards the wall, thoughts of Iman causing her stomach to flutter. She tossed and turned.

'Tarek couldn't fix that fuckin' crossover,' Craig said, rustling noises accompanying his words. 'I've asked the base to send one first thing. Kate's gonna bring it, she wants t' introduce herself t' the company man,' he added.

Ashley tensed down the length of her body. 'Good,' she responded, but the tone was wrong. Kate's image now sat at the front of her mind. The light fluttering that had warmed her chest had turned to full-on stress burning in her solar plexus, and her heart raced. She released her clenched fists and tried to soften her jaw. She'd have to tell Kate sooner rather than later.

14.

'So?' Muhammad asked, staring at his daughter's back as she studied the paperwork in her hand.

She turned to face him, and he placed a cup of tea in her hand. Her heart sank at his heavy lids and flat features, which didn't match the enthusiasm in his voice. He tried to smile, but it was still lacking. 'I need a three-month visa for the training,' she said, pacing the room. 'Or a work visa, which might take six months or more to come through, if I have a job to go to,' she continued.

'We can get you a job,' he offered, sipping his tea. 'If you're willing to wait that long?' It was more than a simple question.

Ash's smiling face, the cute blonde bob tucked behind her ear, and the dark-blue eyes that seemed to expose something intangible stopped her. She sighed at the dull resignation that disturbed her thoughts. 'If I go on the course first then I can start sooner,' she said. He nodded. 'I can come back after the course and apply for a full visa,' she continued. The idea that Ash might have moved on by then struck her, and she moved her hand to chest. Nausea passed quickly, replaced by sharp spasms contracting in her gut. She gripped around her waist, her eyes grasping for something on which to focus, other than her father.

'Are you okay Immy?' he asked softly, placing his steady hand on her shoulder and pulling her into his arms.

She snuffled in response. 'I think so,' she said. 'I just don't know...' She rested in his arms until the sniffling eased.

'Whatever you decide now, you can always choose not to go,' he said, kissing her softly on the top of her head. 'Minds do change.'

She stood taller, comforted by his words, and with renewed determination. 'I need to get lunch across to the base,' she said, dabbing at the corner of her eyes with the edge of the apron hanging from her waist. The thought of seeing Kate at the canteen caused a surge of anxiety, but she breathed deeply, maintaining her resolve to remain professional.

'We can talk later,' he said. 'There's plenty of time, no need to rush into anything.'

She smiled and kissed him on the cheek. 'Thank you,' she whispered.

*

Kate tapped at the keyboard, stopped, deleted, and started again. Finally accepting defeat, she huffed and stood.

The jittery feeling hadn't lifted since Ash had headed out to the rig. She had been desperate to see her, but it had been too soon to arrange a spot check, as they hadn't started testing yet. She'd jumped at the chance to personally deliver the crossover, under the guise of introducing herself to the company man, but now she was feeling even more anxious at the idea of facing Ash!

She rubbed her hands through her hair, massaged her scalp, and rubbed her palms across her eyes. She picked up the mug of coffee, sipped, and winced at the cold, oily texture of the liquid. She placed the cup back on the desk and headed for the base canteen.

She stepped into the room, wiped at the sweat that had formed at her hairline in the short distance from the office cabin, and inhaled the sweet smelling aroma.

'Hi Katherine, can I get you anything?' Iman asked. She hadn't been able to soften her tone or bring herself to use the more familiar 'Kate' that she had adopted from the start of their acquaintance, and her smile lacked its usual openness and warmth, the image of Katherine kissing Ash by the pool clouding her senses.

'Can I get a decent coffee?' Katherine pleaded. 'The stuff from that is woeful,' she said, indicating to the industrial machine at the end of the food counter.

Iman softened at the honest assessment, smiled and nodded. 'I'll make you a proper one,' she said.

'Thanks.' Katherine picked up a tray, selected the falafel, hummus and pita bread and moved down to the sweet dishes, choosing a sticky cookie topped with chopped dates and walnuts. Lunch was drawing to an end, and all bar one table was empty. She sat at the furthest point from the remaining two workers in the room, pondering and picking at the food on her plate.

Iman approached with a steaming pot of freshly brewed coffee and placed it on the table. 'It's good,' Iman said, Kate's pensive look drawing an inquisitive smile.

Kate's eyes held Iman's gaze. 'If you made it, it will be,' she said, her smile tight, her eyes laden with something akin to sadness. Loss? Remorse? Kate stared, her eyes searching. 'Will you sit for a minute?' she asked.

Iman's breath caught, and she paused. 'I...' she started, but couldn't deny the pain emanating from the dark-green eyes. 'Yes, of course,' she said.

'Lunch is finished.' She nodded towards the counter and slid into the seat opposite Kate, waiting for her to speak.

Kate poured the coffee into her cup. 'Would you like one?' she asked.

Iman blinked, rose from the seat and collected a cup from the counter.

'Can I talk to you?' Kate asked, staring into her eyes as she returned to sit.

Iman tried not to avoid Kate, but her eyes flicked around the woman's face, settling on the full lips that were starting to quiver. 'Yes,' she said, keeping the tension in her body from being exposed through her voice. She sat upright, poured a coffee, and sipped from the cup. 'How can I help?' she asked. *Please don't let this be about Ash.*

'I know you know Ash quite well,' she started.

Iman cringed, feeling the heat rise in her chest and the gaping hole that had just opened in her stomach. She sipped at the coffee in her hand without answering the question.

'And she respects you a lot,' Katherine continued.

Iman winced as the coffee shot into her mouth more quickly than she had expected. She placed her cup on the table and a napkin to the burning sensation on her top lip. With her heart racing, she breathed in, the air coming out as a deep sigh.

'Sorry, I was wondering whether you two talk,' she said, dipping the bread into the hummus. 'I was wondering if she'd said anything about us.' She added, looking up from the dip that she continued to prod at, aimlessly.

Iman's mouth opened and then closed. She swallowed down the lump in her throat and took in a breath. 'Um, no, she hasn't. We don't really talk,' Iman said, thankful for the small truth.

Katherine nodded slowly, put down the bread, and sipped at her coffee.

'You look… worried,' Iman said, for want of a more fitting word.

Katherine shrugged and turned to the window. 'We were together for some time,' she said.

Iman's eyes lowered to her clammy hands, fiddling them in her lap, and cleared her throat.

'Sorry, I didn't mean to offend you. I got the impression you were...' Her eyes turned towards Iman, as Iman's eyes lifted. Their meeting provided the certainty Kate had assumed, and she nodded almost imperceptibly. 'I thought so,' she said, turning back to the window. 'Do you like her?' Katherine asked suddenly, her tone shifting to something more defensive.

Iman froze. Her shoulders rose, and her jaw opened as she gasped for breath. She couldn't speak.

'It's okay. I'm not going to say anything,' Katherine confirmed, her tone now flat, sombre even, her eyes still focused on nothing particular on the other side of the window. 'You've answered my question,' she said.

Iman remained silent, fighting the unease that paralysed her. It was a war she would lose.

'You know we made love before she went to the rig?' Katherine said, turning her head as she spoke, fixing her gaze on Iman again. Her dark-green eyes had darkened.

Iman gulped, shifting her gaze to her shaking hands, then out the window.

'I thought so,' Kate continued. 'I thought I saw you at the party, watching us,' she added.

Iman's eyes had started to water, and she rubbed at them, sweeping away the tears that were falling onto her cheeks.

Katherine leaned back in the seat, studying the young woman intently. 'You're in love with her,' she stated.

Iman's chin dropped, her world collapsing under the weight of Katherine's words. She couldn't stop the quivering that was now consuming her whole body. Anything she said would just come out wrong, or make her look vulnerable, or stupid. She stood slowly, turned, and walked with as much grace as she could muster until she reached the kitchen. Placing her hands on the sides of the sink, she stood until the shaking abated, trying not to throw up. The tears dried, and the anger buried itself, leaving her with a greater sense of certainty. She needed to leave Syria, sooner rather than later.

*

'Ya got that pipe tightened?' Craig bellowed.

Tarek's arms halted, the heavy hammer resting precariously in mid-air, sweat streaming down his temples. Damn connections! 'I've got it,' he groaned, his teeth clenched, the veins in his forearms bulging. Letting the hammer drop, the thundering crack of steel on steel vibrated through the ground and he lifted it again. Another crack got lost in the desert.

Craig turned his back, looked at the paper in his hand, then up, his eyes scanning around the site before landing on Dan. 'Dan!' he yelled. Dan looked up and gave the thumbs up. The separator was up and running. He made a mark on the piece of paper and headed for the lab cabin.

Ash yanked on the heavy chain securing the piping to the ground. It didn't budge. She moved onto the next one, and the next. 'Check your chains, Dan,' she yelled over the banging. He looked up giving another thumbs up and started checking the metal rings were firmly attached to the ground. 'You got the Emergency Shut Down stations installed?' she shouted. Dan responded again, and she reciprocated with double-thumbs up. 'Get that last piping hammered in and we're good to go,' she said. Tarek nodded, letting the hammer rest at his feet.

She stood, rubbed at her plugged ears, squinted into the blinding sun, and inhaled the soothing, sweet, earthy, aroma of the clay from the mud-tanks. 'Break,' she yelled. She swiped at the sweat dripping from her hardhat and reached into her coveralls pocket. Pulling out the pouch, she headed for the boundary. As soon as she stepped over the line, she slumped to the ground and lit the roll-up. Craig's long legs were already heading in her direction. She rolled him a cigarette and handed it up to him as he reached her.

'Thanks,' he said, pulling out his lighter. 'So, looks like we're close,' he said.

'Yep.' She drew down, the red tip brightening, sucked in the drug and started reeling off the checklist. 'We're nearly connected,' she said with a wry smile. 'ESD's are all hooked up, separator's checked, and the acquisition network is hooked up to the lab cabin.' She drew down again and blew out slowly. 'And it's still fucking hotter than hell.'

'Briefin' first thing, then we'll move t' shifts. We'll pressure test with Tarek once the wellhead's connected.' he said, puffing out rings and blowing them into the sun. 'No rush, the plan's t' fire the guns-in-hole after the briefin', once the pressure tests are complete. Ya can go to bed now sleepin' beauty.' He sucked, breathed in hard, and blew out a long stream of smoke, which hovered in the heat, before drifting slowly away.

Ash rolled her eyes, stomped on the end of the cigarette and started filling another paper. 'Will Kate be at the briefing?' she asked.

'No. She'll drop the crossover early, then prep for the client meetin'. Ya'll be asleep,' he teased.

She slapped his shin. The adjustment to night shift would take a day or two, but maybe she could hide out in her cabin after the briefing and avoid Kate.

'What?' He failed to sound innocent, and she slapped him again.

'Coffee?' she asked, standing and finishing the cigarette.

'Hell yeah.'

15.

Craig stood up from the choke manifold and spoke into the handheld radio. 'Okay, I got 1,000 psi t' the rig.' He nodded his head as the rhythmical whooshing and pumping came to a stop.

'Got 1,000 psi at the choke manifold,' Tarek confirmed.

'Sensors all look good. Got 1,000 psi all across.' Sayid confirmed from the lab cabin. He recorded the details diligently in the tally.

'Holdin' for 5,' Craig's voice came again. He wiped the sweat from his brow and clicked his neck from side to side, keeping one eye on the gauge. 'Ya can bleed off now.' He watched the pressure drop. 'Okay, we're good. Ya can carry on,' he said to Tarek, heading for the boundary.

It was never the same without Ashley though. He puffed quickly on a cigarette, his mind occupied with his concerns for Katherine. She wasn't going to take rejection well, and as much as he and Ashley were close, he had shared something with Katherine that had bonded them differently. He thumped at his chest with the heel of his hand, but the ache there remained. He buried the cigarette butt with his foot and then headed back to the lab cabin.

Ash lazed on her bed, the clunking and grinding sounds moving beyond her awareness, her mind distracted by more pressing thoughts. She drifted to the night of the party, and the sharp pain that wouldn't go away. The soft click of the cabin door stirred her, and she sat bolt upright.

Kate tiptoed through the door, stopping instantly as Ash's eyes landed on her. 'Sorry, I didn't mean to disturb you,' she said.

'Then why come in?' Ash asked, her tone sharp.

'I…' she approached the bed. 'I've missed you,' she said.

Ash swung her legs off the bed, sat up, and ruffled through her hair. She picked up her watch from the bedside table and studied it. 'You're early,' she said.

'You needed that crossover, and I thought maybe we could do lunch,' Kate said, easing down on the bed, sitting next to Ash and staring at Craig's bunk in front of her. She turned her head and fixed her eyes on Ash, who remained focused on the plain wall in front of her. She smiled at the unruly blonde hair tucked behind her ear, sticking out at the top and back. She wanted to reach out and trace the fine line of her jaw down to her mouth, and tease her finger over her beautifully shaped lips. 'You are beautiful,' she said.

Ash pressed her hand to her chest, wrapping her other arm around her body, the tightness refusing to budge. She fought to breathe deeply, suffocating in the atmosphere she perceived between them. Kate's words were constricting, where they should have softened. She turned slowly, her eyes resisting Kate's dark-green gaze. She had no words to help her. Even her body betrayed her where Kate was concerned. As her eyes settled on the red-hair,

Kate's sudden movement immobilised her. Kate's lips were pressing against hers, and her hands were clasped around her head, pulling her closer.

For a split second, she conceded to the touch. Kate's tongue started to probe, and Ash pulled back suddenly, gasping. She stood, rubbed frantically at her mouth, flicked her fingers through her hair, and paced around the small cabin. 'I can't do this,' she said. 'I can't do this.'

Kate stood, grabbed Ash's arm, and stilled her. The grip was firm, and Ash recoiled from the touch. Kate's eyes narrowed, and she manoeuvred Ash backwards, pressing her firmly against the wall. Ash tried to pull out of the hold, but

145

Kate had grounded her weight and leaned heavily against her. The fire in her eyes flared, and she clashed her mouth against Ash's. Ash tried to move away, but Kate persisted.

Ash's passionate urges were convincing her to take what she needed, enticing her into the passionate kiss, the submission causing Kate to soften her grip. Iman's sweet face flashed in front of her eyes, and she jolted, a rush of adrenaline giving her the strength to duck out of Kate's grasp. 'No!' she screamed. 'Kate, no!'

Kate was panting; her hands clasped at the side of her head. She held out her right hand, palm facing Ash. 'I'm sorry. I'm sorry. I'm sorry.' Her hand moved to the bridge of her nose, squeezing tightly, and her shoulders started to bounce up and down.

Ash watched, reclaiming her breath and allowing her pulse to slow. Kate was sobbing, and it was breaking her heart. *This wasn't Kate.* She took the two short paces and pulled the distraught woman into her arms.

'Sshhh,' she said.

Kate rested her cheek against Ash's chest, allowing the tears to fall silently. The banging, clunking, and grinding noises from the rig slowly increased in volume. 'I'm so sorry Ash.'

Ash released her from the embrace, held her shoulders, and looked her in the eye. 'It's not me you want Kate.' Kate shook her head slowly from side to side. 'Sit down,' she said. Kate sat, and Ash sat next to her on the bed, facing the wall. 'I know we were good together,' Ash started. 'And, you know, when I first saw you in the restaurant all those amazing feelings came flooding back. I thought we might have been good again,' Ash admitted. Kate was nodding.

'But...' She paused. Sighed. 'I've realised...' She turned and cupped Kate's face, holding her gaze tenderly. 'I will always love you. I'll always remember our year together as something amazing.' She wiped away an errant tear from

Kate's cheek. Kate was already nodding in acceptance of the words that she knew were coming. 'Things have changed, Kate. I'm not who I was back then either.'

'I know,' Kate added.

'I can't be what you want me to be.'

'I know.'

*

Iman licked the envelope and sealed the flap. She turned it over, wrote out the address and added the stamp.

'What's that?' Niomi asked.

'My Visa application,' Iman said excitedly, before realising she hadn't meant to say anything. 'You can't tell anyone,' she said sharply. 'And especially not Zack,' she added.

Niomi's eyes dropped. 'I won't,' she said. But that wasn't what was troubling her. 'You're leaving,' she said, her tone subdued, tears pressing at the back of her eyes. She collapsed onto the restroom seat and held her head in her hands.

Iman placed the envelope in her locker and locked the door. 'Not for a while,' she said. 'Maybe six months or more,' she lied.

Niomi looked up, her eyes wet. 'Why?' she asked.

Iman frowned.

'Because of...' Niomi struggled with the word.

'Because I like girls?' Iman asked for her.

'Umm,' she stuttered, averting her gaze.

'See, even you, my friend, struggles with it,' Iman said, gesturing with her arm in the air.

Niomi's eyes dropped again. 'I'm sorry, it's just difficult.'

'I know. But, anyway, it's not just about that. I want to train as a proper chef,' she said, her voice cheery and enthused.

Niomi's head shot back up. 'A chef!' Her questioning eyes searched

Iman, her head shaking as she processed the statement.

'Yes. What's wrong with that?' Iman retorted.

'Why do you need to go away for that?' Niomi asked, shrugging, her hands raised in prayer.

'I want to be the best.'

Niomi's hands dropped to her lap. 'You are the best Immy. You're already the best.'

'Anyway, nothing's decided yet.'

'Well, I hope you decide to stay.' Niomi was fiddling with her apron.

'Want me to teach you to make the best Kanafeh?' Iman asked excitedly.

The dessert of shredded filo pastry and melted cheese soaked in sugary syrup was one of her favourite dishes. 'I'll share my special ingredient,' she added, trying to coax Niomi from her sulk.

Niomi looked up and started to grin. 'Will you?'

'Yes. Let's go and cook.' Iman held out a hand and tugged Niomi to her feet.

'We'll make it all from scratch,' she said. 'You'll need cold hands,' she added, rubbing her sweaty palm after their brief contact.

Niomi giggled and headed for the sink.

*

'Ya's early.' Craig sipped at the coffee that would most likely keep him awake until the early hours, and yawned.

Ash pulled out the chair, sat, and sipped at her mug. 'Yeah, can't see you sleeping through that fucking noise either.' she said, laughing. The oil burner coming alight had jolted her awake, and she hadn't been able to get back to sleep.

'Uh huh.' He scanned her face, lingering on her eyes. 'Everythin' okay?' he asked. 'I saw ya had a visitor,' he added before she spoke.

Ash looked away, then down to the floor. 'I think that's all sorted now,' she said, returning to his face with a tight-lipped smile.

'Her face was blacker 'an midnight under a skillet. Hardly said a word.' he said, sipping, watching Ash's response.

She nodded, breathing deeply.

'So, that it?' he asked.

'Yep,' she said, holding his gaze with the answer he already had.

'Wa'al shit!' he said softly. He turned his attention to the window, the rig lights adding a little illumination to the night sky, but his eyes were vacant. Even the exquisite flaming red waves firing into the darkness held no interest. He continued to stare, sucking softly through his teeth.

'You okay?' she asked.

His dark-brown eyes were almost black when he turned to face her. 'Ah huh,' he said, but she didn't believe him.

She finished her coffee in silence and grabbed another. When she returned to the table, he had gone. She sat in his spot and stared out the same window. Had she upset him? That would be a first. She slouched into the seat, feeling drained. Even Iman's image brought with it a sense of sadness that was unfamiliar to her. It was going to be a very long night.

16.

Ash stood at the boundary, the clunking and grinding noises, a constant assault on her ears even with her earplugs rammed deep, her eyelids weighed down by the long night. She drew in the smoke slowly, released it effortlessly, watching intently the slither of light that spanned the horizon, expanding and rising quickly, into a fiery ball. She shivered, shrugging her shoulders to alleviate the tingling sensation that had descended her spine. It wasn't cold. Her tired eyes pondered the buzzing sand, shaken by the ravaging insults taking place deep below its surface. She smiled at the bug that darted across her boot zigzagging its way across the dune. *Life!*

'Hey!' Craig's upbeat tone jolted her out of her musings, and she turned to face him. He pulled out a cigarette as he approached, his eyes avoiding hers. 'Didn't mean t' skip out on ya last night,' he said, flicking the lighter and inhaling.

She tilted her head to the side and looked up into his weary eyes. 'You're in love with her, aren't you?' she asked. She had spent the night pondering his response, and it had been the only answer she could find. He flushed and fidgeted, and continued to smoke.

'I was,' he said, but his eyes evaded her questioning gaze. He looked pensive. 'Maybe there's still somethin' there,' he said. 'I do care 'bout her,' he admitted.

'Fuck, bud, why didn't you say something before?' Her tone was urgent but empathic.

'Guess I didn't know how I felt. Kate looked happy, and I wasn't 'bout t' get in yer way,' he said, shrugging as he revealed his rationale.

Ash stomped on the end of the cigarette and stood with her hands on her hips; her eyes focused on the mark she'd made in the sand. 'Jeez, I didn't realise,' she said, scratching the back of her head.

'D'ya think she'll be alright?' Craig asked, with something akin to desperation in his voice.

Ash looked up and held his dark-brown eyes and the slight twitch that appeared just underneath his right eye when something was important to him. She'd only seen that look once before, and it had melted her heart then too. She slapped him on the arm. 'I'm sure she'll be fine,' she said. He tried to smile, put out his cigarette, and turned towards the rig. 'Maybe you should talk to her,' she offered.

'Ah huh,' he responded, his eyes drawn to the mouth of the flames flaring up into the desert sky. 'Maybe I will,' he said, looking for the courage he'd need.

'You doing lunch?' she asked, as she stepped into the canteen.

'Ya mean breakfast,' he said, with a coy smile. 'Hell, yeah, I'm starvin'.'

*

Ash staggered through the door of her cabin, leaving her hat and gloves by the door, and undid her coveralls as she walked towards her bed. She glanced at her watch on the table. 2pm. Midnight already seemed too close.

She dropped the coveralls at her feet, collected her towel, and stepped into the shower room. She rubbed at the cramp that tweaked in her stomach; she'd eaten too quickly. *Fucking hot water!* She stepped tentatively into the roasting spray, with no way of cooling the site-generated shower. She rubbed the suds through her hair and into her face and groaned as the massaged skin came back to life. Drying quickly, she threw on a pair of shorts and t-shirt, filled her laundry bag and threw it out the door, and slumped onto her bed. She

151

reached for the cloth coloured tin, her fingers rubbing across its textured surface, a warm feeling tracing her body. She pulled it down onto her bed, turned on her side and wrapped her arm around it, pulling it closer. Her eyes closed and eventually, her fingers stopped exploring as she drifted into a deep sleep, the thunderous noise from the flare fading into the distance.

*

'What about Ashley?'

Iman looked up and stopped whisking the bowl of eggs in her hand. 'What about Ashley?' she repeated. She smiled, pleased with the fact that her visceral response to the question had remained relatively calm.

'I thought you wanted to be with her?' Niomi pushed.

Iman moaned under her breath. Her heart had started to race, her defences were down, and heat was shading her cheeks. 'That's not going to happen,' she said, through a wave of frustration.

Niomi frowned. 'I thought she was... err, liked girls too.' She smiled that she'd managed to get the words out.

'Yes, and she's with someone else.' Iman couldn't bring herself to name the redhead; just the thought of the woman caused her to flinch. *How could someone be so cruel?* An image of Ash flashed into her mind, sat in the 4x4 the morning they had left for the rig, looking as if she'd been dragged through hell and back. Well, now she knew the truth. She put the bowl down and rubbed her hands frantically down her clean uniform. No matter how hard she rubbed though she couldn't erase the thought; Kate had made love to the woman she had fallen for, and that hurt. She picked up the bowl and whisked vigorously, watched closely by Niomi.

'Do you want to go shopping later?' Niomi asked.

'No thanks,' Iman responded, abruptly. 'Let's get this food out; they'll be in for dinner soon.'

'I wish it was for Zack,' Niomi said.

'Me too,' Iman responded sharply. 'Can you do me a favour?' she asked.

'Of course,' Niomi smiled weakly.

'Will you stay front-of-house and I'll prep for tomorrow?'

Niomi's eyelids fluttered, and her smile deepened. She preferred being front-of-house, but it was rare for Iman to give up the position. 'Of course,' she said.

'Oh, and, another thing.'

'Yes.'

'Would you like to serve the base lunches from now on?'

Niomi's jaw opened, and her face lit up, 'Seriously?' she said, clapping her hands together.

'Yes, seriously.'

'Yes, yes.' Niomi stepped into the restaurant, two inches taller.

'Good,' Iman said, but Niomi was already the other side of the door. She watched from a distance behind the porthole window. Kate entered, selected her food, sat at a table on her own, and then left. Something was lacking in her posture, something distant, devoid of her normally confident and vibrant manner. She looked lonely, isolated, withdrawn even. Iman's heart fluttered with the compassion she felt towards any wounded animal. *She must be desperately missing Ash too!*

*

153

Ashley stirred at the opening door. Craig stepped in quietly, but his boots had other ideas and thumped across the floor.

'Fucking hell, twinkle toes.' she groaned, lifting herself up onto her elbows, and squinting. He had dust and grime plastered across his face, his crooked smile shining through the dim light.

'What time is it?'

'Comin' up t' eleven.'

'You wanna do breakfast?' she asked, straining through a yawn.

'Dinner!' he countered with a chuckle.

Rubbing the sleep out of her eyes, she yawned again. 'Give me five, and we can go for a coffee.'

'I'll meet'cha,' he said, marching back out the door.

Ash moved to stand up, and her hand brushed against the sweet tin. Her mouth watered and she smiled. A burning sensation tracked south in her body, and she groaned. She opened the tin, unwrapped a sweet wrapped in gold paper, and popped it into her mouth. Biting down on the chocolate her jaw abruptly stopped. *Toffee. Yum.* She persisted, wriggling her teeth and tongue to soften the solid, slightly bitter, sweet. As she it eased apart, the liquid caramel centre exploded on her taste buds, and she groaned. She placed another of the same sweet onto Craig's pillow and smiled. Pulling on her clean coveralls, boots, and hardhat, she tucked her gloves under her arm and walked the short distance to the canteen, accompanied by the whooshing sound of the bright red flare, and the thunderous clunking noises, filling the night sky.

She dumped her hat and gloves on the bench, entered the canteen, and slumped opposite Craig, who was sipping his coffee. 'Okay, the well's flowin' nicely on 32"/64 fixed choke, H2S's low, oil 'n' gas samplin's done, separator's workin' like a charm... Plan's t' shut-in the well at 2am for the pressure build up. Ya'll have plenty of time t' fool 'round,' he joked. 'Tarek'll give ya the details. That reminds me, H2S stinks,' Craig said, biting into his sandwich with enthusiasm.

'Always does.' Ash smiled. She stretched in the seat, picked up her coffee and sipped repeatedly. 'Fuck that's disgusting,' she said, swallowing quickly. She headed for the counter and came back with two sugar sleeves, emptying them swiftly into the mug.

'I already put sugar in it,' Craig said, with a broad grin.

'Not enough to kill the taste,' she laughed, stirring in the sugar and trying again. 'Much better,' she said, smacking her lips. She'd much rather have the taste of Iman's sweets lingering on her tongue than the acrid flavour of the drink in her hands, but, the delicious sweets would send her into a dreamy sleep, whereas the coffee would keep her awake; and she needed her wits about her.

'What's that 'bout?' Craig asked.

'What?'

'That look?'

'What look?'

'You had a funny, gooey kinda look there for a moment,' Craig said, a mischievous grin revealing the remains of the sandwich he was chomping on.

'Fuck off,' she said, starting to laugh.

'Just sayin',' he said, slurping at his coffee. 'It is,' he added.

'What?'

'Fuckin' disgustin'.'

Ash bit into the pastry on her plate and chewed. 'This isn't much better either,' she said.

'Kill for a beer,' he said.

'Me too.'

'Another coffee?' he asked.

'Yup.'

He placed the filled cups on the table and threw down a handful of sugar sleeves. 'You good?' she asked.

'I'm gonna talk t' Katherine,' he said, with confidence.

'Good. I think she'd appreciate that.' The twinkle in his eyes didn't escape her notice. 'I hope she...'

'Yeah, I hope...' he said, stopping before the words were out.

Rape was the only word on Ash's mind. Craig represented something from which Kate had been trying to escape. 'She will,' she said, hoping for Craig's sake that Kate would be open to exploring something with him.

17.

Ashley relaxed back in the chair and rubbed her eyes at the relative silence. While it was easy to adjust to the constant hum of the generators, the additional thundering from the flare, together with the stress of the well flowing, created a permanent tension that eventually resulted in complete mental and physical exhaustion. With the well shut-in, providing much-needed breathing space, she closed her eyes. With everything on track, they should be able to kill the well by the end of the week. The thought of being able to see Iman again floated into her mind and caused her stomach to somersault. *Jeez!* She sat upright. The surge of excitement surprised her, encouraging a broad smile that seemed to override the tiredness that had caused her eyes to close. She turned to the opening door, trying to compose herself. 'Zack! Everything okay?' she asked.

His sky-blue eyes looked vacant, and his cheeks red. 'Can I talk to you?' he asked.

'Sure. I've got time now. Sit,' she said, pointing to the only other desk chair in the cabin.

He shrugged his already slouching shoulders, his eyes downcast, and slumped into the seat. He looked dejected, and something else. 'It's Niomi,' he said.

Ashley's ears pricked up. *Fuck, she's pregnant!*

He shook his head at her wide-eyed glare. 'No, she's not pregnant. I wish she was,' he said, despondently.

Ashley frowned. 'That my friend would cause you a whole lot of trouble,' she said, with a slight smile, trying to raise his spirits.

He huffed. 'Yeah, I know.' His eyes tracked the cabin floor.

She stood and placed a firm hand on his shoulder. 'It's great you feel that way about her.'

His head rose, tears spilling from his eyes. 'How's that so great when her parents will reject me?' he asked.

She lowered herself and faced him directly. 'There's always a way Zack. Does she love you?'

'She says she does,' he said, wiping his dirty sleeve across his damp cheeks, sustaining her gaze.

'Then you need to find a way,' she said. She looked intently into his glassy eyes. 'Sometimes we need to help our parents move on,' she said. 'They can be stuck in their fears. It's tough, but you need to be strong for Niomi, and find a way to talk to her parents.' She winced, knowing she had failed to live up to her words of advice with her parents, but she wasn't about to share her inadequacies with him.

He was nodding and starting to smile. 'It's fucking lonely as hell out here,' he said.

'Can be,' she said. Her eyes locked onto the metal structures out the cabin window. But it is beautiful here too, she pondered. The flare; dancing, singing, so vast; that was an incredible sight. The darkness of night; so dark, and with thousands of bright stars visible to the naked eye. And then there was the desert itself; wave after wave of red, orange and gold, never beginning and never-ending. 'Can be very awe-inspiring,' she said. He frowned and she pressed her hand reassuringly on his arm. 'You can find a way,' she insisted.

'Yeah,' Zack responded, but he couldn't see how.

'I gotta change the paper charts before the next flow period,' she said.

'Sure.' He stood.

'One more week Zack! One more week.'

'Sure. Thanks,' he said exiting the cabin, though his tone hadn't lifted.

'Hi Katherine.'

'Craig.' The acknowledgement was brief, official; stuffy even, but it still caused heat to enhance Craig's already rugged complexion.

He studied her wavy red locks sticking out randomly, courtesy of wearing a hard hat; and the light-green eyes that seemed to stare straight through him, and smiled. He'd always been captivated by Kate's eyes and the way they shifted in tone. His heart raced, and his hands were beginning to sweat.

'Company man's here already; Jean-Marc,' he added.

'Okay, shall we?' she said, pointing towards the meeting room. She needed to apologise to Ash, but she would still be asleep. *Fucking shifts!* Craig opened the door. Katherine planted her most welcoming smile on her face and strutted into the room. 'Good afternoon Jean-Marc,' she said.

'Katherine,' he responded, taking her hand, his eyes undressing her from top to toe and back again.

She winced and pulled away from his cold, weak grip. 'Right, let's get this meeting started,' she said, moving to take a seat at the small table.

Craig's blood boiled. 'Coffee?' he asked, nudging the company man towards the urn of hot water and coffee powder. 'Hey, we've gone all out today,' he jested. 'We got cookies!'

Jean-Marc leaned across him, grabbing at the cookies on the plate.

'Thanks,' he said taking the offered cup from Craig.

Craig handed out a second cup to Kate, the small hairs rising up his arm when her hand touched his. He cleared his throat. 'Right, let's talk, then we can get started with the inspection.'

Jean-Marc dunked his cookie. 'Merde,' he cursed, as the soggy end plopped back into his cup.

Craig stood, collected the plate, and placed it on the table. 'There's more,' he said. 'Here.'

*

Ashley flicked through the numbers in her book, sipping at the hot drink in her hand. The sun had long since risen into the sky, and the day shift crew were already working. She shovelled a spoonful of bean stew into her mouth and chewed twice before swallowing; any longer and she would have needed to acknowledge the taste. She washed the lumpy food down her throat with more coffee and leaned back in the seat, allowing the yawn to widen her jaw. She groaned as she stretched.

'Mornin',' Craig said, plonking his drink and plate on the table opposite her.

'Evening,' she teased, rubbing her eyes and yawning again.

'Good night?' he asked.

'Zack's struggling,' she said, glancing out the window, her interest momentarily piqued by the increasing density of the grime sitting on the outside of the pane. She turned back and sipped at her coffee.

Craig shrugged, 'That it?'

'What?'

'Well, any details?' he asked, frowning.

'Niomi,' she added.

'Ah huh.' He scooped up a spoonful of beans and swallowed them without chewing, then rapidly picked up his coffee and slurped it. 'Fucking can't wait to get back to some good food,' he said, rolling his tongue around his teeth.

'That too.'

'What decent food?'

'No, getting out of here. He's lonely.'

'Fuckin' rookie,' Craig complained, but his tone revealed more compassion than he cared to show.

'Yeah, he's young. But, he's got a thing for Niomi, and he's a good operative.'

'Yeah, he's a good kid. Reminds me of me,' he said.

'He's barely five-foot-six,' she said, laughing.

'Fuck off.'

'I can't eat any more of this shit. You wanna smoke?' she asked.

He shovelled the remainder of his beans and downed his coffee, rubbing the cuff of his sleeve across his mouth. 'Hell yeah,' he said, clearing his plate and heading out the door.

'How did the meeting go?' she asked, as they walked to the boundary.

'Client's happy, so we're happy.' His smile suggested there was more.

'And Kate?'

His face lit up. 'She's good.' He tilted his head from side to side.

'What?' she asked, looking straight into his eyes.

'Got some work t' do there,' he admitted, but his eyes were shining.

'And you want to, right?'

'Yup.'

She slapped him on the arm. 'Good.'

He placed a cigarette in his mouth then crossed the perimeter line.

'You could get carded for that,' she teased.

'Shoot!' Craig laughed, flicking his lighter and sucking down hard.

*

Niomi skipped her way around the kitchen, a beaming smile lighting up her eyes. 'One more week, one more week.' She grabbed Iman's arm and squeezed it tightly. 'One more week!' she exclaimed. Her excitement was infectious, and Iman's smile broadened, bordering on a chuckle. 'Are you excited?'

'Yes, of course,' Iman responded, though she wouldn't have labelled her feelings that way. Anxious might have been a closer description. She had managed to avoid Katherine since the incident at the base canteen, and she hadn't thought about how she was going to deal with Ash's return.

Niomi studied her friend. 'When are you going to tell her?' she asked, perceptively.

Iman looked up from the bread she was kneading, her eyes vacant.

'You have to tell her,' Niomi responded, shaking her head at the idea that Iman hadn't planned to say anything.

Iman pounded the dough with a heavier hand than required. 'I told you, she's with someone else; so it doesn't matter that I'll be leaving.'

'You don't know that.' Niomi walked around the metal workbench that separated them and stood in Iman's space. She pulled Iman around to face her, holding her gaze intently. 'You can't let her go, just like that,' she said. Water was beginning to pool across Iman's lower lids and trip over the edge onto her cheeks. 'You're in love with her, I can see it.'

Iman closed her eyes and bit down on her quivering lip. Her head tilted backwards, and a low groan escaped her mouth. She opened her eyes. 'I can't,' she said. 'She's in love with someone else. There's nothing I can do about that.' Her arms hung lifelessly down at her sides, then she raised a shaking hand and pressed it against her forehead.

'You don't know that for sure.' Niomi grabbed Iman's hand and squeezed tightly, rubbing her thumbs soothingly across her knuckles. 'I mean, you just might be wrong, that's all,' she said softly. 'I've seen how she looks at you. She doesn't look at anyone else like that.' Niomi's gaze was as tender as her touch. 'I mean it. Even Zack thinks she's hot for you,' she said.

Iman choked and started to laugh through the tears.

'What?' Niomi asked.

Iman was still chuckling. 'It's nothing. It's just funny hearing you talk that way.' She reached out and cupped Niomi's rosy-cheeks. 'Thank you; you're a good friend.' She pulled her into a hug and kissed the top of her head. Niomi squeezed tightly. 'One more week, eh!' Niomi squeezed again.

*

'Hi.'

Ash stopped and looked up from the table. 'Oh, hi,' she said.

Kate strolled across to the counter and filled a cup of coffee, then crossed the room. 'I thought you'd be in bed by now,' she said, sipping the hot drink.

'I was just chilling for half-an-hour,' she said. Ash sighed at the sorrow weighing down Kate's eyes, her own eyes burning from the days of twelve-hour shifts, the ever-present mix of heat and H2S gas, and then there was the insane noise that seemed to infiltrate every cell in her body. She repeatedly blinked, struggling to hold Kate's stare.

'You look tired,' Kate said.

Ash rubbed at her face. She hadn't looked in the mirror since they arrived; she didn't need to. 'I am,' she said, sipping the hot chocolate drink and stifling a yawn. She winced at the strong sugary taste that had never seen a cocoa bean, ever. 'What do you want?' she asked, her voice quiet, weary.

'Can I sit?' Kate asked, pointing at the seat opposite her.

Ash nodded, leaned forward and rested her elbows on the table, her cup poised at her lips. 'You okay?' she asked. There was no malice in her tone, just exhaustion.

'I just wanted to apologise.'

'You already did.' Ash responded, lifting her elbows off the table and leaning back into the seat.

Kate's face twitched. 'I mean a proper apology. I really am sorry. I behaved badly, Ash, really badly.'

'Yes, you did.' Ash stifled a yawn and continued to rub her hand across her face.

'And, I...' She was struggling for the words. 'It's not like me.'

'No, it's not.' Ash smiled weakly.

'I am truly sorry.'

'Apology accepted,' Ash said, sitting more upright in the seat.

'Thank you.' Kate's eyes lowered to her cup on the table. 'I'm going to resign,' she said.

Ash's eyebrows shot upwards. 'Why?'

'I think it's for the best,' she said, rubbing her fingers through her flattened hair, her features remaining emotionless.

'What makes you think that?' Ash asked, unsure whether she should feel compassion for Kate's suffering or annoyance at her victim mentality, and feeling something closer to bemused.

'I need to deal with the past,' she continued. 'And being around you, and even Craig... well, it's not easy.'

Ash pursed her lips and nodded. 'Have you talked to Craig about this?'

'Talked to me 'bout what?' Craig interrupted, beaming a smile at his two favourite women.

'Nothing,' Katherine blurted.

'She wants to resign,' Ash said, watching Craig's face transform at the news. 'Exactly,' she said. 'Right, I've got to get to bed. I'll leave you two to chat,' she said. Her attention on Craig, and her back to Kate, she pulled a face at the Texan, which said, talk to her. Within three paces, she had shut the door and was heading for the boundary, the already prepped roll-up held lightly between her lips.

'What's all that about?' Craig asked. 'Please don't resign,' he said, slumping into the seat Ashley had vacated.

Kate huffed, rubbed her hand across her tense face then tapped a finger on the table. 'It's not that simple,' she said, unable to hold his deep-brown eyes.

He reached across and gently cupped her fidgeting hand. 'I know,' he said, drawing her eyes to him. He smiled warmly, and she responded with a slight movement of her lips. It was enough. 'Ya can talk t' me,' he said softly.

She slid hands out of the touch. 'Not now,' she said, rising from the seat. 'I need to get back to the base.' She put her hand on his shoulder and squeezed, turned to the door, and headed to her car.

18.

'Right, we've started killin' the well. They're reverse circulatin' on the rig floor, and we'll soon be pullin' outta the hole.' Craig bellowed, at the nodding heads and smiling faces in front of him. 'Ain't y'all happy those shifts 'r' over?'

'I'll start working on the report.' Ash said. 'Let's start rigging down the gauges and all the measurement equipment, and, Zack, Aimar, remove the safety slings.'

Zack looked up vacantly. Aimar slapped him on the back and dragged him away. Within seconds the crew had dispersed.

'So, any holiday plans?' she asked, walking up the staircase to the rig floor.

'Greece maybe,' Craig said, with a shrug.

'Nice, mainland or island?'

'Crete.'

'Raft race next weekend,' she said, rubbing her gloved hands together. 'You ready for it?' she asked.

He smacked his hands together. 'Hell yeah, we're gonna win this year,' he said.

Ash laughed, as memories of last year's drowning came to mind. 'You gonna keep control of those legs then?' she asked, eyeing his long limbs as they reached the wellhead.

'There's nothin' wrong with my legs,' he said, squeezing at his thin hard quad muscle to demonstrate a point.

'Not if they're kept out the water, rather than acting like a bloody anchor and tipping us over,' she added.

'Fuck off.'

'You did!' she exclaimed, laughing.

He huffed, suppressing a chuckle. 'Ya goin' away?' he asked.

'Nah,' she said, watching the workers on the rig floor. 'I'll take a bit of time out, then get back to it. Someone's gotta clear up this shit while you're sunning it,' she said.

He assessed her. 'You gonna speak t' Iman?' he asked.

Ash recoiled and banged her hardhat on the metal frame. 'Fuck!' Heat swamped her body, and she wanted to rub her head.

'Those sweets sure 've saved me,' he said, with a wink.

She had placed one on his pillow every day. 'Just sharing the love,' she said, her cheeks flushing.

'Well maybe ya need t' go 'n' get the love,' he said, nudging her in the ribs.

She held his gaze. 'And you?' she asked.

'I'll talk t' Kate when we get back,' he said, his eyes sparkling.

'Good. Now let's go and empty that surge tank, rig down, and get the fuck out of here,' she said.

'Yeah boss,' he teased.

*

'What are you making?' Niomi asked, looking at the charred pencil shaped pastries on the flat tin.

'Choux buns,' Iman responded her hands resting on her hips, biting her lip as she assessed the catastrophe she had just removed from the oven. 'And then I'm going to make crème pâtissière to go inside them,' she added, squinting at the tray.

'Hmmm.'

Both women stared, from the picture on the recipe sheet back to the tray.

'Are they supposed to look like that?' Niomi asked, pointing to the image.

'Yes,' Iman said, poking a fork into one of the lifeless forms. The mixture stuck to the prongs, and she couldn't pull it free without lifting the cake from the tray on which it was stuck.

'Hmmm.' Niomi said again, staring blankly. 'I think something's gone wrong,' she added, stifling a laugh.

'Yes,' Iman said, holding her head in both hands, pondering the steps she had taken. 'I need to start again,' she said, lifting the tray and throwing the buns into the bin.

'Is it some kind of special cake?' Niomi asked.

'Yes. I need to know how to make choux buns before I go on the training course.'

'Oh!' Niomi pondered. 'I thought it was a course to train you how to make them,' she said.

Iman looked up and frowned at her. 'I need to have some basic knowledge,' she said. 'And I've never made them before.' She wandered around the kitchen, collecting more flour, butter, and eggs.

'Wouldn't be for someone special, would it?' Niomi asked, with a twinkle in her eye.

Iman flushed. 'I thought it would be nice for them, after their time away,' she said, with a coy smile.

'Them eh?'

Iman placed the water, butter and sugar into a pan on the stove and waited. 'I'm sure Zack wouldn't say no,' she said, with a mischievous grin.

'Can I make them with you?' Niomi asked, excitedly.

'Of course! When that mixture boils put this flour in,' she said, handing over the weighed ingredient. 'And then stir like crazy with the wooden spoon. It has to be the wooden one. Got that.'

'Yes,' Niomi responded, skipping over to the hot pan. She watched it closely. 'I'm so excited,' she said.

'Me too,' Iman responded, reaching for a vanilla pod and stripping it. She couldn't deny the fact that the thought of seeing Ash again caused her insides to tingle and dance in a funny way. The heady feeling hadn't abated either. Thankfully the sadness had shifted a fraction, with her determination to focus on her career. Maybe she and Ash could be good friends.

*

'Okay, water should be settled by now,' Ash said. 'Let's pump the oil to the flare.' She stepped to the side, and Zack stepped in. She slapped him on the back. 'Thanks, Zack.' He didn't respond. 'You okay?' she asked. His eyes were glazed and his cheeks bright red. She waved a hand in front of his face. 'Zack,' she called.

He looked up, squinted, and then fell to the floor.

'Get me some water and towels,' she yelled through the walkie-talkie. 'I need the medic, now. Zack's collapsed at the surge tank, looks like heat.'

'Medic's on his way,' the voice came back from the lab cabin.

She pulled him into the only shade there was and undid his coveralls. She didn't need to feel his forehead to know he was burning up. His skin was red and dry. 'Looks like you've got heatstroke,' she said.

Zack's eyes opened then closed again. 'My head's fucking killing me,' he mumbled. He was starting to shake.

'It's okay, hang on in there,' she said.

Tarek arrived with wet towels and started placing them around Zack's neck, across his forehead, and under his arms. 'You'll do anything to get out of this place early?' he teased. Zack groaned; his hands clamped to his head.

'Right, let's get him onto this,' Elias said, dumping the stretcher to the ground. He took one look at his patient. 'We need to get him to the hospital,' he said. 'Keep the towels wet.' He stuck a thermometer under his tongue. 'Thirty-nine point eight,' he said, shaking his head.

'I'll get the car,' Ash said, rushing towards the lab cabin. Tarek and Elias followed her, carrying Zack on the stretcher.

Craig met Ashley at the door, keys in hand. 'Is he okay?' he asked, his eyes wide with concern.

'I hope so! We need to get him to hospital ASAP though. I'll take him,' she added.

'Sure,' Craig nodded. 'Aww, hell,' he said, shaking his head. 'You get goin' 'n' I'll fill out the accident report.'

'He just went down like a brick,' Ashley said. 'Looked a bit vacant then bam. He's complaining about headaches and is a bit shaky. Temperature 39.8,' she said, relaying the details for the report. 'We've got wet towels on him, and I'll try and get more water down him in the car.'

'Got it. I'll call the hospital 'n' let 'em know yer on the way,' Craig affirmed.

Ashley raced towards the row of parked cars, flicked the lock, opened the back and lowered the seats. It would be a bit cramped, but he could lie out across the back, with his feet stretching into the boot space.

'We need you to stand to get into the car.' Elias spoke calmly, supporting Zack under one arm, Tarek holding the other.

'Dizzy,' Zack mumbled, raising his head off the flat surface.

'Won't be long mate.' Tarek said.

The two men eased him into a sitting position. Ashley came in through the other side door to help him to lie down then the two men swung his legs around into the boot area and shut the door. She tucked another wet towel under his head, put freshly wetted sheets under his arms, and stuffed another set down his pants legs.

She handed him a bottle of water. 'Small sips, okay!'

He tried to nod and moaned.

'Take these,' Elias said, handing him two small white pills. '500mg of Paracetamol,' he said, for Ashley's benefit.

She nodded and turned up the air conditioning. She would most likely freeze in the next hour, but it would help Zack. Putting her foot down hard, a wave of dust chased them along the road.

*

Ashley pulled up outside the hospital's main entrance, abandoned the car and ran into the reception area. Her favourite man sat at the desk, pondering the computer in front of him and she rolled her eyes, hastily stepping towards him. Before she had reached the desk, two orderlies with a wheeled-bed were approaching the reception, and he pointed them towards her. She smiled briefly and directed them to the car.

'We'll take it from here,' the taller of the two men said. They eased Zack out of the back seat and onto the bed.

'I'll park up,' she said. The tall Syrian man nodded towards her. He had a kind smile and very focused coffee-brown eyes.

'We'll take him through to the emergency room. If you wait in the reception someone will come and get you,' he said. 'He'll be fine,' he added.

The shorter man nodded and smiled.

'Thanks,' she responded. Her legs suddenly seemed to struggle to hold her weight as she made her way to the car. She breathed deeply and sat for a few moments, before turning the engine and parking up.

171

Ash sat in the waiting room, sipping at the hospital coffee, pleasantly surprised at how good it tasted. She'd always thought it tasted awful, but not by comparison with the commercial coffee they used at the rig.

'Hello.'

She turned and smiled wearily at the short wavy hair and brown eyes, dressed in doctor's scrubs. 'Hi.'

'You can't keep away eh?' Giselle smiled. 'You look tired. Are you here for yourself this time?' she asked, assessing Ashley for evidence of an injury.

'No. A colleague. Heatstroke. We were on the rig,' she said, finding it hard to string sentences together.

'You certainly don't look like you were here for that drink you promised me,' she said, squinting at the state of Ash's coveralls and boots.

Ashley laughed. 'I need to find out how he is, so I can get back to the rig,' she said.

'Ah, I'll see what I can do.' Giselle turned to leave.

'Zack Leighton,' Ash said.

'I'm guessing he'll be in a blue coverall,' she said, smiling warmly.

Ashley smiled and relaxed back in the chair. 'Yes,' she said, but the chirpy doctor was already out of sight. She continued sipping her coffee, memories of her last visit to the hospital leading her to thoughts of Niomi. *Niomi! Someone needs to let her know.*

*

'Right,' Giselle said, as she approached. Ashley stood. 'He's been taken to the ward and will be kept in overnight. He should be released tomorrow, or maybe Saturday,' she said. 'They will do some tests just to be sure there's no internal damage, but that's more precautionary at this stage.'

'Can I see him?' she asked.

'You can, but I imagine he'll be sleeping for a good few hours. We've got him under observation, so he's going to be fine,' she added.

'Maybe I'll just get back to the rig then.'

Giselle nodded as if to say she was making the right decision.

'Thanks. I'll be back tomorrow.'

'We'll still be here,' Giselle said, with a warm smile.

Ashley grinned. 'Do you ever get time off?' she asked.

'Not often.' Giselle stood, politely, her comforting gaze on Ashley's tired eyes.

Ash stood, staring.

'I'm sorry, I need to...' She indicated with her hand to the emergency bays.

Ashley jolted out of the sleepy trance. 'Sorry, sure! Thanks again,' she said, heading for the car.

*

Ashley walked towards the boundary. She hadn't stopped since taking Zack to the hospital, and her body was feeling the strain. She slumped down, assessing the half rigged down mess. The flare had ceased, but the sound impression was still present. She rolled the paper around the slither of tobacco, licked the seal, closed the roll-up, and released her shoulders. Lighting the end, she sucked down on the cigarette, spitting out the residual tobacco, and the dust that dried her mouth. As hard as the work was, she would still miss it. Tomorrow they would be heading home. *Home!* The rig was home too. Zack was right this could be a lonely place. The camaraderie that formed over a few weeks of working closely together felt so good at times. But then what? She drew the smoke into her lungs and blew out softly, pondering.

Standing, she stomped on the paper and wandered back to the lab cabin. She needed to talk to Iman.

19.

Ashley jumped into the passenger seat and flopped back. 'Aahhh, thank fuck that's over,' she said, grinning ecstatically. Craig inhaled the cigarette between his fingers and turned the engine. She rubbed her eyes and yawned. 'Soooo tired,' she added, yawning again.

'Yep. But,' he said, with a mischievous grin plastered across his rugged face. 'It's party time.'

Ash groaned. 'Right.' She gazed out the side window at the passing dunes and swirling dust. Iman's image appeared, and she glanced at the empty sweet tin on the seat. The light vibrations in her stomach expanded up and into her chest.

'What's that grin 'bout then?'

'Eh?' She started to chuckle.

'That smile,' he pointed at her rosy cheeks. 'Haven't seen that 'n' in a while. It's ya reeal happy, special, smile,' he added, sending his eyes back to the road.

'Fuck off,' she said, but her cheeks had darkened, and her smile was widening with every kilometre closer to home.

'Iman's a good 'n',' he said, rocking his head and sucking through his teeth.

Ash squirmed in the seat, suddenly struck by the possibility of rejection.

'What if she's not...' she said, with concern.

'Ah huh. I knew it.' He drummed on the steering wheel repeatedly, unaware of her growing apprehension. 'I knew it.'

'I am really attracted to her,' she admitted, massaging her fingers through her hair. She slumped back into the seat, groaned, and picked at her fingernails.

'She sure 's a looker. If she didn't bat for your side, I'd have swept her 'way... Well, if Kate wasn't on the scene I mean,' he added.

Ash's eyes widened, and she sat up. 'How do you know which side she bats for?'

Craig frowned at her, one side of his mouth upturned. 'Zack,' he said, shrugging his shoulders. 'I thought ya knew. Fuck, ya been workin' on the rigs too long,' he added, bringing his focus back to the road.

Ash rolled her eyes and slumped back again. 'What does Zack know?' she asked, dismissively.

'Niomi told him, apparently.'

The butterflies taking flight in her stomach lifted her up in the seat again. She stared out the window, trying to distract her mind from the sensations riding her body. The tingling feeling had shifted to burning and was trying to burst through her chest, and her hands were sweating. Her heart was pounding, and the trembling in her stomach was causing her to shake. The truth hit her squarely between the eyes and landed with a thud. It would be impossible. 'It's forbidden,' she said, trying to bring her thoughts back down to earth.

'Fuck that,' Craig countered instantly, his determination jolting her out of the sabotaging thought. 'Might be forbidden Ash, but she's out t' Niomi, so don't look t' me like she's gonna hide 'way that easily.' He nodded to himself. He was right.

Ash pondered, suppressing the joy that came with hope with the fear of rejection. Her heart ached. But what did she have to lose? Then again, what if something terrible happened to Iman as a result? She couldn't put Iman in that position. She writhed in the seat, tormented by her logical thoughts competing with her heart's desire. And her heart was screaming. Maybe she should take leave, go somewhere and cool off. Her head was winning the battle. Her heart would recover; it had before. She pressed her hand to her chest. Fuck, it hurt.

*

Niomi stepped tentatively across the squeaky floor. Third bed on the right, the nurse had said. She couldn't stop her eyes from straying to the other beds in the room. Men lay still, curtains half drawn. It was surprisingly quiet, but the chemical smells, and a subtle hint of something she couldn't name irritated her nose. Her hand rose to block the odour but dropped away quickly as she locked onto Zack's bright-blue eyes.

'Hey,' he said, pulling himself up and leaning against the large soft pillows.

His beaming white smile caused her stomach to flip. 'Zack!' she said, suddenly overcome with emotion. She rushed to the side of the bed and cupped his face in her hands.

His smile shifted a fraction, and he quickly assessed the other occupants' reactions to the open display of affection. He breathed a sigh of relief, took her hands in his, and lowered them from his face. 'How did you know?' he asked.

'Katherine. I saw her at the base,' she said, with confidence in her voice.

'You look...' His eyes started watering, and she rubbed away the tear that had escaped down his rosy-cheek.

'You need a shave,' she said, her fingers tracing tenderly over his stubbly chin. 'I can't stay long,' she added, knowing there would be consequences if someone she knew spotted them together.

'Close the curtains.'

She did.

'Come here.'

She sat on the bed and leaned towards him, capturing his mouth with urgency. Pulling back, she wiped at her swollen lips and flapped at her flushed cheeks. 'I'm so glad you're safe,' she said.

The depth of Zack's unwavering stare caused her to quiver. 'Marry me,' he said.

She gasped, her hands rushed and covered her mouth, the sparkle in her eyes giving him the answer he needed.

'I've been thinking about it all the time, out there,' he said. He pulled her towards him and kissed her hard.

She pulled away. 'But, my parents,' she responded, struck down by the challenge they both faced.

'We can talk to them. We'll find a way, together.' His intense gaze reached into her soul and she started to shake. 'Will you, marry me?' he asked again.

'Yes,' she sniffled, the smile on her face wiping away the concerns they would need to deal with on another day. Niomi stood, her legs weak beneath her slight frame. 'I've got to go,' she said. She walked shakily, in stunned silence, breathless. Had that just happened, or was she dreaming?

Zack rested his head back on the pillow and sighed. He was still beaming from ear to ear when his eyes shut.

*

Reversing into the parking space outside Craig's house caused the fire in Ashley's stomach to intensify to the point of pain. Excitement and anxiety mirrored her thoughts, and her legs struggled for balance when her feet hit the ground. Righting herself, she stood tall, stamped her feet on the ground, grabbed her bag from the back of the vehicle, and strolled the short distance to her house. 'Catch you later, bud,' she said, remembering Craig.

'Eight 'clock,' he shouted.

She waved a hand but didn't look back.

The shadow that had been cast over the house the night before she left for the rig had left a faint impression. At least Katherine was now in her place, two doors down. She sighed, opened the door, and stared into the emptiness. Her heart sank as she crossed the threshold and shut the front door quietly behind her. The latch clicked. She ambled up the stairs and into her bedroom, her mood lifting as she became reacquainted with her private space. At least her bedroom remained untainted. She dropped the bag and headed for the en-suite.

*

The banging noise seemed to be getting louder, and then Craig's voice bellowed. Ashley stirred, and opened her eyes, still wrapped in the robe from her shower. 'Coming,' she yelled. The banging continued. For fuck's sake! She bounded down the stairs, securing the belt around her waist, unlatched the door and pulled it towards her.

'Why's the door locked,' Craig asked, stepping into the hallway, the aroma of beer wafting on his words. 'C'mon. I'm starvin.' He was hopping from foot to foot.

'Beer's in the fridge,' she said, pointing through to the kitchen. 'I won't be a mo.' She took the stairs two at a time, threw on a dark blue t-shirt, jeans and deck shoes, and was back downstairs before he'd cracked open the second bottle. She took it from him, downed half of it and let out a quiet belch.

'Come on then,' she said. Her stomach gurgled in approval. She slugged the remaining beer and placed the empty bottle on the table.

Ash's heart was racing before they reached the restaurant, and she was out of breath, even though they'd only strolled the short distance. She reached for a tray and placed it on the rails.

Craig placed his hand gently on hers. She was trembling. 'It'll be alright,' he said, softly. He sat his tray next to

Ash's and slid it down the rails, stopping and loading the hummus, baba ghanoush, olives and flatbread onto both trays.

Ash's eyes darted from the food to the porthole window in the door and back again. Her appetite had left the building before she entered it. She could barely swallow, let alone consider digestion. She breathed deeply, her hands resting on the tray. She turned her eyes to the main course dishes on offer. The swinging of the kitchen door alerted her, and she froze.

Iman's eyes locked onto Ash. She staggered, her left hand reaching to the counter and nearly dropping the tray of food perched precariously in her right hand.

Ash's cheeks flushed, and her breath stopped, stuck in her throat, right next to her words. Her mouth opened and closed again. 'Hi,' she said, finding her voice, the heat from Iman's light-brown eyes doing strange things to her senses.

Iman stood taller and took a pace forward, helping to release some of the tension that had struck her. 'Welcome back,' she said, trying to sound professional, the tray landing with less grace than she would have expected. The clanging sound drew a few pairs of eyes from around the room, and she lowered her gaze to the counter.

Ash's smile held compassion as she watched Iman fluster with the food on the serving tray. If she'd had any doubts before, Iman's response had confirmed Craig's rumour. The tingling sensation tracking down her spine told her so too. Iman was definitely into her. And she knew where she stood concerning Iman.

The thought of not being able to have her led to such a dark place, she couldn't set foot near it. There had to be a way, and she would find it. 'Safely,' she added, with a coy smile.

'Thankfully,' Iman responded. 'I'm pleased you all got back safely,' she added, smiling at Craig, before settling her eyes back on Ash. 'Can I get you anything?' she asked. Heat flushed through her, and she blew air up to her fringe. It didn't help.

'Thanks, t' those sweets o' yers,' Craig remarked with a broad grin. 'Wouldn't 've survived without my daily dose.'

Iman smiled sheepishly.

'The sweets saved us both, thank you!' Ash added, blushing at the fact that she'd almost forgotten to thank Iman. 'I think we're fine with breakfast,' Ash said, pointing to the loaded trays. 'No more space,' she said, with a chuckle.

'Well if you need anything else, just ask,' Iman said, holding Ash's gaze.

Ash studied the light-brown eyes intently and another shiver tracked down her spine. 'Thanks,' she said. *How could one word come out so awkwardly?* She picked up her tray and headed for their table, deflating with every step further from the intense eyes at the counter.

'Well that sure was interestin',' Craig remarked, squeezing into the seat, and bashing his knee on the underside of the table. 'Fuckin' kid's seats,' he moaned, rubbing the spot. The aroma emanating from the food on his tray caught his attention, and he dipped a piece of bread into the hummus. He was groaning with pleasure before it hit his mouth. 'Mmmmm. I can see the attraction,' he continued, his eyes shining.

Ash smiled and dipped a piece of bread. But by the time the food hit her taste buds, what was driving her senses wild and causing her to salivate, was something way more tempting. 'Uh huh,' she said, swallowing past the lump sitting high in her throat. She couldn't pull her eyes away from the porthole window in the kitchen door.

'So, the race,' Craig started, through a mouthful of lamb stew.

Ash gazed, entranced.

'The race,' he said again, waving his hand in front of Ash's eyes.

'Uh huh,' she responded, her attention still distracted.

Craig leaned back in his seat and observed. Ash's dishes hardly had a dent in them. His grin broadened. 'Yer reeal into her,' he said, nudging Ash from her reverie.

Her eyes darted around the room skittishly. 'Sshh!'

Craig turned, doing his appraisal of the workers tucking into their food, chatting and laughing, and tutted. 'No 'n' here cares,' he said.

'I do,' she said.

He lowered his eyes to the food and pushed his plate to one side. 'Ah huh.'

She relaxed back in the chair. 'I'm sorry,' she said. 'I didn't mean to fire off at you. It's just tricky.'

'Why don't ya just go out together?' he asked. 'Kinda, like friends.'

She looked him in the eye and frowned. You have no idea how excruciatingly painful that would be. She puffed out. 'It's not so easy,' she said.

'Why?' He was trying to be helpful but failing miserably.

'Because...'

He continued to stare, waiting for the rest of the sentence. When it didn't come, he shrugged. 'Because what?'

'Because, I want so much more,' she admitted. 'You ever wanted someone so bad, being in the same room and not being able to touch them, make love to them, burned a hole in your heart?'

Craig flushed. 'Shit!' that bad?'

'Worse!' She leaned back in her chair and crossed her arms over her chest, each wave of passion passing through her body only serving to increase her frustration.

'Ya'll just need t' talk. Give her a chance to say how she feels,' he said. He had a point.

*

Iman stepped out of the kitchen, not that the air was any fresher on the outside with the balmy night and gentle aroma of the kitchen bins. She turned the corner and leaned against the front of the building, trying to give her attention to the crickets, and even the distant rumbling from the city, but Ash's house continued to draw her eyes. If she looked way out to the right, she could just make out the lights in the city centre, some flickering in the near distance, but nothing seemed to remove the image of Ash haunting her mind. She slumped against the wall and sighed heavily. She should feel happier than she did. Seeing Ash back safely had instantly filled her with joy, dampened only by the physical distance that would remain between them. There was a boiling furnace surging inside her, out of control, desperately seeking, needing, wanting. Ash! Oh to touch her, and to kiss her. And Ash had looked at her differently this evening too. She'd felt it in her heart, and her soul. In that brief moment, she had known without hesitation that Ash had feelings for her. *What about Katherine?*

A groaning noise started to filter into her left ear, getting louder, coming from the other side of the bins. She turned, noticing the familiar raised heel, and swaying leg. She turned away sharply, simultaneously taking a swift, long stride to her right and straight into Ash.

'Shit!' Ash blurted, hopping up and down on one foot, grabbing at the one that had been stepped on. 'Sorry,' she said, holding out a hand in apology for swearing, and starting to chuckle.

'I'm so sorry,' Iman flustered, her hands searching Ash's body at a distance, wanting to touch her but unable to make contact. 'Sorry, sorry, sorry,' she repeated, raising her hands to cover her mouth.

Ash stood still, wiggling the toes on her bruised foot, smiling broadly. She reached for Iman's hands and eased them away from her mouth. 'My fault,' she said, letting go of the fingers that were sending an electric current shooting down her spine. She cleared her throat and rested her hands on her thighs to stop them fidgeting. 'Umm, I was wondering if you wanted to take that trip to the souk,' she said, with a shrug of her shoulders.

Iman's pupils widened, the blood draining from her heart feeding the tingling sensation in her private parts. Her racing pulse pounded through her chest, making breathing difficult. Her white teeth dazzled, and she started shuffling from foot to foot. 'Yes, I'd love to.' She reached out and squeezed Ash around the shoulders, stirred by a rush of excitement, and then released her again, almost pushing her away. 'Sorry,' she exclaimed.

Ash shrugged nonchalantly, her grin lighting up her eyes. She grounded her feet. 'Tomorrow?' she asked.

Iman's head dropped. 'I have to work tomorrow,' she said.

'When you're next off work?' Ash asked.

'Aren't you going on leave like the others?' Iman asked, knowing the expats often deserted the place a few days after finishing on the rig.

Ash lowered her gaze. 'No! No plans.'

Iman raised her eyes. The sparkle had returned. 'Wednesday, I finish at 2,' she offered.

'Wednesday it is. But I'll be in to eat before then,' Ash teased, making a move to turn away and head to the party.

'Ash?'

Ash held Iman's gaze over her shoulder. 'Yes.'

'I'm looking forward to it.'

Ash nodded. 'Me too.' She stood a bit longer. 'Umm, there's a party now, at Craig's, if you and Niomi want to come.' she offered.

Iman smiled. 'Maybe we will.' She watched Ash, her smile tinged with sadness until Ash's back disappeared into Craig's house. Her pulse still raced as she turned back towards the kitchen. Turning the corner, two pairs of eyes were studying her intently. She lifted her head to them. 'Feeling better Zack?' she asked. Their silence followed her through the door.

'So they are an item then,' Zack said, his sparkling eyes matching his broad smile.

'Looks something like that.' Niomi responded, in a more reserved tone. 'I'm going to the party, even if she isn't,' she added, planting her wet lips on his and eliciting a deep groan.

'You are so fucking hot Niomi Dabah,' he murmured, his hands grabbing her buttocks and squeezing hard.

'I'm glad you're feeling better,' she teased, pressing her lips tightly against his.

20.

Ashley cracked open the beer and swigged, coming up for air halfway before swigging again. 'That tastes so good,' she said, placing the empty bottle on the counter and pulling two more from the fridge.

'Boy, howdy! I needed that,' Craig said, belching loudly and taking the offered beer. He stepped outside, and Ashley followed.

It was still relatively early. Tarek and the guys wouldn't be around for a while. They wandered down to the loungers around the pool and sat, leaning their weary bodies into the hard plastic chairs, groaning simultaneously. The gentle whooshing sound of the sprinkler system and the chirping crickets barely registered past the ringing that still reverberated in their ears. It would be a couple of days before that would change.

'I asked Katherine t' come,' he said, supping on the chilled beer.

'I invited Iman and Niomi,' she said, a wry smile forming.

'Ah huh.' He pondered. 'Wanna cigarette?' he asked.

'Nah, thanks.'

He glanced under lidded eyes at her, his lips curled up and he started to chuckle.

'Fuck off,' she teased. 'Just don't fancy it,' she said.

He raised his hands in a peace offering. 'Ah huh. Just can't remember the last time ya turned down a smoke,' he said. 'Just sayin' 's all,' his chuckle turned into a laugh.

She slapped him on the arm, but she too was beginning to laugh. 'Yeah, maybe,' she said, sipping her beer. 'So, you going to speak to Kate then?'

'Yup.' His ruddy cheeks were shining, and there was a fiery quality to his eyes she hadn't seen in a while.

'Good,' Ashley tried to sound more positive about the liaison than she felt. Craig was too consumed by his excited thoughts to notice her reservation. She smiled wistfully. It was good to see him happy. She twitched as she caught sight of Kate approaching from the kitchen. 'Right, looks like that chat's just arrived. I'll get some beers,' she said, standing and heading back towards the kitchen.

Craig turned his head, his smile broadening at the flowing red locks heading towards them.

'Hi,' Ashley said.

'Hi.' Kate seemed distracted. She tilted her head and pursed her lips. Her smile was tight, but at least it was a smile.

'I'll leave you two,' she said, indicating towards the crooked grin and bright eyes gazing in their direction. 'You wanna drink?' she asked.

'Maybe later.' Kate turned and continued towards Craig.

Ash nodded and stepped into the kitchen. *Fingers crossed!* She pulled a glass from the cupboard and filled it from the water cooler. She'd give them some space and then take Craig another beer. She stood in the doorway, watching them, sipping from the glass.

Kate was shaking her head, her hair swaying, and then she was nodding. Craig's head lowered and he too started shaking his head. That's not going well. He slouched back in his chair, squirmed, and then sat upright, holding his head in his hands, as Kate spoke. He reached across the short space between them and tried to take her hands, but she eased away. He was rubbing his eyes. Her hand rose to her hair, and she ruffled it before covering her eyes and pinching the bridge of her nose. He looked tense. So did she.

'Hi.'

Ash swung round at the soft sound. One small word, and yet, its impact so immense it could have floored her there and then. She tried to swallow but her mouth was dry, and she stood wordless, motionless on the outside, her insides shaking with the voltage passing through her nervous system. Iman stepped closer. Ash stood, immobilised, speechless, consumed by the intensity of her feelings. 'Umm, hi.' The words croaked their way out, and she raised her hand to her head, running her fingers through her hair and tucking the side around her left ear.

'Can I get a drink?' Iman asked, with greater clarity in her voice than Ash could muster in hers.

'Oh, err, yes. Sorry.' She was bumbling and Iman started to giggle. Ash's smile grew, and she opened the fridge. 'What can I get you?' she asked.

'Iced tea please.'

'Sure.' Ash emptied the chilled drink into a tumbler and handed it over.

Iman took the quivering glass, her warm fingers lightly brushing against Ash's hand. Agghh! A bolt of lightning grounded itself through Ash's core, and she wasn't sure if the moan in her own ears had also reached Iman's.

Iman smiled sweetly, and delicately sipped at the refreshing tea.

Ash tried to breathe, unable to pull her eyes from the soft lips caressing the rim of the glass. She sipped at her drink, standing awkwardly, waiting. She winced as the cold water slid over the lump in her throat. 'Want to sit outside?' she asked.

Iman nodded, her eyes gazing over the top of the tumbler resting on her lips.

Ash gulped, turned and stepped into the early evening heat.

Iman froze. The blow to her chest, delivered by Kate's presence, stunned her, and her hand started to shake violently.

'What's wrong?' Ash asked, searching Iman's face with concerned eyes.

She turned her head towards the object of Iman's attention. *Kate!* Ash moved to touch Iman on the arm, then withdrew. 'Is everything okay?'

Iman turned her head. 'I'm sorry,' I shouldn't have come here,' she said. Turning swiftly, she placed her glass on the wall and stepped back into the kitchen, leaving Ash standing.

Ash's shoulders dropped, along with the boulder that now sat in the pit of her stomach. Then, the fire began to rise. *What the fuck has Kate done?* She glared at Kate, still talking to Craig. Something had spooked Iman, and she needed to know what that was. She raced towards the talking couple, her heart pounding; slowing as she reached the table. Craig looked up, his eyes red and swollen. 'Sorry, I...' She looked from Kate to Craig and back again.

Kate's eyes were bright, glassy.

'It's okay, I'm gonna get a beer,' he said, standing and striding towards the kitchen.

'I've told him,' Kate said. Her tone subdued, oblivious to Ash's outrage.

Confronted by the sympathy that now invaded her senses, Ash tried to stem the rising anger. 'What did you do to Iman?' she asked, trying to balance the warring emotions in her tone.

Kate's eyes dropped to the table, and her hands cradled her head. 'I'm sorry. I need to apologise to her,' she said, raising her eyes to meet Ash's. 'I said something to her,' she continued.

Ash rose up to her full height, hands pressing on her hips, staring at the night sky, and she sighed deeply. 'What the fuck, Kate!' She lowered her eyes and stared intently, not letting Kate escape.

'I implied you, and I were together,' Kate said, speaking softly.

'Jeez,' Ashley spat. 'How could you do that?'

Kate's head was rocking back and forth, her eyes unable to sustain Ash's glare. 'I'm sorry. I need to speak to her.'

'No Kate, no! You need to fucking stay away from her,' Ash yelled, raising her index finger threateningly at Kate's face.

'Yes,' she whispered. 'I am sorry.' Ash had turned and disappeared before the words were out.

Ash stormed out of the house and back to her room. She groaned loudly as desperation and desire coursed through her body, feeding different parts of her. She screamed out an altogether different noise, as Kate's conversation with Iman played on her mind. She threw herself onto her bed and shouted into the pillow until no more sound would come. Eventually, fatigue took her.

*

Iman studied the course confirmation paperwork in her hand. It wouldn't sit still so she could read the words she had read so many times already, so she placed it on her dressing table. She would travel to Paris.

Her hand, pressed against her chest, moved with the steady beat of her heart. The fluttering sensation in her stomach wasn't the same airy feeling that she had when thinking about Ash. There was more density, and weight, to the sensations associated with the trip, but Paris was the right thing to do. She couldn't continue to maintain false hope. Confused, and drained, she looked at the document once again. *I'm going to Paris*.

She gazed out her bedroom window into the darkness, and to the southeast, in the general direction of the expat houses that sat out of reach. The excruciating pain that had consumed her, moments ago, had been replaced by a hollow, empty feeling. Had she been so foolish as to think that Ash felt something for her? She placed the document in the top drawer of her dressing table and undressed. Slipping beneath the sheets, her eyes wouldn't shut, and her mind wouldn't quiet. The chanting came and then faded, only the crickets remaining to listen to her thoughts.

21.

Ashley leaned into the restaurant wall sipping her coffee. She hadn't stopped to peruse the breakfast options, instead, darting through the room and out the back door. She fiddled with the roll-up paper, which wasn't complying, screwed it up, and threw it to the floor.

'You'll get carded,' Craig teased.

His drawl brought the shadow of a smile to her face. She stared into his red-rimmed eyes. 'Fucking Kate!' she blurted.

He handed over his pack of cigarettes. She shook her head and sipped her coffee. 'What's she done?' he asked, inhaling the smoke and blowing out slowly. He yawned wearily and sipped his drink.

'She told Iman that her and I were together.'

'She's had it rough,' Craig defended.

'I know, but still.'

Craig tilted his head. 'She told me 'bout the rape,' he said, his voice croaky.

'Uh huh.' Ash stared, waiting for more words.

He stood taller and tensed. 'I jes wanna kill the fuckin' bastard who did that t' her,' he said, his fiery anger fuelling the tears welling in his eyes.

'Hey, bud.' She reached out and pulled him down to her head height, closing her arms around his neck. 'I'm glad she told you,' she whispered.

He eased out of the hold. 'Yeah, I guess.' He drew down on the cigarette. 'I'm gonna need t' give her time,' he said, thoughtfully.

Ash blushed. Maybe she needed to give Kate time too. 'You're right. I need to cut her some slack too.'

'Iman's in the kitchen on her own at the moment,' he said. He took a long drag of his cigarette and blew rings into space above his head.

'How do you know?'

'Just seen Zack 'n' Niomi headin' t' his room,' he said, with a coy smile. 'Did ya know he proposed t' her?' he asked.

'No shit! Good on him.'

Her smile broadened as she crossed the restaurant and gazed through the porthole window. She studied Iman's back, admiring her shapely curves, her hands occupied by something she was making on the workbench. Warmth invaded Ash's body, and her pulse raced through her chest. Taking a deep breath, she pushed the door and stepped confidently into the kitchen.

Iman turned at the unexpected squeak and jumped. She turned back to the workbench and continued piping the pastry mixture onto the tray, fighting the shaking in her hands.

Ash stepped closer, circled Iman's back, and faced her across the table. She watched as the unsteady hands tried to control the end of the piping bag. What was coming out was a long thin wriggly worm-like stripe of the mixture that didn't have a chance of forming a bun. Ash's smile turned into a giggle, but she stopped instantly at the sight of Iman's puffy eyes. 'Can we go somewhere and talk?'

Iman dropped the bag onto the top, wiped her hands on her apron and directed Ash into the restroom, closing the door behind her. Ash hadn't moved far enough into the room, leaving her occupying Iman's personal space as the door clicked shut. Iman gulped at the blazing heat between them.

Ash took a step closer, her fingers tentatively searching for Iman's trembling hands, her eyes intently focused on the glassy light-brown pools that remained steadfast. As their fingertips connected, Iman shuddered, and her lips parted. Ash brushed her thumbs tenderly across the soft surface of Iman's hands. 'Are you okay... with this?' she whispered. Iman nodded, biting down on her dry lips.

'I thought...' Iman started to say.

'Sshh!' Ash released her right hand and softly pressed her index finger to Iman's lips. 'I'm sorry. I think Kate...' Her eyes lowered, breaking the intensity, allowing Iman to breathe. 'Kate said things that were... well, untrue.' Iman's lips twitched against her finger, sending goose bumps down her spine. She stepped back a fraction, her heart aching at the smallest increase in space between them.

Iman stared. The woody scent infiltrating her senses had her captivated. She couldn't stop staring. Her heart pounded in her chest, and her stomach felt jittery. The soft touch of Ash's finger caused her lips to tingle, and the private place between her legs to throb so hard that she was struggling to breathe. *Kiss me.* The thought was on repeat and causing her to ache with desire. Ash was standing so close, the warmth of her breath caressing her so tenderly, her eyes so...? So, compassionate. So, passionate! The absence of the finger on her lips only served to increase her desperation, drawing a guttural groan. Ash moved away, and Iman closed the gap. Slowly she inched closer until she could feel Ash's warm breath on her face again, and hear her heart beating. Or was it her own?' Then all thoughts stopped, suspended in a space and time that would never exist again. The soft sweet sensation of Ash's lips against hers sent a rush of blood to her cheeks, and wave after wave of electricity pulsing through her body.

Ash eased back. 'Are you...o?'

Iman swept the word from her mouth, her lips crashing down on Ash's. This time, there was a greater sense of urgency and undeniable confidence, the kiss conveying so much. Ash released a groan and Iman pulled back, her concerned eyes searching Ash for reassurance.

Ash cupped her face. 'Don't take this the wrong way,' she said softly, holding Iman's worried look. 'But I need to go before we both get into a lot of trouble.'

Iman studied the soft focus, holding Ash with such tenderness. Ash had released her face and was tracing an index finger from her temple, over her cheekbone, and down to her lips. The sensation seemed to be firing up every cell in her body. She started to fluster, unable to extract herself from Ash's penetrating smile.

Ash took her hand and squeezed tightly, staring longingly into the light-brown, fiery eyes. 'Can we date?' she asked.

Iman's smile broadened. 'Yes,' she said, unsure of where to put her quivering body.

Ash leaned in and placed a chaste kiss on her lips.

Iman's fingers lingered on the tingling spot, as Ash opened the door and exited the restroom.

*

'You look... happy,' Niomi said, knowing that wasn't the word she wanted. She studied Iman through a sideways glance, trying to work out what was so different about her friend's demeanour. 'Did you get your place on the course?' she asked, wrapping her apron around her waist and washing her hands. She looked back at Iman and the faint aura that appeared to surround her. 'You making those French cakes again?' she asked, assessing the perfectly shaped piped buns sitting on the tray.

Iman put the piping bag down and placed the tray into the oven. 'I hope so,' she said with a broad, dreamy grin. She glided around the kitchen collecting ingredients, closely observed by Niomi's inquisitive gaze.

Niomi tipped a bag of flour onto the metal surface, swept out the centre to form a doughnut shape then filled the space with a mix of yeast and cold water. Lifting the flour into the centre, she started to work the mixture into a ball. She slapped it, sprinkled a layer of flour and stared at Iman. 'I'm getting married,' she announced, watching for a response. Iman's hands stopped working, and she met Niomi's beaming smile with a broad grin. 'Zack let it slip last night at the party, but you'd gone by then,' she added.

Iman's hands rose to her cheeks. 'Oh, wow.' Her joy instantly shattered by the reality of their circumstances, 'What are you going to say to your parents?' she asked. Niomi's parents were nowhere near as liberal as her own. On the contrary, they could easily abandon her for disgracing the family. 'What about Joram?'

Niomi's smile disappeared. 'I know,' was all she said. 'I haven't worked out how to tell them yet,' she said, her hand beginning to manipulate the ball of dough.

'Joram?' she asked again.

'I haven't seen him in a while,' she said. 'I think he got the message when I told him he had no balls,' she shrugged. Iman sniggered, encouraging Niomi to laugh with her.

Niomi looked up from the dough. 'Will you help me?' she asked.

Iman flinched. The idea of facing Niomi's parents, given her own relationship status, caused her heart to stop. 'I can speak to my parents, see if they can help,' she offered.

'Would you?' Niomi asked, reaching for Iman's shoulders and pulling her into an enthusiastic hug. Iman allowed herself to be squeezed, her mind racing to work out how she would address Niomi's situation with her parents. Even though they knew each other, both sets of parents came from different perspectives. It would be a miracle if her father could talk them into accepting Zack. 'Thank you,' Niomi said, releasing her and returning to her work. Iman smiled. Love felt so good; surely it couldn't be a sin? She picked up an egg, cracked it into the bowl and started whisking.

'We kissed,' Iman said, her eyes staying with the whisk in her hand.

Niomi gasped, her hand powdering her face with flour. She started to giggle, clamping her hand to her open mouth. 'What was it like?' she chirped.

Iman looked up; her eyes were bright, her tone serious. 'So amazing,' she said, a starry-eyed grin across her flushed cheeks. 'And it was...' she paused, looking to the ceiling for the right word. 'Excruciating.'

Niomi frowned. 'Excruciating?'

Iman started laughing. 'Yes, excruciating, to have to stop kissing her, and excruciating to not be able to touch her.'

Niomi's cheeks flared, and her eyes widened, but she was laughing excitedly. 'Oh my heavens,' she said. 'You really kissed her. You really are a lesbian.'

Iman laughed loudly at Niomi's first use of the word. 'Yes, I really did, and yes, I really am,' she said, starting to whisk again, distracted by the electric sensation pulsing between her legs. *Excruciating!*

22.

Amena sat at the kitchen table, her eyes scanning above the line of the book in her hands, with a broad smile on her face. 'You look happy,' she quizzed. 'A different kind of happy,' she added. Iman always looked happy when she was baking, but there was something about her demeanour that had shifted; lightness in the way she moved, a romantic aura surrounding her. She always held herself with graceful allure, but there was something else, something subtle and deeply fascinating. Iman looked up, the softness in her eyes caressing Amena, causing her to giggle. 'You have, haven't you!' she stated, making sense of her sister's look.

'Have what?' Iman asked, with a coy smile, toying with the ingredients in the bowl in her hand.

'Done something?' Amena lowered the book to her lap and studied her sister carefully. The sensual way the flour sifted through her fingers, with the lightest of touch. 'You have, I can tell,' Amena said, sitting up excitedly.' What did you do? Who with?' she pressed.

Iman balked at the second question, before starting to giggle. 'Ash of course.' She shrugged trying to look nonchalant and looked anything but, as a wave of exhilaration caused a sharp intake of breath.

Amena's hands swept to her mouth but failed to stifle the gasp. She jumped to her feet and raced across the kitchen, squealing with delight. 'Tell me, tell me, what was it like?' She grabbed Iman and squeezed her. 'I'm so excited for you,' she babbled, hopping up and down and squeezing again. Iman pondered dreamily, unsure where to start or how to explain the exquisite sensations that had revealed themselves in the brief kiss. Her lips tingled, and her face burned at the physical memory. 'Come on, tell me,' Amena pressed, impatiently.

'It was so sensual,' Iman said, with a deep sigh, her index finger lazily sliding back and forth across the block of butter that sat next to the bowl. The silky texture started to stimulate her skin, and the intensity of her finger movements increased.

Amena coughed loudly. 'Huh hum.' She nodded her head towards the butter, smiling wickedly. Iman jerked out of her dream and wiped her hands on her apron. Amena started giggling.

'Sshhh,' Iman chuckled, her eyes scanning the kitchen-diner. Even though they were at home and their parents were out, the wary response was ingrained.

Amena grabbed her hands. 'Tell me more,' she insisted.

Iman immersed herself in her memory of the kiss, her fingers blending the butter into the flour. 'Her lips are so soft and gentle. They caress you like the softest silk. Then there's this delicious woody scent and salty sweet taste. It's like she touches you in all the right places, even though she's not touching you.

Amena stood, watching her sister's every movement, her mouth open, and her cheeks darkening. 'Wow!' She exclaimed softly, reaching her fingers to her lips, vicariously engaging in the sensual experience Iman was describing. She had never been kissed in that way before. 'Oh my.' She watched, transfixed until Iman removed her hands from the bowl and moved to the sink to rinse them. 'Are you going to tell Dad?' she asked.

Iman's eyes lowered to the sink, rubbing her fingers together to remove the sticky mixture. She started to rub more furiously, splashing water and beginning to grumble. 'Ahhh!' she screamed, slamming her hands down on the sink, succumbing to the frustration that had risen swiftly and consumed all the good feelings.

'What's wrong?' Amena asked, closing the gap between them and placing her hand on her sister's tense back. 'Immy?' she begged.

Iman turned, her eyes darker, her focus narrowed. 'I... I...'

'Hey, it's okay.' Amena swept the wavy hair out of her sister's eyes.

'What is it?' she asked.

'Paris!' she said.

Amena released a deep sigh and smiled. 'And?'

'What if...?' Iman couldn't bring herself to pose the question. She couldn't face the possibility that Ash wouldn't wait for her, or be there with her.

Amena reached up and cupped her sister's cheeks firmly. 'You don't have to go,' she said.

Iman mumbled. 'But what if I don't go and then...?'

'Immy.' The voice was strong, certain, and confident.

Iman backed down and nodded sheepishly, waiting for the admonishment on her sister's lips.

'Stop. You are worrying about things that may not happen. Speak to Ash.'

Iman continued to nod, tormented by her fears, unsure as to how she should broach the subject of Paris, and unwilling to face rejection from Ash.

'What if...?' she started again!

'No Immy! There are no what if's. If you love each other you will find a way to be together,' Amena continued fervently.

Iman's face softened, and a weak smile started to form. She pulled Immy into her arms. 'I love you so much,' she said, squeezing her tightly. Something about her sister's unwavering confidence settled her. 'We're going to the souk later,' she whispered, with a hint of optimism.

Amena released the hold and stared into the light-brown pools, searching. 'Don't be afraid of loving her,' she said.

Iman released an uncontrolled chuckle, as the truth landed with a resounding thud in her chest. She held Amena's intensely dark eyes. 'How did you get to be so wise?' she asked, with a tender smile.

Amena frowned.

Iman leaned in and placed a kiss on the lines that had formed on her forehead. 'Thank you.'

'Enjoy the souk,' Amena said, a sparkle returning to her eyes and her cheeks colouring as she spoke.

'I will.'

*

Ash paced across her bedroom floor, and back again. She'd never given what she wore to the markets any consideration when she had gone with Craig and a couple of other expats. Now though, nothing in her wardrobe seemed appropriate. She picked up the open-necked white shirt, studied it, and threw it down on the bed, blowing out the air that seemed to restrict her lungs. She dug deeper into her wardrobe and pulled out a pair of black linens that had more creases in them than a camel's backside. *Fuck! Where's the iron?* She threw the trousers on top of the white shirt and dived into her chest of draws.

'Black jeans, where are you?' she mumbled to herself, scrabbling around, one drawer after another. She pulled out the folded jeans and stepped into them. Struggling for balance, she hopped around until the jeans were past her knees. She hoicked them up over her hips and did up a couple of buttons. 'Fuck!' she exclaimed, as the banging on the front door hit her ears.

She leapt down the stairs, pulled open the front door, and gulped, immediately crossing her arms over her partly exposed chest. 'Umm.' A bolt of lightning shot down her spine, and her words were stuck in her throat.

Iman flushed instantly, and averted her gaze, though her eyes insisted on tracking back to the bare shoulders, and tracing down the arms that obscured her view, and then down to the taut stomach and the half-buttoned, jeans. She emitted something between a chuckle and a groan, her eyes gaining confidence with every second that passed. Her hand moved to her mouth, and the tip of her index finger rested at the edge, between her lips, toying with her teeth.

Ash gulped, her eyes fixed on the soft lips and tongue that teased the fingertip mercilessly, and she stopped breathing. *Fuucckk!* Her mouth opened and then closed again.

Iman's hand dropped to her side, and her smile widened. 'Can I come in?' she asked.

Ash convinced her feet to move, and she stepped back from the door, avoiding Iman's intense gaze. 'I'll finish getting dressed,' she said in a broken voice, turning swiftly and scampering up the stairs.

Iman released a long breath, and a slight moan, as the sense of burning desire that had shifted from the racing of her heart to the butterflies in her stomach, now flamed low in her core. She didn't want to resist the temptation any longer. She stepped into the kitchen and poured herself a glass of water, her hands shaking. Swallowing the cold liquid did nothing to reduce the feelings or stifle the blazing heat that was controlling her body.

'Hi.' Ash bounced into the kitchen, fiddling with the top button of her white shirt.

Iman jumped and let out a squeal. She turned to face Ash, suddenly feeling more self-conscious, her mind providing the caution that her body lacked. 'You're dressed!' she said, frowning.

Ash's smile turned into a laugh. 'Umm, yes.'

'You look lovely,' Iman stuttered.

Iman's eyes seemed to be assessing every part of her, undressing her, touching her, and dressing her again. Ash struggled to swallow, her feet following her instincts and stepping closer.

Iman put the glass down on the table, willing Ash to take another pace towards her. She did.

'You look beautiful,' Ash said, taking in the three-quarter length, flowing cream dress, with a black cotton pattern, delicately embroidered. Subtle. Elegant. She took another pace closer. With a shaking hand, she traced the material sitting across Iman's collarbone, her fingers coming to rest in the centre point, directly below her chin.

Iman flinched, goose bumps sprinted down her spine, and raw heat burst through her skin. She willed her eyes to close but they refused, locking onto

Ash, and there was nothing she could do but surrender to her.

Ash's fingers remained in place, her eyes fixed intently on the brown irises, their colour shifting through shades from light to dark hazel. She could feel Iman shaking beneath her fingertips, her pupil's craving, begging. She could feel it in her own pulse racing out of control, and the vibrations that she could no longer contain in her stomach. Her fingertips traced back up to Iman's neck.

Iman gasped as Ash's fingers moved from her dress, tenderly sliding across her skin, leaving a burning trail that fuelled an intense desire to close the gap between them. Her feet refused to comply, and she remained frozen to the spot.

Ash teased the soft lips that had rendered her speechless just moments ago and released a stifled groan as a deep sigh. She started to ease closer, her eyes never lifting from Iman's. Then, her hands dropped to her side suddenly, and she shifted backwards.

Unable to resist any longer, driven by something stronger than she could control, Iman refused to allow Ash to back off. Desperately, she closed the gap, and her lips landed clumsily on Ash's.

Ash groaned at the contact that caused her legs to weaken, and her mouth connected with a sense of urgency she hadn't experience in a long time. Forever even. She had opened to Iman, and let her touch something so profound she might drown. She was drowning, and there was no escape.

Iman's eyes closed, her senses overwhelmed by the hunger in the kiss, as she explored Ash in a way she had never explored anyone. The pain of oppression, she had lived with for so long, now consumed by a passion so wild, there was no taming the desire inside her. Years of waiting for this moment: hoping, dreaming, the denial and frustration; and then the realisation, and the wanting. Her tongue delved into the warm wet space. Her lips searched, and for a long moment, she forgot to breathe. She pulled away, and opened her eyes, gasping for air. Ash was staring at her, and she was smiling, the intensity in her dark irises penetrating straight through to her core and settling effortlessly in her soul.

Ash's heart still raced through her chest, her hands still shook, and she had no explanation for the dizziness that was making it hard to focus. They couldn't move that quickly. She needed Iman to be sure. But, jeez did she want to take her to bed right now. She took a deep breath and released it slowly, reached for Iman's hands and squeezed them tightly. 'You okay?' she asked, eventually finding her words. Iman nodded, wide-eyed. 'Shall we go to the souk?' Iman nodded again. 'Are you going to breathe?' Ash asked, a soft smile forming as she swept Iman's hair to the side and lightly traced her fingers down the side of her face.

Iman released a long breath and smiled. She had never felt so utterly vulnerable and insanely happy at the same time.

Ash stepped closer and pulled her into her arms. She held her tightly, enjoying the warmth of her cheek against her chest. 'You sure you're okay?' she asked.

Iman eased out of the hold and cleared her throat. 'Yes,' she said, in a broken voice. 'It's just so intense!' She was still smiling, and her hands were still jittery. 'I didn't expect to feel like this,' she said, rolling her eyes.

Ash started to chuckle. 'Yes, I didn't expect to feel like this either,' she said. Iman's smile turned into a giggle. Ash cupped her cheek, moved closer and placed a tender kiss on her lips. 'Let's go shopping,' she said.

23.

'When did you know about yourself?' Iman asked, lowering her eyes to the porcelain cup of mint tea in her hands. The quaint café, in the centre of the souk, doubled up as a stall for local artists. Handcrafted gifts sat as centrepieces on the three small tables and strips of cloth, transformed into beautiful pictures for tourists, hung from purposefully constructed rails to draw the eyes of passers-by.

Ash studied Iman's genuinely inquisitive gaze, distant memories flooding her mind. She hesitated. A fruity odour from hookah smoke lingered in the air, momentarily distracting her thoughts.

'Sorry, I shouldn't have asked.'

'No, it's okay.' Ash breathed in the heady aroma filling the small space, turning the delicately patterned cup in her hands. 'I was thirteen when I realised for sure,' she said.

Iman's eyes widened. 'That's young,' she responded.

'Maybe,' Ash shrugged. 'What about you?'

Iman started to flush. 'Well, I think I had a crush at school but didn't realise until just recently.'

Ash flinched. 'Wow, really?' She sat back in her chair and considered the hungry eyes, staring at her.

'Does that matter?' Iman asked, suddenly concerned that Ash might think poorly of her.

Ash started to reach across the table, desperate to make physical contact, but Iman moved away, and Ash retreated quickly. 'Sorry, I just...'

'I know. I want it too, but...'

Ash nodded. An impulsive act could land them in a lot of trouble. 'No, it doesn't matter at all,' she answered. 'As long as you're sure?' She held Iman's pure, innocent face, the pain of not being able to touch her tugging at her heart. God this was agonising. All she wanted to do was hold her, and kiss her.

'I am sure,' she said, a soft smile forming, her eyes flickering in the sunlight.

Ash sighed, mirroring the smile that seemed to increase the longing between them. 'Good.' She sipped her tea, pondering in the brief silence. 'Do your family know?' she asked. Iman nodded. Ash released a sigh. 'That's good.'

'What about your family?' Iman asked.

Ash bit down on her lips and her eyes dulled. 'That's a long story,' she said, her tone curt. Sitting up in the seat, alerted, her eyes started scanning the market stalls.

'We have all afternoon,' Iman said softly. 'I'd like to know a bit more about you,' she added, sipping her tea.

Ash let out a deep breath and relaxed back into the chair. It was a fair request, and her reaction had been uncalled for, except for the fact that talking about her childhood tended to warrant such an emotional response. 'I was adopted at the age of 7,' she started.

Iman's eyes fixed on her as she spoke.

'My adoptive parents, well Jason actually, was a religious man and worked as a vicar in our local church.' She pursed her lips before continuing.

Iman shook her head back and forth, not quite understanding the significance, but sensing there was more to come.

Ash fidgeted in her seat. 'When I told them I was a lesbian, they, well he, gave me a choice. Either to correct my ways or he would kick me out of the house.'

Iman gasped. 'What about your Mum?'

'Sandra,' Ash corrected. 'She couldn't say anything against him. He would have beaten her.' She was picking at the nail bed of her finger, raised it to her mouth and bit down on the skin. It started to bleed, and she continued picking at it.

Iman reached across, forgetting herself, and took Ash's hand in hers. She picked up the small paper napkin and dabbed it at the bloody spot. 'I'm sorry,' she whispered.

'It's okay. It was a long time ago,' Ash said, but her eyes remained distracted by the unwelcome memories.

Iman held her gaze, with fire in her eyes. 'No, it's not okay Ash. It can never be okay.'

Ash studied the look she hadn't seen before. She smiled weakly and shrugged. 'Maybe.'

'Did he hurt you?' Iman asked, holding Ash's dark-blue eyes with apprehension.

'Once.' Ash's irises had darkened, and her jaw tensed.

Iman's chest tightened. She squeezed the hand in hers, willing Ash's past to go away. 'What happened?' she asked.

Ash looked away and pulled her hand out of the warm, safe touch.

'Sorry, I shouldn't have asked,' Iman said, sitting back in her seat. She picked up her cup and sipped it, trying to swallow past the constriction in her throat.

Ash turned back to face her. 'No, it's okay. It was just a very long time ago and a long time since I've spoken about it.'

Iman nodded, her eyes lowering to the table.

'I was sixteen, and he caught me kissing another girl. He was drunk, as always, and he beat me,' she continued. 'Sandra pulled him off me and for once in her life threatened to call the police and report him, so he agreed to stop. He continued to beat her instead though, so I moved out of their house anyway. She found out who I work for and has sent me a birthday card every year since, and every year I return them, and that's about it.' She shrugged. As her focus landed on Iman, her breath hitched. Iman was so beautiful, so kind, and such a compassionate woman, so removed from the ugly world she had had to endure as a child. The intensity emanating from her light-hazel eyes burned low in Ash's belly. *What if something happened to Iman because of their connection?* She swallowed hard as the worrisome thought imposed itself, interfering with her honest reflections of the woman she was falling in love with. The warmth of love had turned quickly into anxiety and was jabbing in her gut. She couldn't let anything terrible happen to Iman.

Iman gazed quizzically at the blonde bobbed hair and deep blue irises, and her body yearned to be close. She needed to hold Ash and remove the distress from the past. Ash was staring straight at her, but something had shifted between them. There was a palpable distance now that hadn't been there before Ash's revelations. Hurt maybe? She sat upright, with determination to shift the energy back again. 'Shall we wander?' she asked, her smile jaded by the weight of the conversation.

Ash smiled back, but it was a weary effort and lacked the passion they had shared back at the house, momentarily tarnished by a reality she knew they would have to accept. She rose to stand and held out a hand to help Iman to her feet. The brief contact elicited a deep sigh, and the warmth eased its way back into her chest. As their eyes locked together, Ash's smile deepened.

They ambled in silence along the cobbled street; the heady aroma of burning incense and scented soaps; the vibrant colours of fabrics hanging from the high rails; and the smell of a thousand spices wafting in the motionless air, drawing their attention, and causing them to stop. Iman stood, perusing the large open-topped bowls of spices, lifting each to her nose and inhaling their scent. 'Here, taste,' she said, holding a pinch of the bright red spice to Ash's mouth.

Ash's lips parted, the brief contact with Iman's fingers causing her gut to tighten, momentarily distracting her from tasting the spice. She recoiled at the lemony flavour hitting the back of her tongue, confused by the colour that didn't match the taste.

'It's sumac,' Iman said, chuckling at Ash's frown and tight lips.

'Wow, that's tangy,' she said, smiling at Iman's delight. 'You have a real passion for cooking,' Ash said, with a look of admiration watching Iman dive into another spice.

Iman's smile dropped from her lips. She needed to tell Ash about the training course. Later. She turned to face Ash, a pinch of something greyish between her fingers. 'Try this.'

Ash took the spice, her lips lingering on Iman's fingers.

Iman pulled away quickly and flustered as Ash bit down on the seeds, deliberately scratching Iman's fingertip in the process, and sending a tingling sensation down her arm.

She frowned at the spicy sweet flavour with a hint of something that seemed familiar, but she couldn't name. 'What is it?' she asked, finding it hard to swallow as her eyes locked onto Iman's fiery gaze.

'Caraway,' Iman said, softly, but it was her sharp focus that was causing Ash's heart to race.

Iman was biting down on her bottom lip, and it was wreaking havoc with Ash's nervous system. Bolts of electricity spiralled down her back, and the fluttering in her chest was heading south and kicking off the throbbing sensation in her core. She couldn't find a thought to stop the emotional rollercoaster that was now overtaking her body. 'You wanted to show me the shawl shop,' she said, wiping at the beads of sweat that were trickling down the side of her right cheek.

Iman held Ash's gaze a fraction longer before she gathered herself to answer the question. 'Sure, follow me.' She turned on her heels and scooted into the bustling market, Ash in tow. She stopped suddenly, turned swiftly, and faced an incoming Ash, who stopped just short of a collision. 'Would you take me home, please?' she whispered.

Ash shuddered at Iman's breath against her ear and shivered again as the warmth disappeared. 'You okay?' she asked, trying to assess the reason for Iman's shift in mood and the thumping sensation trying to escape her chest. 'Have I offended you?' she asked, having found nothing else on which to pin the transformation.

'No.' Iman locked onto Ash's dark eyes, her voice ragged. 'I just want to be alone with you,' she said.

Ash couldn't breathe. A sudden rush of uncertainty threw her off balance. She tried to reason with why they should take it slowly, or even just be friends, but any thoughts she had scattered like confetti, and made little sense to her. 'I don't know if that's a good idea,' she offered, but the rebuff was half-hearted. Her legs were losing strength as quickly as her will, and Iman's smile told her she knew as much too.

'Please?' Iman stood, inches away from the lips she desperately wanted to kiss; the mouth she wanted caressing her body, and the hands she wanted to feel against her most sensitive parts. The constant flow of desire she had had to battle with, to stop herself rushing in, was winning. 'I need you,' she said, her voice fractured, her lips quivering.

The tightness in Ash's chest released itself, allowing her racing heart to beat freely. She nodded, and they turned back to where they had entered the souk, oblivious to any eyes that might have been judging them.

The clicking of Ash's safety belt broke the silence between them. Iman reached her hand across and placed it on Ash's, and squeezed tightly. 'I'm twenty-six Ash, not a teenager. I know what I'm doing, and I've never been surer of anything in my life.'

Ash swallowed hard, heat flaming her cheeks. She had no response. Iman was right. Turning to face the road, she shifted the 4x4 into gear and headed home.

'Would you like a drink?' Ash asked, heading for the kitchen.

Iman clicked the lock on the door. 'No.' The word was barely audible, and the lower range stopped Ash from moving any further. Iman closed the gap between them before Ash had turned to face her, the fire flaming through her veins seeking only one thing. Ash!

'I...' The wet heat consuming Ash's mouth killed all thought, and she stumbled backwards under the force of Iman's passion. Iman's soft lips were working her effortlessly, her tongue probing, dancing, exploring. Her teeth were biting down, pulling tenderly at the delicate flesh, before consuming her hungrily, and Iman's hands had already found the top button of her jeans. Ash groaned and any sense of self-control she had hoped to apply got lost in the impassioned kiss. Her hands reached up, and eased through Iman's hair, pulling her closer, all the while her body demanding more direct contact. She eased back. The black eyes staring back at her had only one thing in mind. Ash reached down, took Iman's hand and walked her up the stairs and into her bedroom.

Iman stood watching Ash watching her, as she unbuttoned the white shirt she had wanted to remove since she'd set eyes on it. Ash let the shirt slide down her shoulders onto the floor, and Iman marvelled at the goose bumps forming on the smooth skin beneath her fingertips. She lightly traced the line of Ash's bra from the strap on her shoulder to the front of her pert breasts, her heart racing and her breath faltering at the of effect of her touch on the blue-eyes gazing at her.

Ash stood, captivated by the intensity of Iman's light touch and the tingling down her spine. Iman was staring so intensely into her eyes, tracing down between her breasts and across her taut stomach to the opening in her jeans. Her heart skipped a beat as Iman moved lower, slowly undoing her jeans' buttons, and releasing her trousers to the floor. She was trembling, feeling strangely vulnerable to the imbalance in their state of dress.

Iman reached for the button at the top of her dress and undid it. Ash's hands cupped hers, bringing them closer, and she gasped. Ash was continuing to unclip the row of small buttons along her back, her fingers creating a fiery trail as they moved across the skin beneath the dress. She couldn't stop the tiny groans she released with every unlocking, her eyes fixed on Ash's dark gaze.

Ash slowly eased closer, taking Iman's parted lips with sensitivity. Tenderly, she captured her top lip, then her bottom, savouring the sweet, sensual surrender as Iman gave herself completely. Her tongue teased across Iman's teeth, probing, then delving deeper. She groaned as Iman's fingers passed across the skin at her waist and tracked up her back. Ash pulled back and released the dress over Iman's shoulders revealing a lacy white bra and her full breasts.

'Ahhh,' Iman moaned, as Ash's lips teased the fleshy top of her left breast, and then the right. She gasped as Ash's hands reached around her back and released the clasp of her bra, allowing it to slide to the floor. Her eyes wild with passion, she smiled seductively. She clasped her hands around Ash's head and drew her mouth onto her rigid nipple. She gasped again as fire infused her, her hands becoming more frantic; burying Ash's head more firmly against her breast.

Ash massaged and flicked at the raised bud, the texture on her tongue guiding the erotic vibrations down to her core. Iman released a scream as her teeth scraped lazily across the sensitive area, fuelling her desire. She pulled away, undid her own bra and removed her knickers.

Iman removed her underwear and threw herself into Ash's space. Ash's mouth was on her again and pushing her towards the bed. As her legs pressed against something substantial, she lost her balance, bounced onto the soft mattress, and started to giggle.

Ash smiled, sweeping the hair from Iman's face. 'You will let me know if you want to stop?' she asked in a whisper, not knowing how she might manage that request and hoping she wouldn't need to.

Iman cupped Ash's cheek with one hand and stared at her concerned gaze. Pulling Ash down on top of her and claiming her mouth again with increasing urgency, she answered the question. She moved her hand down to Ash's small, perfectly formed breast, her thumb seeking out the rigid nipple, and started to massage.

'Urrggghhh,' Ash groaned, her body involuntarily jerking under the passionate touch. Iman pulled her hand back and studied Ash's dark stare. Ash took the hand and placed it back on her breast, her eyes closing briefly at the contact. When they opened again, Iman was grinning, her fingers teasing the spot, her eyes absorbing Ash's erotic response. Ash bit down on her lip to prevent herself from screaming out, the flaming fire running a direct line from her nipple to the burning sensation in her clit. 'Urrmmm,' she groaned. She shifted them further up the bed and lowered herself down on top of Iman, claiming the mouth that had already claimed her heart.

Iman groaned at the changing texture of Ash's nipple against her thumb, aware that her movements seemed to cause a reaction in Ash that was then driving her own senses wild. The surreal sensation intensified the spasms low in her core, and she bucked when Ash's leg eased between hers. She could feel her warm wetness pressed against Ash's soft skin, and Ash's firm thigh against her throbbing centre. She gasped. Ash had moved from kissing her lips and was now tracing a path with her tongue, down to her breasts. The pulsing in her sex was growing stronger, obsessing her, and increasing her desire to be touched, taken.

Ash pulled up from Iman's breasts. She wanted to slow things down, but Iman's wet heat on her leg, and her intoxicating scent, were drawing her in, drowning her. She held Iman's dark eyes, her fingers lightly caressing and slowly easing lower, watching for any signs that she should stop. None came.

Iman groaned as Ash's hand slid between them.

'Mmmmm,' Ash whispered, parting Iman tenderly, confidently. She studied Iman attentively. Her eyes were shut, and she looked lost in the sensations riding her body. Ash's eyes closed as she became immersed in the feel of Iman's wet heat on her fingers. She gently caressed the silky folds, tripping over the bundle of nerves that had Iman jolting. She continued rhythmically circling, easing into the warm space, created by the movement.

Iman screamed out, and her head lifted sharply off the bed, as Ash's fingers eased gently inside her. Her head fell back, her body arched and she clamped Ash's hand with her legs, as she adjusted to the fierce burst of fire that had just flamed through her.

Ash stilled inside her, waiting, sensing every small movement. She could feel Iman slowly relax in her hand, encouraging her to continue. Exploring, delicately, tenderly, slowly, she made love to her.

Surrendering to the gentle movements, new sensations gripping her body, Iman cried out. Unable to control the overwhelming feeling, for which she had no name, rising into her chest, tears released themselves onto her cheeks.

Ash eased out of her, resting her fingers at the soft wet entrance, and pressing tender kisses to her breast, her other hand reaching under her back and around her waist, pulling her closer.

'Don't stop,' Iman whispered.

Ash pulled at Iman's nipple with her teeth, traced circles with her tongue, and sucked at the surrounding puckered skin. Iman was bucking and groaning under her deft touch, enticing her and giving permission for her fingers to explore again. Slowly, sensitively, she slipped inside her, eliciting a guttural groan. Rhythmically she eased in and out, the palm of her hand brushing tenderly across Iman's clit. She rocked her hips, and her fluids seeped hot against Iman's leg, providing perfect friction.

Iman's hands covered her eyes. Consumed and confused by the fire coursing through her body, insecurity struck her, and she lifted her head off the pillow. She pulled Ash up towards her and kissed her urgently on the lips.

Ash eased out of the salty kiss, smiled softly, and trailed a finger down the side of Iman's face, her eyes caressing the flushed cheeks and wide sparkling eyes.

Iman's gaze softened, and a tentative smile started to appear.

Ash moved further up the bed, pulled Iman into her shoulder and kissed the top of her head.

Iman wrapped her arm around Ash's waist, and snuggled into the warmth, turning her face into Ash's neck. Comforted by the familiar woody scent, she breathed softly, silently.

Ash held back the chuckle sitting on the tip of her tongue, but couldn't stop the beaming grin that graced her face. She pulled Iman closer and allowed herself to dream.

Iman pulled away a fraction and looked up into the deep dark-blue irises, her heart burning.

Ash leaned down and kissed her tenderly on the lips, with every ounce of restraint she could muster, her heart racing at the light contact.

Iman resumed her place in Ash's arms and snuggled up again. 'Mmmm.' The soft sound lingered in the electric silence between them. She kissed the side of Ash's bare breast, eliciting a slight flinch. 'Mmmm,' she repeated.

You have no idea. Ash groaned, knowing her heart had taken a leap from which she could never return.

24.

'Well?' Amena sat up in her bed, dropped her book by her side and clapped her hands with excitement.

Iman closed the door quietly, the exhilaration that radiated through every pore in her body, balanced by the sense of overwhelm that had rendered her speechless. If she voiced the joy in her heart, as she wanted to, she would wake her parents. Wake the world!

Amena patted the space next to her. 'Come, come! How was it?'

Iman drifted across to the bed and slumped lazily next to her sister. 'It was... incredible,' she said, still riding the high that she didn't ever want to come down from. 'Soooo intense,' she continued, her fingers lightly tracing her lips, connecting her with the lingering touch that remained. Tears of joy welled in her eyes. 'So...' she couldn't find the words that would do justice to the sensual, loving experience she had shared with Ash.

Amena's eyes widened, and her hands clasped together in her lap.

'Wowww!' Her mouth sat agape as she studied the shift in Iman's demeanour. She was in love.

Iman's smile spanned her face as she held her sister's inquisitive gaze.

'We touched, and kissed, and...'

'What? And what?' Amena pushed, eager to hear the details.

'And, it was all so incredible, so out of this world,' she said, softly. 'Her lips taste like the finest chocolate you could find. And the woody scent she wears just melts inside my chest. And, when she touches me, it's so tender, so assured; so sensitive. Like she knows me intimately. And then, the way she looks at me with those intense blue eyes. She's so beautiful!' She started fiddling with her fingers, mindful of the arousing feel of Ash's nipples stiffening with her touch. Heat flamed in her cheeks.

'Wow,' Amena said again, unable to raise her jaw to close her mouth.

'I know. It was so awesome and so intense,' she said, as she reflected on the tender, warm feeling that still lingered in her sex.

Paris? Amena refused to air the question on the tip of her tongue, unwilling to burst Iman's bubble, and hoping that Ash might give her sister a good reason to stay.

*

Ash lounged by the pool in her shorts and t-shirt, entranced by the shimmering on the near-still surface of the water, the crickets chirping loudly. She sipped at the beer in her hand. Its chill didn't cool her, and the alcohol wasn't doing much to numb the sensations that were making her body restless and driving her mind senseless. *Had she pushed Iman too far?* The intimacy they had shared had been beautifully painful for her also, and she hadn't anticipated that she would react so strongly. She slammed the empty bottle onto the table. 'Aaahhhh,' she groaned. She'd gone too far, too quickly. And, yet, she was left wanting, craving, and something else that she didn't want to face. She headed for the kitchen and cracked open another beer.

It was so late; she almost missed the light knocking sound. She padded through the kitchen and pulled the front door open. 'Kate!'

'Sorry, I wasn't sleeping, and I saw the light on and, I wondered if you wanted a drink.' Kate stood, her arms wrapped around her body, her eyes unsettled, shifting from

Ash to the kitchen beyond. 'Unless you have company?' she asked.

Ash held out the newly opened beer and stepped back from the door. 'Come in,' she said. Kate stepped past her, taking the drink and sipping from it as she walked through to the kitchen. Ash followed her and pulled out another beer from the fridge, continuing through to the garden and reclaiming her seat by the pool. Kate sat next to her, and they gazed, silently together. 'You okay?' Ash asked, eventually.

'I think so,' Kate said, still staring into space. 'I saw Iman leave earlier,' she added, after a moment's reflection.

Ash sat up in the seat, a surge of adrenaline preparing her for the fight she expected was coming. She slugged on the bottle in her hand. 'Yes,' she said, but her tone was harsh.

'I'm pleased for you Ash.' Kate smiled. Her eyes held genuine warmth, and when she reached out and squeezed Ash's hand, Ash relaxed to the point of smiling back.

Ash wanted to talk to Kate, share her joy, but didn't have the words to express how she felt. Struck by a thunderbolt didn't even come close to it. Vulnerable yes, very open, very raw. Frustrated, yes, but for an entirely different reason. Worried that her heart would be broken, yes, and fighting the urge to retreat and hide. Kate was the last person who had elicited something similar in her, and even then, this was a thousand times more intense. So intense she felt she might explode. 'Thanks,' was the only word that came out though, and the burning sensation flared deep inside her chest, again.

'I'm going to see how things go with Craig,' Kate said, sipping her beer, staring across the pool.

'That's great,' Ash responded. 'He's a good man, and he really cares about you,' she added.

'He is. And I like him too.'

'Well, that's a good start.' Ash clunked her bottle against the one in Kate's hand, and as their eyes met, they smiled.

'It is,' Kate said, knowing no one would ever replace the blue eyes staring back at her, and accepting that that part of their journey together was now history.

'Want to swim?' Ash asked, jumping out of her seat and running straight into the pool. She'd hit the water before Kate had had the chance to answer. When her head emerged, Kate was laughing. 'Come in. It's fab.' Ash dived under the water, and swam to the other end, unhindered by the wet t-shirt dragging against the water's resistance. Perhaps a few lengths would tame the fire inside her.

Kate downed her beer and stood. 'I'll head off,' she said, as Ash surfaced again. 'Thanks for the drink.'

Ash wiped the hair from her face. 'You're welcome,' she said. Submerging, she swam another length. When she rose from the water, Kate had disappeared. She puffed out hard and continued swimming.

25.

The thumping on her front door stirred Ash from a deep sleep. She squinted into the darkness. Four o'clock. *What the fuck!* She had still been stargazing at two o'clock. The banging came again. 'Urrgghh,' she moaned, pulled herself out of bed and staggered down the stairs. Wiping at her eyes, she opened the door and focused into the darkness. Her heart stopped, then raced. Goose bumps raced down her back, and she was shaking.

'Is everything okay?' Ash asked. Iman's intense glare answered the question.

Iman stepped across the boundary and closed the door behind her, her eyes drawn to Ash's bare legs. 'I have an hour before I start work,' she said, stepping into Ash's space, and pulling her into a deep kiss. Taking Ash's hand, she led her to the bedroom she had left only a few hours earlier. Iman had dropped her skirt and pulled off her shirt before she reached the bed. She released her bra and pulled down her knickers, and stood naked. As Ash approached, Iman reached for her t-shirt and pulled it over her head. As their lips collided her hands swiftly removed Ash's underwear, and in one effortless movement, she landed Ash in the middle of the bed.

The taste of Iman's minted breath on her tongue excited Ash's senses, the tingling in her sex creating a sense of urgency that it seemed they both shared. She deepened the kiss without reservation, her tongue delving, and dancing with Iman's, aware that Iman's hands were exploring her body. Massaging her breasts, tweaking her nipples and sending electric pulses to her throbbing centre. She groaned out, 'Fuck me,' and opened her eyes to catch the wild look on Iman's face.

Iman lowered her hand to the hot space between Ash's legs and groaned. Driven by passion and instinct, stronger than the nerves that challenged her to stop, she allowed her fingers to explore the wet heat. 'Ahhmmm,' she groaned again at the silky sensation on her fingers. She continued to toy, effortlessly exposing Ash's centre, pressing tenderly, and easing her open.

Ash jerked, her eyes focused intently on Iman, the fire in her belly mounting with the steady increase in pressure.

Iman smiled with the confidence of a competent lover. Holding Ash's fiery gaze, she plunged into her, groaning again at the sensations pulsing through her fingers, up into her chest and down to her core.

Ash could feel herself contracting and releasing with each thrust. She didn't want it to stop, but she needed to touch Iman too. She reached down to the legs astride hers and found Iman's sex. Circling slowly, drawing her silky fluids, sliding between her folds and pressing gently, she tenderly caressed her.

Iman groaned at the heightened sensations in her core and the feeling of Ash on her fingers. She tried to focus on her fingers, but something was stopping her, clouding her mind, and preventing her from moving. Ash's movements were getting faster, stronger. She was teasing inside her, outside her, her thumb dancing with her clit, and it was burning so exquisitely. She was shaking, low in her centre, and the fire seemed relentless. Space and time had stopped. Nothing moved, except the energetic explosion that was now causing her to spasm. The world had narrowed into a single point of focus, and that was directing the fireworks and sparklers that were shooting from her core up through her chest and up her back, and to Ash, the woman doing this to her. 'Aahhhh,' she screamed out, collapsing on top of Ash, wave after wave of aftershocks continuing to pulse through her body, accompanied by a guttural groan that had no end.

Ash pulled her up into her arms and placed kisses on her eyelids and down her cheeks, lingering on her soft, swollen lips.

Iman dived into the kiss with a resurgence of energy, her hands beginning to retrace their steps. She lowered herself down to take Ash's breast into her mouth, teasing the puckered skin and nipple with the flicking her tongue. She cupped the other breast tenderly, her thumb teasing the rippled surface, causing the nipple to rise at her will. She moved across, to give it the same attention with her tongue.

Ash released a groan and her back arched.

Iman moved away a fraction, a mischievous grin spreading across her face. She was enjoying this very much. She eased her hand down and found Ash's sex, forming circles with her forefinger, straying into the warm wet fluids, her arousal rising with every delicious contact. Ash's hips were moving with her, encouraging her to enter her fully. She kissed her way to Ash's belly, tickled her belly button with the sensitive movements of her tongue, and entered Ash with her fingers.

'Fuucckk,' Ash cried out, as Iman continued to penetrate her, rhythmically delving deeper. The energy building low in her core was rising rapidly, begging for release, and she had lost any will to contain it. She came hard against Iman's still thrusting fingers.

Iman continued to explore, unsure whether to stop or not. She tried to move with Ash, whose body was in spasm. Slipping out of her, she caressed and teased Ash's clit tenderly, drawing a long, soft moan as Ash started to move rhythmically in tune with her again. Drawn into a trance by Ash's musky scent, she eased into her and gently penetrated, deeply, twisting her fingers, exploring the silky wet centre. Lost in the sensual touch, the guttural scream that Ash released caused her to freeze momentarily. The hot fluid now bathing her hand caused the bubbling sensation to rise in her chest, but it was the wide-eyed, deep smile on Ash's face that resulted in the uncontrolled giggle that followed.

Ash pulled Iman into her with such passion that it took her breath away. Her lips were on Iman's, with the hunger of a starved animal needing to be fed or die.

The laughter that had bubbled up a moment ago in Iman's chest had transformed into something entirely different. An awareness of the intense connection between them, a sense so fierce it burned a hole in her heart. Tears rolled down her cheeks merging with those from Ash. Even the salt tasted sweet. She eased back slowly from the kiss. Neither was smiling. The message that passed between them was something that existed beyond the realms of happiness. 'I think I'm in love with you,' Iman said.

'I'm in love with you,' Ash responded, softly.

Iman placed a tender kiss on Ash's lips. When she pulled back, she was grinning, and Ash's face had softened too. 'I need to get to work,' she said.

'Yes! The shower is through there,' Ash whispered, pointing to the door to the en-suite.

Iman rose from the bed, pulled Ash to her feet, and led her into the bathroom.

*

Ash picked up the tray and set it on the rails, her heart racing. It was a feeling she was starting to enjoy. Even though the breakfast dishes looked good, as always, her appetite for food had deserted her, having been replaced by something a lot more satiating. She still had the mischievous grin on her face when Iman bounced through the kitchen door, with another tray of food in her hand. 'Morning,' she said, her voice ragged.

Iman's cheeks darkened in an instant, and the smile on her face beamed to the whole world that she had just made love with this woman. Fortunately, the dining room was still empty. 'Do you want to give me a hand?' she asked, with a flicker of her eyes.

'Sure. Do I get a decent coffee too?' Ash asked, sporting a huge grin.

'Yes, I'll show you where everything is.' She followed Iman through to the kitchen. 'This way,' Iman directed, heading into the dark pantry. As soon as Ash stepped in behind her, Iman pinned her against the wall and planted a deep, lingering kiss on her lips.

A bolt of lightning shot down Ash's spine and exploded in her core. 'Jeez, don't do that, seriously,' she said, but she was laughing.

Iman opened the door fully, picked up the ground coffee and set off towards the canteen. 'Come on slowcoach,' she teased. Ash recovered her legs, blew out the breath that had been stolen from her, and followed Iman to the machine. 'Do you want to come to my house for dinner on Friday?' Iman asked, as she filled the machine with water and turned on the percolator.

Ash gulped with the sparks that ignited in her gut. 'Ummm,' she hesitated. Iman's wide eyes caused another sensation, pricking at her chest. 'Are your parents okay with that?' she asked, swallowing hard. She hadn't thought as far as meeting Iman's parents. Even though she already knew Muhammad and Tarek, this was a whole different kind of meeting. Being an engineer was one thing, being a lover was something else. And, the thought was causing untold pain to shoot from her solar plexus into her chest, and mess with her brain. *What if Iman's Mum didn't like her? What if Tarek thought wrongly of her? Or Muhammad? Jeez!* She breathed deeply to control the trembling in her stomach and allowed her attention to drift to the gurgling coffee. She poured a large mug and added two sugars.

'Are you okay? Iman asked with a concerned tone, watching Ash fluster. 'They already respect you,' she added, with a smile.

'Uh huh,' Ash said, trying to smile and instead grimacing.

'They do. My sister's excited to meet you too,' Iman said, wincing slightly at her sister's real motivation behind the meeting. 'And if she asks you any personal questions, remember you don't have to answer them,' Iman confirmed. 'She can be quite direct and excitable,' she added.

'Ah huh.' Ash frowned.

'She's just curious,' Iman clarified, the heat rising to her cheeks as she spoke.

Ash cleared her throat, but it didn't stop her blushing. 'Ah huh,' she said again, sipping at the hot, bitter coffee and following Iman back through to the kitchen. 'So, what do you want me to do?' she asked, jumping at the chance to change the subject.

'Put this on, and I'll teach you to make bread,' Iman said, reaching the apron around Ash's waist, and pulling their bodies close. 'You smell good,' Iman whispered, biting down on her lip, her voice broken.

'You're gorgeous,' Ash whispered back.

Iman crossed the cord behind Ash, brought it round to the front and tied it in a bow. 'Bread,' she said, smiling seductively.

'Bread!' Ash repeated, chuckling, waiting for the next instruction.

*

227

Zack stood tall. If he stretched up as far as he could, he would reach five-feet-seven-inches. The collar around his neck, while the ideal resting point for the sweat trickling down his neck in forty-degrees of heat, did nothing for his capacity to breathe. He fiddled his fingers, to create some space for his Adam's apple to move freely when he swallowed. That said, his mouth was dry, and his throat had constricted long before he had put on his shirt. He looked over his shoulder, brushed at the flicker of dust sitting on his dark blue jacket, and turned to face the door. His clenched fist focused on the front door; he swung forward. The door opened before he made contact, and the weight of the move threw him over the threshold and into the chest of Mr Dabah. He wasn't smiling.

'Mr Leighton, I take it.' There was a softness to his bearded face that seemed to take the edge off his gruff voice.

'Err, yes, sir,' Zack mumbled, standing up again. He held out his hand. Dayoub nodded for Zack to follow him, ignoring the dangling limb.

Zack dropped his arm and walked a pace behind the stocky man, down a short dark hallway and into a room full of books. A solid wooden desk sat in the corner of the room, adjacent to the window, but otherwise, the room was dark and uninviting. Even the large patterned rug in front of the couch didn't add to the ambience.

'You wish to speak to me?' Dayoub asked, taking the seat at the desk, and facing into the room. He glanced over at Zack, assessing him.

Zack stood to attention a few paces short of the desk. A trail of sweat was tickling its way down his back, but he daren't move. 'Umm, yes, sir.' His voice was as determined and confident as he could make it, while his legs had taken on the texture of jelly, and his stomach churned. If it hadn't been for Iman's parents, he wouldn't be here at all. He took in a deep breath and summoned his courage. 'I would like to ask you for permission to marry Niomi, sir.' The words had come out relatively well, not least because he had rehearsed the line at least fifty times on the short journey to the house.

Dayoub started coughing and continued to the point of near choking. Zack's gut wrenched, and he moved to take a pace backwards. 'Wait.' Dayoub held his hand up, palm outwards, his other hand on his chest until he had finished spluttering into his handkerchief. 'You want to marry my daughter?' he confirmed.

'Yes, I do sir. I will give her a good life… and I love her.'

Dayoub's eyes bored into Zack, who instantly retracted physically. 'You think she will not have a good life here?' he asked.

'I'm sorry sir, I didn't mean…' Zack's eyes searched for the words. 'We will live wherever Niomi wants to live. I don't intend to take her away from her family,' he added.

'So, you think she will not have a good life abroad?' Dayoub's eyes had softened, but his question caused Zack to flinch.

'I don't know, sir.' His eyes lowered to the floor and were beginning to burn. 'I love her, and she loves me,' he said, in a softer tone.

'Ah, good, so you have an honest heart,' Dayoub responded, pulling a tissue from the box on his desk and handing it to Zack.

'Thank you, sir.' He wiped at his moist eyes and pocketed the tissue.

'Muhammad tells me you are a promising young engineer,' Dayoub said, fiddling with a piece of paper on his desk. 'Do you promise to take good care of my daughter too?' he asked.

Zack's bright eyes rose from the floor. 'Yes, I will, forever, I promise.'

'Good. I am an old man Zack, and I will not be around for a long time, and while I do not agree with these new ways, I am also too tired to fight this battle. I need to be sure that Niomi is with the man she loves and while I think Muhammad is too liberal with his son and daughters, he is well respected, and he highly recommended you as an honest man and potential husband.'

Zack's mouth opened, and then closed again, and heat rushed into his cheeks.

'If it is Niomi's wish, then you have my blessing,' he added.

Zack blinked. Had he heard the old man correctly? Dayoub looked up from his desk and smiled warmly. Zack beamed his widest grin. 'Thank you, sir.'

'You may call me Dayoub,' he responded.

'Thank you, sir, Dayoub,' Zack blurted, fidgeting his feet.

'No, young Zack, I don't think your Queen has bestowed that title upon me yet,' he chuckled. He stood and took the two paces into Zack's space. He held out his hand, and when Zack took it, he pulled him into an embrace, slapping him firmly on the back. 'We had better go and let them know,' he said, indicating towards the door.

Zack swallowed hard past the lump in his throat. He hadn't thought that far!

26.

The soft click of the latch caused Ash's head to rise from the kitchen sink, and her lips to curl upwards. She had hoped Iman would come by after work. A warm feeling in her chest, a smile on her face, and tingling in her stomach, she turned.

'Ya wanna beer?' Craig's drawl killed the joyful sensation. Feeling exposed, she wrapped her arms tightly around her robed body. 'Ya 'll right?' he asked, eyeing her suspiciously, continuing on his path to the fridge. He pulled out two bottles and cracked them open.

Ash rubbed the heel of her hands into her eyes to clear the vision she had hoped would appear. 'Yep.' She took the offered drink and sipped, twiddling her feet and keeping one eye on the front door.

'Ya expectin' someone?' he asked, an amused smile cutting across his face.

'Yep,' Ash responded, avoiding eye contact with him.

'I thought ya might want t' talk through our tactical plan for Saturday,' he said, taking a long glug of the beer.

Ash turned and locked eyes with him, tilting her head to the side.

'Really?'

He squirmed. 'Well, and t' check yer okay. Haven't seen you for a couple days,' he said, with genuine concern.

Ash allowed a smile to form. 'I'm fine, honestly.' She hadn't deliberately been avoiding him, but with taking a short break from work at the base, there hadn't been any reason to interact either. And, she had found better things to do with her time!

'Iman?' His crooked teeth jumped out of his mouth with the chuckle that followed.

Ash's cheeks darkened. 'She's been teaching me to cook,' she said, starting to laugh.

'Is that what it's called in Syria?' he responded, his eyebrows rising.

'Fuck off,' she teased, slapping him firmly on the arm.

'So yer full on then?' he asked.

She held his eyes with her own, revealing the vulnerability she felt.

'Shoot!' he said, assessing her, but there was something else.

Ash's eyes darkened, and she sipped at the beer in her hand. 'I am worried,' she admitted.

He dropped his eyes to the floor. 'Uh huh.' His tone was reflective, sombre even.

'Did you hear about the two guys in Damascus?' she asked. She hadn't realised she was shaking until the rim of the bottle touched her lips.

Craig's eyes rose to meet hers. 'Yes,' he said.

He never said yes, always yep, or uh huh, never yes. There was something deeply affirming about the word that revealed his concern for the situation. She nodded, sipped her beer, and averted his gaze.

'What ya gonna do?' he asked.

She sighed deeply and shrugged, sipped again, and pinched the bridge of her nose. 'I don't know,' she said softly, pressing against the stinging in her eyes. She wasn't willing to face the obvious solution: the one that would break her heart irreparably. 'Her parents are supportive,' she added.

'And worried for her safety,' Craig reiterated.

Ash looked up and stared into his eyes.

'Tarek,' he confirmed. 'We got t' talkin'.' He was trying to sound nonchalant, though his stomach churned as if he had been cheating on her, talking behind her back. 'I'm worried too.'

'Fuck!' Ash's heart dropped with a heavy thud. The reality needed to be faced. 'Fuck, fuck!' she moaned.

Craig took a pace forward and pulled her into his arms, his large hand clamping her head into his chest. The position was comforting, but it didn't stop the searing pain in her chest or a tear from trying to form. He swept his hand lightly through her hair and kissed the top of her head. 'There has to be a way,' he whispered, as if to himself.

Ash pulled back, wiped the frustration from her eyes and studied his pensive gaze. 'There is, and that is to leave Syria. But I don't want Iman to feel she has to run away to be who she is.'

'What 'bout what she wants? Whether it's ya she falls in love with or 'nother woman, she should decide, don't ya think?'

He had a point. Ash nodded. She pinched the bridge of her nose to stem the red mist from forming in her mind. 'It's so fucking insane,' she blurted.

'What is?' Iman stood in the doorway to the kitchen, staring from Ash to Craig and back again. Ash avoided eye contact. 'What's wrong?' she asked, with increasing apprehension, crossing the room and reaching for Ash's arm.

Ash retracted a fraction.

Iman froze, a flash of something unpleasant gripping her chest.

Ash looked at Craig, who was frowning and sighed. She rubbed at her eyes, erasing the image of the minor rejection she had just inflicted. Reaching out, she pulled Iman into her shoulder. 'Nothing's wrong, it's just work,' she lied.

'Ah huh, I'll leave y'all to it,' Craig said, downing his beer and leaving his bottle on the side.

Iman pulled out of Ash's shoulder and cupped her cheek, forcing her to look at her. 'Don't lie to me,' she said.

There was no doubting the conviction in her voice. 'Ash...' She spoke the name slowly, sternly, her gaze unwavering.

Ash broke eye contact, put her arms around Iman's waist and held her close. Iman's hands rested lightly on her chest. 'Two men were badly beaten today,' she started. Iman tensed. 'They were gay,' she added.' Iman shuddered.

She released one hand and pulled Iman's head into her chest, fingering tenderly through her hair. 'There is a real danger here Iman. People like us, we can get badly hurt, by people who are ignorant or frightened.' Iman was breathing heavily, and the heat of her breath was causing Ash's skin to tingle. When Iman pulled away and held her gaze, her breath hitched in her throat.

'I love you.' Iman's fingers traced tenderly down Ash's temple and around her ear, toying with the soft lobe, and then tracing down her neck.

Ash stared into the light-brown gaze. 'I love you too,' she said. 'But what if it's not safe for you... for us?' she added.

Iman answered her with the touch of her mouth. The supple flesh enveloped Ash's lips, slowly encouraging them to part, and her tongue gently explored, connecting them on a level beyond the physical realm. Iman's fingers pulled at the belt around the bathrobe, and it slid to the floor. Her fingers traced down the small gap at the front, drawing the robe apart, and she pressed her body into the space. Her fingers traced up Ash's side to the eager breast, and she flicked her thumb across the erect nipple.

Ash gasped and deepened the kiss, her hands pulling Iman's head into her, devouring her.

Iman groaned at the sensation of Ash on her fingers and the bittersweet taste of the beer on her tongue.

Ash pulled back, her eyes dark, wild, all-consuming. She started to unbutton Iman's dress, then stopped suddenly. She took her hand, walked to the front door and flicked the latch. She tested the handle to make sure it wouldn't open, and walked Iman up the stairs and into the bedroom.

Iman intently watched, as Ash slowly discarded her robe to the floor, revealing her perfectly formed breasts, toned body, and her enticing sexual centre, pulling her in; captivating her. She stepped closer, feeling Ash's heat invade her body and instruct the somersaults in her stomach.

Ash flipped Iman around and continued to unbutton her dress, unhooking the bra as she descended. She swept the long wavy hair to one side, kissed down Iman's neck, and traced her tongue down her spine, eliciting goose bumps along the trail. She pulled off the unwanted clothing, lowering to the floor, revealing Iman's soft bare flesh. Slowly she turned Iman back around, and taking in the sweet scent emanating from between her legs; she placed a tender kiss on her crotch. She moved her mouth across to Iman's hip, up to her belly button, and then up towards her breasts. Rising to stand, she took the dark nipple into her mouth and started circling and flicking her tongue across the stiffening bud. She kissed up Iman's neck, finding her mouth with an increased sense of urgency, encouraged by the guttural noises hitting her ears. Iman's hands were pulling her closer, and as they touched along the full length of their bodies, she deepened the kiss, exploring, sensing. Iman's fingers were tracing a line down her back, and cupping her tight ass. The feel of Iman's crotch pressing directly to hers caused her mouth to part and her tongue to quiet. 'Fuucckk!' she groaned, diving back into the kiss and pulling Iman down onto the bed. As they crashed onto the mattress, Iman's light-brown eyes opened. Ash's heart stopped, her breath stolen by the intense brown eyes piercing her heart. Paralysed, she continued to stare.

Iman smiled, but her eyes didn't shift from Ash's. Her hand started to explore the breast that had tempted her lips for too long, and she caressed the area tenderly, biting down on her lip, her eyes flickering at the sensual feel of Ash's nipple on the palm of her hand, and then her fingertips. She couldn't restrain any longer. Her mouth crashed onto Ash's breast, her teeth biting, grating, and her tongue teasing the sensitive point, savouring the shifting texture and sweet taste hitting its surface. 'So delicious,' she groaned, taking Ash in her mouth again, with the most tender of touches.

Ash moaned, her back arched, and her sex throbbed with the fire pulsing from her nipples to her core. Powerless, she drifted absent of thought, immersed in the effect Iman was having on every sense in her body.

Iman sat astride her, her thumbs taking over from her tongue, so she could study the woman she loved. Her fingers moved sensitively with Ash's rhythm, naturally responding to the familiar display of eroticism building in her beautiful face. Watching Ash had that delirious effect on her again, sending the tingling sensation down her body, accumulating and pulsing between her legs. Ash's hips were rotating rhythmically, connecting them when her pubic bone touched Iman's wet centre, her bundle of nerves reacting to the pressure that threatened to cause her to explode.

Ash groaned with the tension building between her legs and Iman's wet heat covering her sex. The absence of pressure was excruciating and driving her wild. But, she needed something else even more than the quick release. She shifted, tossed Iman lightly onto her back, pulled one leg out from underneath Iman, and eased them together; her sex to Iman's.

Iman jolted at Ash's sudden movement, finding herself thrown back onto the bed, creating an unwanted space between them. She was about to complain, but Ash's wet centre pressing against her own silenced her. Consumed by the rising heat filtering through to her core, her eyes closed, and she found herself moving effortlessly with Ash, tenderly caressing herself on Ash. And Ash was groaning. The lightest, and most delicate form of pressure, on her sex, seemed to be having the deepest and most profound effect on her heart. Iman jolted, the pressure on her clit increasing. Ash's thumb was delicately teasing her with their fluids, and sending exquisite spasms through her lower-lips and up into her belly. 'Aahhhmm,' she groaned, as the intensity overwhelmed all other senses. The gentle vibrations were expanding, wave after wave causing her hips to buck and thrash. The sudden rise in tension low in her belly brought her body to a halt, and for a moment the world stood still. Tipping over the edge, she shook uncontrollably, releasing a long gasp. She rested the back of her hand on her forehead, and her eyes remained closed, biting her lip, groaning, smiling until the shuddering eased.

Ash extracted herself and eased her way up the bed, resting her elbows either side of Iman's head, and softly kissed her. The tender touch caused Iman to shudder again. Softly, Ash caressed her with light kisses.

Iman's eyes opened slowly, and her smile deepened. Her hand reached up, swept the blonde bob behind Ash's ear, only for it to fall back down again. Cupping her face, she drew her down into a languid kiss. 'Mmmm, you are insanely sexy.' Iman licked tenderly along Ash's top lip. She eased the swollen lip into her mouth and played with it between her teeth. With increasing urgency she deepened the kiss, her hands re-acquainting with Ash's body. With one heave and a lack of resistance from Ash, she flipped her onto her back.

Ash smiled through dark eyes. She would never grow tired of this feeling, or the tongue that was exploring her body again and causing her nerves to fire and her sex to pulse.

Iman released Ash's nipple from her mouth. Smiling mischievously, seduced by her intoxicating scent, she kissed down Ash's taut stomach. She needed to taste her. Ash rose up and tried to slow her progress, but Iman shrugged off the

237

effort, slid down swiftly and landed a kiss on Ash that threw her backwards.

'Ahhhh,' Ash groaned, biting down on the back of her hand, her clit exploding at the feel of Iman's tongue and lips. Sucking her in, flicking, pulling, and teasing her relentlessly. She groaned again.

Iman settled between Ash's legs and inhaled the musky odour, groaning at its impact on her increasing sexual appetite. She pulled back a fraction, admiring Ash's beautiful sexual centre. She eased Ash apart, revealing the vulnerable, wet flesh and slid her tongue lightly across its surface. Ash bucked and gripped her firmly, holding her in place. She probed more deeply, savouring the delicate silky fluids that gathered on her tongue. With increasing confidence, her fingers joined the exploration. She flicked her tongue relentlessly across Ash's clit and entered her simultaneously. The cry that hit her ears fuelled her, and she thrust deeper, sucked harder, until the final scream stilled her.

'Fuucckk!' Ash's head flew up from the bed as she rode the orgasm that had her body thrashing uncontrollably. Iman's soft brown eyes stared up at her, a beaming grin on her face. Ash pulled her up, and claimed her mouth hungrily, holding her close, connecting along the length of their bodies. 'I love you,' she whispered.

'I love you more than life,' Iman responded, easing up and holding Ash's bright smile.

27.

'Are you sure I look okay?' Ash asked, licking and flicking her fingers down her dark blue jeans, and pulling down on the front of her white shirt.

Iman stepped up behind her, kissed the back of her neck and let her hands lazily trace the front of Ash's shirt, thumbing across the nipples that had sparked up.

'That's not helping,' she groaned, placing her hands over Iman's and increasing the pressure on her breast. 'Fuck!' She pulled Iman's hands off, turned in her arms and clasped her head in her hands. Drawing her close, she placed a tender kiss on Iman's full, red lips. 'Seriously! Do that, and we'll never get to your parents,' she said. When she pulled away, her gaze was intense, her smile tense.

'Are you okay?' Iman asked with concern, her fingers tracing Ash's taut face.

'A little nervous,' Ash admitted, with a tilt of her head. But there was also the other issue that Iman seemed reluctant to discuss. Ash's eyes dropped. She cupped Iman's hand and kissed the palm. 'Shall we go?' she asked.

'Arrgggh,' Iman groaned, with a mischievous smile. She ran her thumb down Ash's lips, down her chin, her neck, and across her breast. 'I could think of...'

Iman's fiery stare and sensitive touch sent a bolt of lightning through Ash that caused her chest to crush. 'Jeeeezzz, you are dangerous,' she said, with a wicked grin. She grabbed Iman's hand and squeezed. 'Later,' she said, racing down the stairs and opening the door before she could change her mind.

*

'We can go through the back,' Iman said as Ash pulled into the large driveway at the front of the house. She stepped out of the 4x4, walked around the side of the building, and through an ornate metal gate. Ash followed her, maintaining a respectable distance between them. 'That's Amena,' she said, as they approached the occupied garden seat on the lawn.

The proximity of her lips as she whispered caused Ash to shudder. White-grey smoke wafted into the sky from the brick construction close to the house, and the aroma of cooked spicy meat drifted on the heady evening air.

Amena threw the book down on the seat and bounded to her feet. 'Hi, I'm Amena, she said, holding out her hand excitedly.

Iman chuckled at her sister's display of enthusiasm, settling the quivering in her stomach.

'Hi,' Ash said, though the word was croaky, and her eyes couldn't settle on the dark-brown eyes that were gazing dreamily at her.

'Cute,' Amena blurted, and a flush of heat rushed to her cheeks. She started giggling, her hand covering her mouth.

'Ammy,' Iman admonished, but she too was chuckling.

Ash flushed, wide-eyed.

'Where is everyone?' Iman asked, her eyes scanning from the outdoor kitchen to the house.

'Mum's getting ready. Dad's doing some salad thing and Tarek's helping,' she said, rolling her eyes.

'Tarek!' Iman laughed.

Ash wriggled her hands, unconsciously picking at the skin around her fingernails.

'Come on,' Iman said, reaching for Ash's hands and pulling them apart.

Ash followed her across the garden and into a door leading to the kitchen, her heart thumping through her chest. Her shoulders dropped as her eyes caught Tarek's; whose distinctive light-brown irises bore a striking resemblance to Iman's, the kind smile on his face, giving her permission to breathe. 'Hi,' she said, with a tilt of her head.

'Welcome,' he said, continuing to shred the carrot in his hand.

'Ah, Ash!' Muhammad appeared from the pantry with a covered dish in his hands, a cloth hanging over his arm. 'Welcome.' He placed the plate on the kitchen surface and approached Ash with open arms.

Ash stiffened initially, then folded her arms around him and patted his back. 'Thank you.' She could feel a surge of warmth rising in her chest, and her eyes were starting to burn.

'Marla, Ash is here,' he called, into the house.

Within seconds Iman's mother appeared, in an elegant, flowing royal-blue dress with embroidered gold trim. Iman's brown wavy hair cascaded down her back, and Amena's dark eyes smiled at her. 'Hello Ash, welcome.' She held out her hand, and Ash took it.

'Thank you for inviting me,' Ash said, feeling her chest expand with their kindness.

'Immy, show Ash around the garden.' Muhammad instructed with a wave of his hand. 'Would you like a drink?' he asked Ash. 'We have beer,' he added, with a broad grin.

'Later, thank you.'

Tarek smiled at Ash's apparent restraint.

'This way,' Iman said. Ash nodded, extracting herself slowly from the three sets of eyes that seemed intently focused on her.

*

'She seems sweet,' Marla said, approaching her husband and placing a chaste kiss on his cheek.

'Iman is smitten,' he responded. The crow's feet had disappeared, replaced by the lines between his dark eyes. He sighed.

'I worry for her too,' Marla said, nodding her head. 'Maybe Paris will be just what she needs,' she added.

'I hope so,' Muhammad said, picking up the covered dish and taking it to the outdoor kitchen.

Marla turned to Tarek. 'I'll make some bread,' she said.

Tarek kissed the top of her head. 'You make the best,' he said, sentimentally.

Marla pushed him away with a huff. 'Immy makes the best bread,' she corrected, with a forthright smile.

*

Iman led Ash across the lawn to a cobbled path. Taking the track leading away from the house, they sauntered down the lane, bedded flowers and designed shrubs on one side, small trees on the other. The aromatic sweet scent of white jasmine lingered as they walked, the flowers still hiding from the heat of the day. A burst of lilies wafted across their path and then a hint of rose.

'It's beautiful here.' Ash's eyes lingered on Iman. She wanted to hold her hand and lean on her shoulder as they walked. The sadness in her heart reflected in the shift in hue in her blue eyes.

Iman stepped closer. 'No one can see us,' she whispered, reaching for Ash's fingers and interlocking their hands.

Ash fought the surge of anxiety pricking the back of her neck. 'Are you sure,' she asked, searching through the thick foliage.

Iman took her chin, turned her face and held her gaze. 'Yes, I am sure,' she said. Her soft smile widened, and then retracted as she closed the space between them.

Ash's lips parted, and when her eyes closed all she could see, all she could feel, was Iman. The sweet aroma and slightly salty warm taste on her tongue, and the lightness of her fingers that exposed her painfully. The trembling sensation in her chest and the light-headed dizziness dancing in her mind weakened her legs. She could barely breathe. Iman slowly released her from the kiss, leaving her wanting, needing, and mesmerised.

'Come and see the lake,' Iman said, squeezing her hand and dragging her down the lane, enthusiastically.

Ash hadn't recovered herself by the time Iman turned into a gap in the treeline and squeezed out the other side.

Iman eased her way down the uneven bank onto a small sandy verge bordering the large, dark-blue body of water. Tall trees lined its boundary as far as the horizon.

Ash followed Iman down the slope and sat on the sandy bank. 'Wow,' she exclaimed, entranced by the reflection of the descending sun dancing on the water's surface. 'It's spectacular.'

'I used to come here a lot when I was a kid,' Iman said. 'We used to take a boat out too, and fish, over there.' She pointed.

Ash lowered her eyes. *How could she ask Iman to leave this behind? And yet, how could they stay?* She rubbed at the tightness in her chest, her throat constricted, and a silent tear fell onto her cheeks.

'Hey, what's wrong?' Iman asked, clasping Ash's face in her hands. She kissed the tear away. 'Baby, what's wrong?' Iman begged.

Ash shrugged, finding it hard to know the right words to say. The pain burning in her eyes as she locked onto Iman was excruciating, and the thought of leaving her, even more agonising. 'I...' she started to speak, but the words wouldn't come.

'Ash, please, you're scaring me.' Iman's worried eyes skittered across Ash's face, seeking answers, seeking reasons.

'I'm worried about you.' Ash said, fighting for her composure.

Iman sighed deeply, pulling Ash's head into her chest. Holding her tightly, she squeezed as if she would never let her go. Then a penny dropped. 'Please don't say... please don't do this...' The red rage of injustice warred with the deep sense of grief that had just pierced through her heart. Ash pulled out of the hold and Iman released her reluctantly. Iman's eyes darted from Ash to the sand, to the water, to the setting sun. 'I won't let you go,' she insisted.

Ash nodded, her hands clasped in her lap. 'I know,' she said. 'But, times are changing, and it's getting tougher here.'

'I know,' Iman responded, reaching for Ash's hand. 'We can live abroad,' she added, too quickly.

'You would leave your family, and your home... all this?' Ash asked, her arm indicating to the surroundings and beyond.

Iman's eyes dropped, and her heart sank with them. 'Yes,' she said. An image of the course details, sitting on her dressing table, hit her mind's eye, but the joy that she had previously experienced at the prospect of training to be a chef didn't appear. The idea of time away from Ash cast a dark shadow and her stomach churned. She had been running away when she originally signed up for the course, and now she didn't want to run.

Ash watched the stream of consciousness playing out through Iman's facial expressions. 'You don't seem sure,' she said, reaching for her cheek and caressing the soft flesh tenderly. 'I need you to be sure if that's what you want. Living in another country, where everything is different. It won't be easy.'

'It's not just that,' Iman said, her eyes searching Ash. 'I... I applied for a Chef's course in Paris, so I planned to go away, at least for a while.'

Ash's jaw dropped, her eyes blinked repeatedly, and her brain tried to make sense of her visceral response.

'It slipped my mind, because...'

'I, I didn't realise,' Ash said softly, staring vacantly, her mind spinning.

'It slipped my mind because I don't want to go now,' Iman said.

Ash locked onto Iman's piercing eyes. 'You must go,' she said, trying to ignore the stabbing pain in her chest. 'It's the right thing to do. It's exactly what you need to do.'

'No, it isn't. I don't want to be away from you,' Iman pleaded.

Ash sat upright, trying to formulate her thoughts. 'I could get some time off and...'

Iman was shaking her head. 'I can't be away from you for one second,' she said. 'It would hurt too much.'

'But at least you would be safe,' Ash said, trying to find some enthusiasm for the plan that made obvious sense.

'Alone, dying inside, that's not safe Ash.'

Ash paused. Holding her head in her hands, she pressed hard against her temples. 'You were going to leave,' she stated.

'That was before... us.' Iman said.

Ash released her head and stared at Iman. She had no desire for them to be apart either.

'I would leave for us,' Iman said, answering the question in Ash's eyes. 'But not without you, and, at a time of our choosing.' She breathed out slowly, feeling lighter for the conversation, even if it hadn't resolved the underlying issue of Iman's, or their, safety.

'We need to be careful,' Ash said. 'What do your parents think?' she asked, staring out at the horizon.

'They want me to be happy,' Iman responded, with an affectionate smile. 'And safe, of course,' she added.

'I still think you should do the course,' Ash said.

'No.' Iman retorted, rising to stand. 'Come on; food will be ready.' As Ash rose, Iman pulled her close. 'I'm not leaving you,' she said, placing a tender kiss on her lips.

The touch left a scar where it burned.

28.

The loud thumping on the door jolted Ash awake, and she turned into the cold side of her bed. Leaving Iman at her parent's house, she'd felt the emptiness. She cursed as the banging from downstairs reverberated through the floorboards again. 'Alright,' she shouted, knowing full well Craig would be bouncing up and down on the other side of the door, with a crooked grin on his goofy face.

'C'mon, c'mon,' he said, bounding through the door. 'We need to get the raft over to the river.' He handed her a mug of coffee.

'Thanks, bud.' She sipped at the hot drink and tussled with her bed-hair.

Craig gazed up the stairs inquisitively, and she slapped him on the arm.

'What?' he teased.

'She's not here,' Ash confirmed, with a coy smile. 'Give me ten,' she said, slowly making her way back up the stairs.

'I got pastries,' he shouted, heading for the kitchen.

She jumped into the shower, avoided wetting her hair, jumped out; threw on her shorts and t-shirt, collected her coffee and made her way back downstairs.

'Eight minutes! Yer good,' Craig said, with a wink, munching into a sticky sweet cake.

Ash scanned inside the paper bag and lifted a sugar-coated pastry triangle to her lips, knowing that the soft almond paste would dance on her tongue. 'Yum.' The sweetness went some way to filling the void that occupied her chest. She wanted to feel the joyous sensation of the love that she and Iman shared, but the shadow of truth was too strong. She had seen the love between Iman and her family too. Pulling Iman away from her home, her life. What if Iman resented her for it, eventually? She sipped at the hot drink, the bitter taste bringing her back to the sound of Craig's voice.

'Everythin' okay?' Craig asked, observing her. Ash's eyes caught his, answering the question. 'Anythin' I can do?' he asked, frowning.

Ash puffed out a breath, stood taller and sipped her coffee. 'Yeah, let's go win this race,' she said, braving a smile.

Craig's crooked teeth appeared, but there was still a concern in his gaze.

'Ya ready then?'

'Sure, let's do it.'

*

Niomi ran excitedly into the kitchen, drawing Iman's eyes from the crème pâtissière she was working on. 'They said yes,' she screeched with delight, her cheeks rosy and her eyes sparkling. 'They said yes. Can you believe it?' She danced around the kitchen, humming a tune. 'What can I get your parents…? To thank them,' she said.

Iman shrugged. 'I don't think they'd expect anything,' she said, smiling warmly. 'I'm so happy for you.' She held out her arms and Niomi fell into the embrace. 'When are you getting married?' she asked, suddenly aware that she might not be around for the wedding if they had to leave the country.

'We haven't set a date yet. Zack wants to date me properly,' she said, her chin rising, with a tilt.

'That's lovely.' Iman gazed at her friend, the gripping sensation niggling in her gut reminding her that she would never be able to share her joy openly in the same way. She sighed deeply. 'You going to help me with the party food for the race?' she asked, redirecting her attention.

Niomi clapped her hands in front of her chest. 'Yes, I can't wait. It will be such fun watching them this afternoon.'

Her eyes glazed and she swayed where she stood. 'I hope they win.'

Iman threw her an apron. 'Come on then. We've got a lot to do,' she said, the thought of creating something unique lifting her spirits.

'How's Ash?' Niomi asked as she walked into the pantry.

Iman's heart fluttered, momentarily replacing the dull feeling that accompanied any thoughts of needing to leave the country, or being apart from the woman she loved. 'She's wonderful.'

Niomi placed the semolina flour and syrup on the workbench. 'Are you going to Paris?' she asked, her tone reflecting the lack of enthusiasm that Iman felt.

'No,' Iman said. Her eyes lifted, with her smile. Niomi was grinning and her eyes alight with excitement.

'What will you do?' Niomi asked.

'About what?'

'Ash... and you?'

Iman stared straight through Niomi. 'I don't know,' she said.

'Will you move abroad?' Niomi asked, her tone suddenly serious.

Iman stood, staring into a space in her mind. Her hands were shaking, even though her heart was full of hope. 'If we have to, I guess,' she responded, with a sigh.

'What about your family?'

The question fractured her heart, and her eyes stung. Her father had always given her choices. Options. Even saying she could change her mind about the course if she didn't want to go. Amena had been even more resolute in offering her perspective; she didn't wish for Iman to leave. Tarek hadn't said much, but his smile had taken on a different quality since she had talked openly about her and Ash. Her mother had

249

been the only one who had been firm about her going to Paris, insisting that it would be for the best, and even that was out of concern for her safety. She had seen it in each of their eyes. The moment her sexuality had become more than just a fantasy. She would never be able to live openly here, in Syria, and, she didn't want to run from her life, her family, and all that she had ever known. And then there was Ash: the beautiful, amazingly sensual, Ash. She had never known such intense feelings towards anyone. To let her go wasn't an option either. 'It will be hard,' she said, her eyes glistening.

'The injustice is so wrong,' Niomi said, shaking her head.

'Yes, it is.' Iman responded, smiling through the sadness.

Niomi stepped around the bench and pulled Iman into her arms. 'We can look after each other,' she said.

'Yes,' for now. Iman cupped Niomi's face. 'Thank you for being a good friend.'

Niomi blubbered. 'I will die if you leave,' she said.

'No. You will get to make more sweets,' Iman teased, pressing a light kiss to her forehead. 'Come on, let's cook,' she said, shifting the energy.

*

'What the fuck ya doing, Zack? Grab that fuckin' corner 'n' put some beef behind it.' Craig rolled his eyes, but the grin on his face caused Ash to chuckle.

Zack gave him the finger, and shifted across two paces, trying to get a firm grip on the barrel.

'Ya got it yer end?'

'Yep,' Dan responded, though he too was struggling to get a good purchase on the round metal, weakened further by the laughter rumbling in his chest.

Ash stood from having been bent over the raft for too long, waiting for the men to sort themselves out, and stretched her back. 'When you lot are ready, call me,' she said, heading for the cool-box. They'd had mechanical support to get the raft onto the truck, so there wasn't any wonder in her mind that it was taking them a bit more effort to manually shift it onto the shore. She cracked open a beer, leaned against the truck and slugged. She chuckled as she watched other teams struggling; rafts of all shapes and sizes were being lifted, dragged and slid into position on the water. A loud jeer sounded downstream as a competing company's raft splashed into the river.

Zack and Dan abandoned their positions and joined her.

'For fuck's sake,' Craig complained, still holding his corner of the raft. He threw off his gloves and stepped up to the cool-box. 'So how we gonna shift this mule?' he asked. Three pairs of shoulders shrugged at him. He pulled out his cigarettes and offered them up to Ash. She refused. 'Ya stopped?' he asked.

She pulled away from the truck and headed to the water's edge, 'Seems so,' she said. She hadn't had any desire to smoke since they had returned from the rig. She couldn't explain it. It was like a switch had gone off, and although she had had moments when she could have easily picked up a cigarette Iman's image in her mind's eye had somehow prevented her.

'Fuck!' Craig mumbled, inhaling deeply, scratching his head.

Ash walked downstream studying the bank below the water. 'Here,' she called. 'If we can back the truck into the water, it will be on a tilt, and we might be able to lever it directly in.' Splash! Another jeer went up. It was going to be a competitive race. She grinned.

'Where the fuck's Tarek?' Craig grumbled, jumping into the driver's seat and turning the engine. Three pairs of eyes scanned the area. Nothing. Craig pulled the truck forward, aligned the rear end with Ash's instructions and reversed slowly.

'Keep coming,' Ash said, standing on the bank, waving her hand, watching the back wheels slowly submerge. 'Stop,' she yelled, but the 4x4 kept moving. 'Stop,' she yelled again, banging on the side of the truck, bringing it to a halt.

'Here's Tarek,' Dan said, pointing at the silver 4x4 heading in their direction.

'Thank fuck,' Craig mumbled.

Tarek ambled over, assessing the partly submerged truck. 'How you gonna get that out?' he asked.

'No idea 'n' I don't care,' Craig said. 'Let's get this bloody raft into the water before the race starts.'

Tarek started laughing. 'Won't take an hour,' he said.

Ash rolled her eyes. Craig's passion was getting the better of his temperament.

Tarek climbed onto the back of the truck and assessed the raft. 'Is this meant to be attached?' he asked, unhooking one of the straps that had secured the raft for the journey from the base to the river.

Craig's cheeks darkened.

Ash broke into a full belly laugh, Dan shook his head, and Zack rolled his eyes. 'Right, let's get this baby landed then,' Ash said, 'now that it's unhooked,' she added. Even Craig was laughing. 'You ain't gonna live that one down bud,' Ash said, chuckling.

Craig mumbled, but he was still laughing.

Another jeer went up as their raft hit the water.

Craig jumped into the driver's seat of the partly submerged 4x4 and turned the engine. The truck spun on its wheels, and the crew from Exxon jeered again.

'I'll pull it out,' Tarek said, with a wry smile. He meandered over to his car and reversed it towards the stranded vehicle. 'You just keep hold of that raft,' he shouted to the others. 'I'll hook her up.'

29.

Ash pulled herself onto the raft. She swayed with the rocking motion and moved carefully to fix the rudder to the back. Dan and Zack pulled the ropes taut to try to stop the raft shifting. Tarek and Craig had parked the vehicles up and were heading over with the cool-box, and something else.

'Ready.' she yelled. Craig beamed a grin and handed over a stick with a flag attached to it. Ash started laughing. 'Where's that going?' she asked.

'I made a hole for it,' Craig responded, pointing to the point on the raft that she hadn't had time to notice.

She placed the tapered end into the hole and pushed the pole firmly in place. The white, unmarked, sheet hung limply in the absence of any breeze.

'Great design,' she teased sarcastically.

Craig chuckled. 'I didn't have time t' paint it,' he said.

Ash slapped him on the arm and nodded to each of them. 'Grab the paddles,' she said. Zack released the rope to pick one up, and the raft tilted sharply. 'Jeez, we'll be lucky to get to the start line,' Ash teased.

Craig grabbed the rope, instructing the others to board first. Dan sat, tentatively at one side. Craig released the string and made a dive for the raft, causing it to heave. Lifting his weight up onto the planks caused it to lean even farther. Dan lost his balance and tumbled into the water. 'For fuck's sake!' Craig complained, grabbing the rudder and taking his position at the back of the raft. Dan spluttered as his head bobbed out of the water. Zack took his arm and pulled him back onto the slatted surface; Ash doubled over with laughter. 'Right, we need t' get this over there,' he said pointing towards the starting area. Dan was flicking the water out of his ears. 'Get paddlin' boys,' Craig ordered.

'Aye, aye Captain,' they responded, in unison, through fits of giggles.

Leaning over the boat, paddling upstream, they made their way to the starting area. 'Fuck, this is knackering,' Zack complained. His arms were shaking, and his back burned from the hideously uncomfortable, crouched position.

'Yep,' Craig responded, sitting back and sipping the beer in his hand.

'No fucking chance Johnson.' The shout from a competitors raft had Craig giving the finger with a broad grin on his face.

'Fuck off Edwards,' Craig responded, raising the beer in his hand. 'I'll see ya when yer get that heap o' junk pulled outta the water,' he jested.

The man called Edwards raised his beer with a laugh. 'In your dreams.'

A loud jeer went up. One of the smaller rafts was already sinking.

'It'll be easier when we're going downstream,' Ash said reassuringly, patting Zack on the back and handing him a beer.

'Is it very deep?' Dan asked, looking at the water, his face pale.

'Just keep your jacket on,' Ash responded. She was starting to wonder if they would get off the starting line themselves, let alone to the finish line.

Shouting over a megaphone, interrupted the banter, and the booming of a gun initiated the frantic paddling that ensued. Less than twenty yards into the race and another raft was breaking up.

'Go join the shellfish,' Craig yelled, laughing hysterically at his own joke as the Shell team started to flounder.

Ash's head was down and she was paddling hard, enjoying the physical exertion. She felt strong, exhilarated, and able to take on the world. And, she couldn't wait to see Iman at the finish line.

'C'mon Ash ya slackin',' Craig reprimanded, with a beaming grin.

He turned the rudder a fraction, having little effect. The boat was still heading to the right.

'Fuck off,' she teased. She looked up, dipped her paddle into the water and held it firm, redirecting the raft. The boys looked exhausted, and they'd only moved fifty-yards. 'Let's let her float for a bit,' Ash said, downing her paddle and heading for the cool-box.

'No.' Craig whined. 'Shifts. Do it in shifts,' he begged. 'Look, fuckin' Edwards' got twenty-yards on us already.' He waved his arm downstream, his head on the same tilt as the raft he was observing. 'Looks a bit unstable mind.' He chuckled.

Ash ignored his plea, pulled out the beers and handed them around. Tarek took a long glug and lazed back on his elbows. 'Shift's is a good idea,' he said, a glint in his light-brown eyes.

'Give me a minute,' Ash said. She slugged her beer, regaining her breath. 'We'll take the first shift,' she said, indicating to Tarek. The younger boys looked wasted already. She leaned over the boat, scooped up some water and splashed it on her face and neck. 'Fucking hot as hell.'

'Good reason t' win early,' Craig said, with unwavering focus.

Ash puffed out a couple of breaths and nodded to Tarek. In silence, they picked up their paddles and got to work.

'Ahoy there,' Craig called out, waving like royalty, as they passed the sinking Texaco raft. The crew in the water were struggling to breathe, laughing hysterically as they scrambled to the shore.

'Right, swap,' Ash said, pulling her paddle from the water and rubbing her burning forearms. 'Jeez,' she complained, shaking her right arm. Zack and Dan leapt into place and started to paddle. As she and Tarek shifted to the back, the raft tilted violently, and Zack lost his balance. Splash!

'For fuck's sake,' Craig cursed again, leaping forwards on the raft to hook him out. The boat swayed again, and Ash slid in. Splash!

As her head surfaced, the water trickling down her face from the river merged with the tears of laughter. She allowed herself to drop down into the cool again, before pulling herself back onto the raft. 'Will you fucking sit still bud, or you'll drown us again,' she teased. Tarek was bent over laughing, as memories of last year's event came flooding into his mind's eye. Dan and Zack looked blankly at each other.

'Dan, you steer for a bit,' Ash said. 'Right boys,' let's paddle.

'C'mon; we're catchin' 'em,' Craig bellowed, his eyes firmly on Edwards' boat.

Ash looked up and pointed. 'They're sinking,' she laughed.

Craig studied the craft, just a few yards ahead of them. 'Aha,' he yelled. 'Fuckin' heap a junk,' he bellowed. A raised middle finger came back at him, and he laughed.

Easing off with the paddling, they cruised up to the sinking raft. 'Ya wanna beer Edwards?' Craig asked, handing a bottle to the man in the water.

'Cheers man,' Edwards said, with a broad grin, taking the beer. 'You in good shape?' he asked, eyeing their raft from water level.

'I reckon,' Craig responded. The nearest craft to them was about ten-metres back, the suspension bridge was visible, and the finish line was just beyond the bridge.

'Go win this thing man,' he said, leaning across a piece of wood, sipping from the bottle.

'Go catch a fish,' Craig responded, giving Edwards the thumbs up. 'Right, let's win this race, team.'

Ash and Tarek assumed their positions at the front of the raft and started to paddle hard. 'Let's get some distance between them and us,' she said, indicating to the Alco raft making ground on them.

The fire in Tarek's eyes transferred to his arms. 'Too fucking right,' he said. He never swore.

*

'I can see them, I can see them.' Niomi was jumping up and down, pointing from the suspension bridge. 'They're winning,' she squealed, grabbing Iman's arm and squeezing it as she jumped.

Iman started hopping up and down with her. Was it the adrenaline pumping through her veins that was causing her to feel quite giddy, or the sight of Ash's blonde hair and toned body, paddling fiercely? She giggled. Her brother on the other side of the raft seemed to be struggling to keep up with Ash's pace. She started waving both hands furiously, and Niomi joined her.

'Come on Ash,' Iman yelled, unable to contain her excitement.

'Come on Zack,' Niomi yelled, simultaneously.

The man with dark-slicked-back hair, sucked slowly on the cigarette in his hand, observing from a short distance. He took a long sip from the drink in his hand. His eyes refused to move from the two women, celebrating on the bridge. His ears didn't register the other screams and shouts from loyal supporters, though they afforded him the concealment that enabled him to hear her voice, screaming for another: not him. He sucked down on the cigarette, studied the occupants of the raft, the red rage building in his head. How could she do that to him? How dare she?

Niomi and Iman continued to wave. Ash and Tarek had stopped paddling for a moment and sat back on their heels. Ash was wiping her forearm across her forehead. Tarek did the same. Craig and Zack were paddling, crouched just behind them.

Ash scanned the bridge hungrily, and it didn't take long for her eyes to register Iman bouncing up and down and waving like crazy. Her heart skipped a beat. She could see Iman's smile, and it was getting wider. She looked over her shoulder briefly and then to the finish line just beyond the bridge. The buzzing in her chest told her they were going to win. She waved. 'Look, Iman and Niomi,' she said.

Tarek held his paddle above his head, making a pumping action.

Zack looked up, a beaming smile accompanying his waving arms. 'We're gonna win,' he yelled.

'Keep paddlin',' Craig hollered.

Ash started laughing. 'They're nowhere near. Just you keep your fucking body in the boat bud. That's the biggest threat to us now,' she chuckled. Tarek wiped the tears of laughter from his cheeks.

'Fuck off,' Craig teased, but his eyes carried the shine of victory. Only one thing was missing. Kate! At least she'd promised to be at the after race party.

'I love you,' Zack shouted up, as they passed under the bridge.

Niomi blushed, her hands cupping her cheeks.

Iman felt Ash's smile, deep in her chest. She hoped Ash felt her smile too.

The man drank from his cup, lit another cigarette, and ducked into the crowd.

Raucous cheers, clapping, and whistles filled the afternoon sky as Craig, Ash, Tarek, Zack and Dan, landed their raft. Even Dan couldn't shake the beaming smile from his face as he disembarked cautiously.

Ash slapped him on the back. 'You okay?' Dan's grin disappeared. He turned, leaned over, and heaved. Ash started laughing. 'Don't fucking volunteer for offshore,' she said, patting him on the back.

'Told y'all we'd fuckin' win.' Craig slapped her on the arm and handed over a beer. 'Cheers,' he said, raising his bottle.

'Cheers.' She clinked her bottle and sipped.

'What's with him,' Craig said, finally noticing Dan's head between his knees.

'No sea legs,' she said, with a wry smile.

'Don't fuckin' volunteer for offshore,' he said with a tilt of his head.

Ash laughed. 'Yep,' she said, her eyes scanning the path leading from the bridge.

'Party time,' Craig said. 'Right, let's get this baby outta the water,' he added. 'Tarek!' he yelled, waving his arm.

30.

'Hello, Iman.'

Iman jumped, and her heart raced. The voice came from the left-hand side of the kitchen bins. She froze. 'Joram.' Her shaky voice, controlled by her instinctive sense of concern, surprised her. His timbre was as she remembered, even though it had been a while since she had seen him, but something in his tone caused unpleasant goose bumps to ride down her spine. His body must have been obscured from view when she had entered the kitchen moments ago, darkened by its orientation to the hotel, and out of reach of the descending sun. She tried to breathe, but her chest was too tight. She wanted to move, but her legs were weak.

Joram took a step into her path, his face just inches from hers, his eyes flaming. 'You did this, didn't you?'

Iman tried to take a step back, but the wall stopped her. She tried to speak, but his hand moved violently and smothered her mouth. The strong smell of stale tobacco and alcohol caused her to wriggle, to try to free herself, but his rough hands just pressed harder.

'You. You drove her away from me.'

Iman's stomach lurched at the thunderous look in his eyes. The sudden shift, from the giddy excitement she had felt as she locked the door to the kitchen heading for the party at Craig's house, was causing her body to convulse.

'Open the door,' he demanded, spittle flying from his foaming mouth. Iman reached for the keys and held them out to him. Pinning her to the wall, with her covered mouth, he snatched at them, turned the key in the lock and pushed her into the kitchen restroom. 'Do not scream,' he commanded.

Iman nodded, standing still, willing the tears that were forming in her dazed gaze not to spill out. 'I don't...'

'Shut up.' He stepped into the room, dominating the small space with his angry presence. 'Why did you turn her against me?' he asked, rubbing his hands through his greasy, styled hair.

'I didn't,' Iman whispered, drawing her head back from him as she spoke.

'She's marrying an infidel. How did you get her parents to agree to that? They're weak, just like yours.' He spat, looking down his nose at her. He didn't want answers that he wasn't willing to hear.

Iman stared, wide-eyed. Any excitement she had felt for her friend drowned in the fear that had her heart thumping in her chest. Joram's eyes were scanning her, tracing slowly down her body. Her skin shuddered as he stopped at her breasts and then again at the point between her legs. She couldn't swallow, couldn't breathe.

'Riffat always said you were odd,' he smirked. The strong scent of tobacco, as his hand reached up and toyed with her hair, caused the bile to rise in her throat. 'Are you?' he asked, taking a pace back and assessing her again. 'You look like a real woman to me,' he said, lost inside his warped perspective.

'No.' The word came out as a squeak, her head recoiling from his touch.

His hand moved down to her neck and squeezed her throat. 'Not a sound.' His wild glare lacked focus, but his intention was clear. He pressed her roughly against the locker wall, and she moaned as a shooting pain ripped through her shoulder. His hand moved down to her breast, and he started to squeeze roughly. 'See you like this,' he said.

Iman gasped, her head spinning, and her body frozen. The red rage building inside her mind just seemed to lodge itself in her chest, going nowhere. The power she needed to fight was lost, between her fear and physical inadequacy. She wanted to scream, but her voice wouldn't come either, and there would be repercussions if it did.

'You like this feeling? Did Riffat do this to you too? Did you fuck him? Or are you odd Iman? Are you a woman lover Iman? This is what Riffat thinks, but maybe you just need a confident man, eh? Sometimes a woman needs a strong man. See, you like this I can tell.' His coarse fingers were manipulating her nipple, underneath the flimsy dress.

His questions barely registered, and the only sensation passing through her body was revulsion. The stench from his breath, too close to her face, was causing the tension to rise in her spine and shoulders. She needed to relax to be able to break free, but if she did, he would take it the wrong way. 'Please get off me Joram,' she said, appealing to the better nature she had seen, in the years she had known him.

'You need a real man, Iman, to teach you the proper way,' he whispered, his rugged face pressing against her cheek.

'Joram, stop. This is not right.' She tried to push against his chest, but he leaned into her, pressing his rough lips into her neck, his free hand scooping up her dress. 'Joram!' She screamed out, and he silenced her firmly with his mouth, his tongue trying to penetrate the space, and her teeth refusing entry. He grabbed at her throat, forcing her chin up and her mouth to open. His tongue probed the small gap and his hand grasped between her legs, ripping at the thin cloth that offered no protection.

The groan emanating his foul mouth caused her senses to close down; recoil into the space and time of another dimension. Her body was falling, as the weight that had been pressing against her suddenly lifted. Her eyes remained closed while her ears registered the rustling sounds, and then groaning. A man was cursing, and then there was another crunching sound, and a familiar voice crying out. She tried to open her eyes but they refused, and she remained curled up against a locker, her arms wrapped around her knees. Then there was silence.

'Iman.' The tender touch on her arm caused her to flinch and retract, but the voice opened her eyes, and she stared, momentarily confused.

'Kate!' The pain in the dark green eyes that stared at her allowed the tears to fall on her face.

Kate kneeled in front of her, anger trying to burst through her chest, every ounce of her will, fighting the desire to stand up and finish off the job she had started. She wanted to reach out, hold Iman, reclaim her own inner child, but Iman had flinched away, and she understood only too well how that felt. The man on the floor was holding his head, blood pouring from a deep cut to his face, and his legs folded, his knees up to his chest. Whatever damage she had inflicted, it would never be enough. 'I'll call the police,' she said.

'No!' Iman's hand braced down on her arm. 'No, we can't,' she insisted. Her glassy eyes averted Kate's gaze. 'This is Joram, Niomi's ex-boyfriend,' she added as if the details should make a difference to Kate's comprehension.

Joram groaned as he tried to straighten his legs.

'Did he hurt you?' Kate asked, her voice stern as she focused her attention on the prostrate man on the floor.

'No.' Iman's voice was vulnerable, but she was shaking her head. 'No, I'll be fine. I'm just...' She was trembling violently.

Kate studied the pitiful man on the floor. 'Get up,' she demanded, driven by something profound, something repressed for too long.

Joram scrambled to sit and glared from Iman to Kate and back again. 'Fucking women whores!' He spat on the floor in front of Iman. Kate rose up and finding the strength she didn't know she had, pulled him up by his collar, her face inches from his. 'You...'

'Don't, please.' Iman's words stopped her, and she released her grip. Joram retracted at the threat and hit the wall behind him. 'Get out,' Kate said, through gritted teeth. 'You stay away from her. You stay away or I will...' The words sounded weaker than she wanted.

Joram smirked. He looked down at them both and stared through the top of his eyes. 'You need to watch out,' he threatened, with a raised hand. 'You're sick, and you will be punished.' His deliberate pronunciation and dark tone affirmed his place in his society - on the right side of the law. This was Syria. He scampered out the door.

Kate slumped to the floor. 'Are you okay?' she asked, her voice betraying the sudden onset of the trembling in her body.

Iman rested her head against the locker, unable to move from the floor. Her hair was ruffled, and her breast and shoulder still felt tender from the assault, but she had been lucky. 'How did you...?' she asked.

'I saw the door open. I was on my way to the party, and then I heard a scream.' Kate wiped at the tears that eased down Iman's cheeks. 'I'm so sorry Iman.'

Iman moved onto her knees, facing Kate. 'You saved me,' she said, holding Kate's watering eyes with tenderness.

Kate brushed her hand across her forehead, willing the tears to abate.

'You're bleeding,' Iman gasped, catching sight of the red graze covering the back of Kate's hand.

'I smacked him hard,' she said, a wry smile forming.

'Good.' Iman nodded, but she wasn't smiling. 'I need to find Ash,' she said, in a whisper.

'Yes.' Kate stood slowly and offered Iman a hand up. Iman swayed as she stood, and Kate pulled her into her arms to steady her. 'You okay?' she asked, releasing her and watching her balance.

Iman nodded. She moved slowly. Locking the kitchen door behind her she pocketed the keys, and they walked across the road in silence.

*

'Hey Kate,' Ash said, chirpily, as the redhead stepped into the kitchen. Ash held her gaze. Kate's silence and stern green eyes sent a chill down her spine. 'What's wrong?' she asked, looking frantically over Kate's shoulder.

'What's happened?'

Kate stepped closer and placed her hands on Ash's shoulders, drawing her entire focus. 'Iman...'

Ash pulled away, violently, trying to escape the firm grip.

'She's fine, Ash.' Kate was trying to hold Ash's jittery eyes but to no avail. 'Ash, listen to me.' Kate held her more firmly.

Ash stared at her, breathing deeply to try to control the anxiety that flared inside her. 'What's happened, Kate? Tell me.'

'There's been an incident.' Ash squirmed. 'She's fine. 'Apparently, it was Niomi's ex-boyfriend. He tried to assault her. He got what he deserved,' she added, her jaw clenched, her eyes on her grazed knuckles. 'She's fine Ash, and she'll explain to you. She's at your house.' Ash wriggled free and stormed out of the house. Within seconds she was through her front door.

'Iman,' she yelled, the swell of tears pressing hard at the back of her eyes. Iman stood at the kitchen table, and Ash rushed into the room, and into her arms. 'Are you okay?' she whispered, unwilling to release her hold, clasping Iman to her chest. Iman was shaking, sobbing, and the stabbing pain piercing Ash's heart was intolerable. If it continued, she would surely pass out. She squeezed Iman tightly and repeatedly kissed the top of her head. 'God, I was so scared,' she whispered, her pulse slowing a fraction with the knowledge that Iman was at least safe. 'Did he... hurt you?' she asked, slowly releasing Iman and staring into her dark eyes.

Iman shook her head. 'I got lucky,' she said. 'Kate came in before he...' Iman struggled to get the words out.

Ash's features tensed. 'Bastard!'

'I'd like a bath,' Iman said in a softer voice.

Ash puffed out a deep breath, and then another. 'I'll go and run one,' she offered. She made a move, but Iman clung on to her. 'In a minute,' she added, pulling Iman closer again.

Iman started to breathe without sobbing and gently eased back. She couldn't think of any words to say as her mind replayed the touch of Joram's hands on her body, over and over again. Her skin crawled, and her stomach churned. She averted Ash's eyes, her thoughts competing with her need to be held, loved, and caressed, by Ash. She stepped out the kitchen and started up the stairs. Ash followed.

'There's a robe,' Ash said, pointing to the back of the bathroom door. She turned to leave. 'I'll wait...'

'Please come in with me,' Iman said. Her dark eyes lowered to the suds forming with the running water.

A soft smile appeared on Ash's face. 'Are you sure?' she asked, moving to close off the taps.

Iman looked up and locked onto the dark-blue irises, laden with sadness. 'Yes.' Iman reached out and traced a line down Ash's cheek, sweeping the hair around her ear. She leaned in and placed a tender kiss on her lips. 'I want you, Ash. I cannot change that fact, no matter what happens. I will not change that,' she said. There was no uncertainty in her tone.

Ash smiled, but her eyes didn't lighten. She nodded, her vision clouded by a reality they both needed to face.

Iman eased into the bath and slid her body down beneath the water, cleansing the assault from her skin. As she emerged, she swept her hair behind her, squeezed the water from her eyes and opened them. The flowery scent was already soothing her mind, and the warm suds were softening her body.

Ash stepped into the bath behind Iman and started soaping her back with more suds and rubbing softly, massaging her shoulders and down her arms. She continued to apply the rose scented soap, up Iman's neck, down her shoulders and across her collarbone. Taking great care to tenderly caress the top of her breasts, her own breasts pressing into Iman's back, she placed a soft kiss on the exposed neck and immediately regretted doing so.

Iman flinched. She hadn't meant to and didn't want to. It had just happened, and a surge of something uncomfortable spiked in her stomach. She tensed in Ash's arms.

'Sorry,' Ash whispered.

Iman turned her head to face the wet, blue eyes. 'No Ash! It's not you.' She leaned back and placed a tender kiss on Ash's lips.

The fire that burst through Ash's chest caused her eyes to wet.

'Take me to bed.' Iman said, wiping away an errant tear.

'I need to take you home,' Ash retorted, staring, seeking.

'No.' Iman was shaking her head, and there was warmth in her eyes, that seemed unaffected by the sadness in Ash's heart.

'What about your parents?' Ash asked.

'I told them I was staying with you tonight.' The smile that appeared went some way to alleviate the sorrow that had befallen them both. 'And, I think they are going to need to get used to me not being around,' she added, mournfully.

Ash sighed. 'Are you going to do the course?' she asked, softly.

'Yes.' Iman leaned in and pressed her mouth tenderly to Ash's. She eased slowly out of the kiss and locked onto Ash's eyes. 'Will you hold me in bed please?' she asked.

'Yes.' Ash responded.

31.

Ash turned towards the sweet scent, enticing her to open her eyes. She moved closer, spooning behind Iman, her arms wrapping tightly around her slim waist, her mind unwilling to face the fact that Iman would be in Paris by the evening.

Iman sighed, refusing to wake. She moaned softly, at Ash's warm breath on her neck. 'Mmmm,' She mumbled, wriggling her bottom back into Ash's belly.

'Mmmm,' Ash responded. Her hand slowly moved up, crossed Iman's chest and cupped her breast, holding her close; protecting her.

The contact felt comforting, reassuring, and so very sensual. Iman drifted, absent of thought, fear, and expectation, immersed in the tranquil space that had no beginning and no end.

Ash eventually eased out of the hold, her hand moving up to Iman's shoulder and beginning to explore the tense muscle running from her arm to her neck. She stopped. 'Stay here,' she whispered, easing herself gently from the hold. Slipping out of bed, she stepped into the bathroom.

The slightly smoky, woody scent of cedarwood filtered into Iman's awareness as Ash's oily hand resumed its position on her shoulder and started to apply gentle and consistent pressure. She eased down onto her belly, her arms resting either side of her head. Her eyes remained closed, her senses diverted to the aroma and the shifting contact point under Ash's soft touch. She drifted back into the trance.

Ash straddled her waist, her palms tracing the long muscles each side of Iman's spine, easing along her shoulders, and then tracking down the outside of her back, her fingertips trailing lightly across the exposed part of Iman's breast. She repeated the path, adjusting the pressure in her hands with each cycle as she tuned into Iman's needs. She swayed her body with the sweeping motion across Iman's back, occasionally stopping at her neck, for her thumbs to ease up to the base of her skull.

Iman drifted deeper into a trance, lost in the sensual massage.

Ash steadily increased the pressure with her thumbs, on the tight spots her palms had discovered, coaxing them to relax.

Iman remained silent, breathing softly.

Ash continued to work around Iman's shoulders and down her arms, capturing her hands, and caressing them, loving them. Then she massaged up her spine again, and into the back of her neck. Applying the pressure through her forearms, she shifted the sensation down Iman's back to something more languid, connecting them beyond physical touch.

Iman remained under the hypnotic spell.

Ash shifted again, her fingers easing through Iman's hair, seeking out the subtle dips and pressure points on her head.

Iman released a soft sigh.

Ash eased down Iman's body and leaned forward, resting her chest on Iman's back, her lips softly touching her exposed neck. Her arms wrapped around the top of Iman's head and clasping her hands; she lay perfectly still.

Iman breathed softly, enjoying the exquisite sensation of Ash's breasts against her, the heat on her back, and the supportive feeling of Ash's arms and hands, cradling her head. She had never experienced anything as intimate and comforting. The warmth of the massage had soothed her, its effects swept through her and purified her body, cleansed her soul; and drawn them closer. She didn't want the feeling to end, but she knew it would, all too soon. She fought against the sadness rising into her chest, but the silent tears still wetted the pillow beneath her head. Whatever the future held, though, no one could take this moment from her.

*

Ash placed the suitcase in the back of the 4x4.

Iman pulled her father into her arms, but it was his embrace that provided the strength she lacked at that moment. 'I'll miss you,' she said, unable to control the tears from spilling onto her cheeks.

'We'll miss you too,' Muhammad said, wiping at his own damp eyes.

Tarek pulled his sister into his arms and slapped her on the back. 'You're the best chef and don't let them tell you any different,' he said, squeezing her tightly. His irises had darkened before he released her, and his eyes scanned the sky as Iman moved towards their mother.

'Bye Mum,' Iman said softly.

Marla pulled her daughter close to her chest, though her embrace maintained the familiar tension it always had and didn't reflect the pain in her breaking heart. 'Be safe Immy,' she said, holding back the tears.

'Ammy!' Iman approached her blubbering sister with open arms and pulled her into a tight embrace. 'I'll be home soon,' she whispered. Amena nodded against her chest but continued to cry.

'I'm going to miss you,' Amena sobbed, pulling back and wiping at her blotchy, puffy face.

Ash's eyes tracked the ground at her feet. The crushing feeling in her chest wouldn't lift. Watching Iman saying goodbye to her family intensified the pain in her heart as if life itself were seeping through her fingers. Iman turned to face her, her red eyes adding to the profound sense of grief she already felt. 'Shall we go?' she asked, barely able to utter the words.

Iman nodded. She turned to face the four pairs of glassy eyes. Iman was still sniffling. 'I'll be back soon,' she said, but the words hung in the uncertainty surrounding their reality. Iman opened the passenger door and climbed silently into the car.

Ash eased the driver's seat and turned the engine. 'You ready?' she asked. Iman's teary eyes answered the question, and Ash turned her attention to the road, stemming the tears burning behind her eyes. Even the thought of Iman's safety in Paris didn't come close to filling the pit of despair in which she now found herself. Whichever way she looked at their situation, there was uncertainty. Except for the intense love they shared. In those moments of togetherness, everything was crystal clear. She eased her foot down on the accelerator. 'It's gonna be a hot one,' she said, staring vacantly.

Iman remained silent, gazing out the side window.

Ash drove.

Iman continued to stare. As they approached the familiar souk that they didn't get to see, a sad smile formed on her face in the shadow of her dark eyes. 'Do you think we'll ever be together?' she asked softly.

Ash struggled to answer, unwilling to consider any other scenario. They'd been over this time and time again, since the incident. 'Yes, we will. I'm going to take leave in a couple of weeks and come to Paris. We can take a look around, and I'll see if I can get a transfer.' She looked across to Iman, and then to the road ahead. The anguish in Iman's beautiful eyes ripped through her again, and she struggled to breathe through the sharp pain in her heart.

'I'll miss my family so much,' Iman said, rubbing her wet eyes. She'd told herself she wasn't going to cry, but the promise was just an illusion. She didn't feel brave.

'I know.'

They travelled in silence.

'You got your passport?' Ash asked as they approached the airport.

Iman released a huff. 'Yes...unfortunately.'

The silence continued.

'Do you want children?' Iman asked.

Ash flinched. 'What makes you ask?'

'I was just thinking about the world we bring them into, and how cruel it is.'

The words cut through Ash. She was struggling to hold it together. 'Life's tough,' she said, her voice breaking under the strain.

'I hate it,' Iman responded. 'I hate the injustice.'

'Yes.' Ash steered the 4x4 into the Dier ez-Zor airport car park. She switched off the engine and sat, her hand refusing to undo the seatbelt. Iman moved first and exited the car with urgency. Ash followed, grabbed the suitcase from the boot and rushed behind her, into the small departure lounge.

'I'll check in then.' Iman's dark eyes lowered to the ticket in her hand.

Ash moved to take Iman's hands but retracted immediately. The inability to touch the woman she loved was causing her head to burst and her heart to fracture: killing her.

'Call me when you get there,' Ash said, grasping for something positive on which to fix her attention.

'Please come soon,' Iman begged.

Ash swallowed hard, fighting the pressure in her head. 'I will. I'll speak to Kate about a transfer as soon as I get back from here,' she said, trying to smile.

Iman nodded. 'I'd better go,' she said. She took a step closer and put her arms around Ash's back. The contact was brief, wholly inadequate, and left her wanting, and crying inside. Releasing her, she took the handle of the suitcase and dragged it through to the check-in area.

Ash couldn't watch any longer. She turned and ran.

Iman stood in the line, her mind foggy and unable to focus. Consumed by an overwhelming sense of loss, she waited, stepped a pace forwards, and waited again. She moved to an empty check-in desk, and the woman smiled at her, but all she could do was watch the process that was taking place in front of her.

'Passport please.'

She handed it over.

'Place your bag on here please.'

She lifted her case onto the conveyor belt and watched it dive into the hole, on the other side of the curtain.

'Have a nice trip.'

She took her passport back and placed it in her pocket. She wandered through to the next step in the process, and eventually found herself sitting at the departure gate, staring at the aircraft that was taking her away from everyone she loved.

*

Ash thumped her hands down on the steering wheel. 'Nooooo!' she screamed, without a care for who might be watching her. She pounded again. Even though she would take leave and go to Paris, the reality still struck her. What then? The dark, soulless gaze in Iman's eyes as she'd said about missing her family, and the profound sense of grief that had hit her as Iman had walked away. It was wrong. It was all so wrong. Yes, they could make a life together in Paris, or anywhere else in the world. But, that was only one half of the problem. 'Fuucckk!' she screamed. Driven by the red mist in her mind, she slammed the 4x4 into gear and sped out of the car park.

Iman stared at the large white metal object out the window. She couldn't relate to it, or its purpose. The crew were embarking, and all she could do was watch their movements as if stuck in a time warp. She couldn't compute the scene playing out in front of her eyes and started to fidget. She glanced around at the smiling faces, occupying the small space, waiting to fly. *How many of them were running away?* She scanned each one. The cheery family with the young baby: maybe a holiday? The grave, young, suited man, a business trip maybe? The young Syrian couple, gazing into each other's eyes lovingly, a honeymoon? Even they seemed to maintain a respectful distance, but at least they were allowed to be honest with their affections. She slumped back into the padded chair. Life wasn't meant to be like this! She rose from the seat and paced the small area.

Ash screeched the car to a halt and jumped out. She'd driven the longest route back that she could, but that hadn't helped to assuage the emptiness or the loneliness in Iman's eyes that haunted her. She slammed through the front door and dove into the fridge. Cracking open the beer, she took a slug and swallowed. The beer wasn't going to be enough to alleviate the pressure in her head or fill the void in her heart. She placed the bottle on the kitchen surface and searched the cupboards, pulled out a bottle of Cognac and poured a large glass.

Stepping out into the garden, glass and bottle in hand, she tried to breathe in the balmy air. The sun still beat down, the crickets were still chirping, and the beeping of car horns would always rumble in the distance, but nothing else remained the same. She sat watching the slight movement on the surface of the swimming pool and took a long slug of the burning fluid, allowing it to wallow in her mouth. The joy of the raft race, only a few days ago, seemed a distant memory. And even if Craig hadn't gone on holiday, if he'd been there for her now, it still wouldn't have helped. He couldn't work that kind of magic! She swallowed hard. The searing heat down the back of her throat was far more preferable than the excruciating pain accompanying her thoughts, and a welcome distraction. She leaned into the plastic chair and allowed her eyes to close. Perhaps that would help? It didn't. Maybe she'd go to work after all. She took another slug. *Fuck it!* It was too late in the day to bother. She'd just get drunk. She poured another glass, leaned back and closed her eyes again, willing for not this!

*

'I didn't know you drank Cognac.'

The illusion of the voice caused Ash's eyelids to shoot open. Her heart raced in her chest, and she jumped up in her seat. 'Jeez!' She stood, staring, stunned. No words could express the sensations coursing through her, as she locked onto the light-brown smiling eyes.

'I couldn't do it,' Iman said, stepping into Ash's personal space, cupping her cheeks, and placing a languid kiss on her open lips. She eased out of the kiss, maintaining the contact between them: her forehead against Ash's. 'I'm not running away, Ash,' she said softly, but with absolute determination.

Ash couldn't speak, her mouth wouldn't move. Her heart still racing, she tried to swallow. 'I...' The spinning sensation in her head had nothing to do with the Cognac, most of which still sat in the glass on the table. The quivering in her stomach was rising through her chest, and her hands were shaking. She stared at the beautiful woman in front of her, who was continuing to justify herself, and grinned.

'I'm not doing it, and that's final. I refuse to run. If I... If we go anywhere it will be because we choose to and we do it together when we decide. I already called Dad from the airport, so they know where to find me...'

Ash's grin broadened. 'I love you so much,' she said. Finally, she could breathe.

Heat rushed to Iman's cheeks. She'd expected Ash to argue. 'I...' Her words were swept away by the soft mouth tenderly caressing her lips. Her heart fluttered, and her mind quieted at the soothing strength of Ash's hands in hers. This was right. She groaned, falling deeper into the telling kiss.

Ash eased out of the kiss, resting her cheek against Iman's. 'Will you make love with me?' she asked, in a whisper.

'Always,' Iman whispered back, biting down on Ash's earlobe, and eliciting a shudder.

'Fuucckk,' Ash groaned.

Other Books by Emma Nichols

Visit **getbook.at/TheVincentiSeries** to discover The Vincenti Series: Finding You, Remember Us and The Hangover.

Thanks for reading and supporting!

About Emma Nichols

Emma Nichols lives in Buckinghamshire with her partner and two children. She served for 12 years in the British Army, studied Psychology, and published several non-fiction books under another name, before dipping her toes into the world of lesbian fiction. You can contact her through her website and social media:

www.emmanicholsauthor.com
www.facebook.com/EmmaNicholsAuthor
www.twitter.com/ENichols_Author

And do please leave a review if you enjoyed this book. Reviews really help independent authors to promote their work. Thank you.

Manufactured by Amazon.ca
Bolton, ON

25966537R00160